/EL

SILVER and the Sunday Cypher

NEW YORK TIMES #1 BESTSELLER TONY LEE writing as

JACK GATLAND

Hooded Man MEDIA
INSPIRATION • PRODUCTION • PUBLICATION

Published by Hooded Man Media.

Cover design by L1graphics

First Edition: September 2025

PRAISE FOR JACK GATLAND

'This is one of those books that will keep you up past your bedtime, as each chapter lures you into reading just one more.'

'This book was excellent! A great plot which kept you guessing until the end.'

'Couldn't put it down, fast paced with twists and turns.'

'The story was captivating, good plot, twists you never saw and really likeable characters. Can't wait for the next one!'

'I got sucked into this book from the very first page, thoroughly enjoyed it, can't wait for the next one.'

'Totally addictive. Thoroughly recommend.'

'Moves at a fast pace and carries you along with it.'

'Just couldn't put this book down, from the first page to the last one it kept you wondering what would happen next.'

Also by Jack Gatland

DI DECLAN WALSH BOOKS

LETTER FROM THE DEAD

MURDER OF ANGELS

HUNTER HUNTED

WHISPER FOR THE REAPER

TO HUNT A MAGPIE

A RITUAL FOR THE DYING

KILLING THE MUSIC

A DINNER TO DIE FOR

BEHIND THE WIRE

HEAVY IS THE CROWN

STALKING THE RIPPER

A QUIVER OF SORROWS

MURDER BY MISTLETOE

BENEATH THE BODIES

KILL YOUR DARLINGS

KISSING A KILLER

PRETEND TO BE DEAD

HARVEST FOR THE REAPER

CROOKED WAS HIS CANE

A POCKET FULL OF POSIES

CHEATING MY DESTINY

STAND AND DELIVER

WE PLAY WITH DEATH

HIS DEAD MAN'S HAND

TOM MARLOWE BOOKS

SLEEPING SOLDIERS

TARGET LOCKED

COVERT ACTION

COUNTER ATTACK

STEALTH STRIKE

BROAD SWORD

ROGUE SIGNAL

SNIPER ALLEY

SHADOW THREAT

SENTRY POINT

ELLIE RECKLESS BOOKS

PAINT THE DEAD

STEAL THE GOLD

HUNT THE PREY

FIND THE LADY

BURN THE DEBT

TAKE THE KING

LIAM HARPER BOOKS

FINAL STRIKE

BLOOD RIDGE

TRACK SHIFT

CARLYLE & SILVER BOOKS

SILVER AND THE SUNDAY CYPHER

SILVER AND THE CHRISTMAS CAPER

DAMIAN LUCAS BOOKS

THE LIONHEART CURSE

THE EXCALIBUR QUEST

STANDALONE BOOKS

THE BOARDROOM

As Tony Lee

STANDALONE

TWELVE TASKS

THE PLAYING CARD WAR

KNAVE OF SPADES

QUEEN OF BLADES

CHARMING

LAST PRINCE STANDING

HAPPILY NEVER AFTER

For Mum, who inspired me to write.

For Tracy, who inspires me to write.

CONTENTS

PROLOGUE

HARRY FARRELL HAD WALKED THESE LONDON STREETS FOR THE better part of twenty years, and he knew when he was being followed. This wasn't the paranoid suspicion that occasionally gripped retired intelligence officers – God knew he'd seen enough of his former colleagues jump at shadows cast by perfectly innocent postmen, or dog walkers – no, this was different. This was the real thing, a knowledge of what was about to happen, as he turned off Gloucester Road onto the quieter side streets of Smithfield.

He'd tried the usual tricks. A sudden stop to tie his shoelace outside a bakery, using the shop window's reflection to scan behind him. A quick detour through the covered market, doubling back to see if anyone followed. Took a taxi a few streets, only to see a black sedan already on his tail. Even tried the old standby of crossing the street twice for no apparent reason, but it sorted nothing out. Anyone who was watching him, or even watching the follower watching him, would have seen he'd tried everything here. But it was to no avail...

Someone was definitely back there.

Scaffolded buildings lined the narrow road ahead, their metal frameworks creating a maze of shadows and hiding places. Old churches sat beside small shops selling everything from artisan cheese to mobile phone repairs – you know, the sort of London street that had developed organically over centuries with little regard for architectural harmony.

Harry risked another glance over his shoulder, keeping the movement casual.

There.

About thirty yards back, a young man in his twenties wearing the sort of slim black suit that screamed *undertaker* or *Mormon missionary*, with short hair, side parting, and a bored, expressionless face that belonged in a corporate headshot rather than wandering around Smithfield on a Tuesday afternoon.

The uniform, Harry thought with grim amusement. *They really couldn't help themselves, could they? Might as well hang a sign around their necks: "Creepy Cult Member – Please Maintain Distance."*

This was *Mister Wednesday,* maybe *Mister Thursday,* though the boy looked barely old enough to order a pint, let alone serve as a weekday operative for an organisation like *The Calendar*.

Harry quickened his pace, muscle memory from his US army days kicking in despite his sixty-eight years. He had a plan that only a small amount of people knew, but he had to be in the right place at the right time for it to work. He could slip down the alleyway between the cheese shop and the florist, walk the covered passage that led back towards the main road, even use the side entrance to St. Bartholomew's Church if things got truly desperate.

Too many civilians around, though.

That was both protection and problem. The Calendar preferred their operations to appear accidental – a heart attack, a slip on wet pavement, a tragic encounter with London traffic. Hard to manage with witnesses milling about, taking photographs and asking awkward questions.

His hand moved instinctively to his inside jacket pocket, confirming the small package was still there. Not the one they *thought* he had – that was already gone, safely delivered before they'd picked up his trail. This one was different. *Personal insurance,* you might say.

For Rebecca, when he didn't make it home for dinner.

The thought of his wife made his chest tighten in a way that had nothing to do with his cardiovascular health. Twenty-seven years of marriage, most of which spent keeping secrets she'd never deserved to carry, every morning she'd make his tea just the way he liked it – two sugars, splash of milk – and every morning he'd wonder if today would be the day his past finally caught up with him.

Their breakfast that morning felt like a lifetime ago now – Rebecca pouring tea while sunlight streamed through their kitchen window, catching the silver threads in her hair. He'd almost told her everything then – about The Calendar, about the years he'd spent documenting their activities, about the evidence he'd finally gathered that could alter everything, and change the balance of power forever...

About how she'd probably never see him again after he left.

Instead, he'd kissed her goodbye and told her he was off to his club for lunch.

The regret sat in his stomach like a stone.

The Calendar called themselves that internally, though Harry doubted many people outside the highest levels of government knew the name. Elegant in its simplicity – operatives designated by days of the week, each with specific roles and responsibilities. Monday through Saturday, anyway.

No one would discuss Mister Sunday, which said everything anyone needed to know about where the real power lay. It'd been five years since the last known one had left, Harry wasn't even sure if they'd gained a replacement yet.

Although it was very likely.

A nursery rhyme as the foundation for an international intelligence network; it would have been amusing if they weren't so devastatingly effective at what they did.

The package he'd delivered that morning was purely to bring a long dead asset back to life and reveal secrets long forgotten. Which meant Mister Thursday back there wasn't following him to intercept intelligence, as that opportunity had already passed.

This was clean-up.

Harry paused at a newsstand, pretending to browse the headlines while using his peripheral vision to track his tail. The vendor, a cheerful gentleman who'd probably been working this corner since the Thatcher years, looked up hopefully.

'Afternoon paper, sir? Got the latest on the football if you're interested.'

'Not today, thanks,' Harry replied, offering a smile that felt more natural than he'd expected. Strange how normal conversations could feel like small luxuries when you suspected you might not have many left. 'It's only bad news today.'

He continued walking, deliberately slowing his pace. If Mister bloody Thursday was going to make his move, better it happen here in public than somewhere isolated. Crowds had a way of asking inconvenient questions and taking unwanted photographs.

Unless of course there were *two* of them. *Was that the operational process these days?*

Harry's pulse quickened as he scanned the street ahead. It looked to be the usual London afternoon crowd, with office workers grabbing late lunches, tourists consulting maps with the look of people determined not to admit they were lost, mothers pushing prams while simultaneously managing mobile phones and shopping bags.

Nothing obviously suspicious. *Yet.*

St. Bartholomew's Church loomed ahead on his right, its medieval stones a testament to the sort of stubborn endurance that had made London what it was. Harry had always appreciated old buildings – places that had witnessed centuries of human drama and somehow kept standing despite everything history threw at them.

Rather like himself, really, though he suspected his own endurance was about to be tested more severely than usual.

Harry had spent his entire career understanding that some battles couldn't be won through official channels; too many departments had been infiltrated, too many operations compromised by people who appeared respectable on the surface but served other masters in the shadows.

Here was where Harry Farrell would try to cheat death.

Across the street, a young couple emerged from an electronics shop. The man – mid-twenties – laughed at something his companion said. He pointed towards the old church, then convinced her to strike a pose while he fumbled with what appeared to be a newly purchased SD card, sliding it into his camera.

They definitely looked like locals rather than tourists, comfortable with their surroundings in the way only Londoners could be. Just ordinary people having an ordinary afternoon, completely unaware they were about to witness something rather *less* ordinary.

It was time.

A figure stepped directly into his path; another black suit, this one worn by a man perhaps ten years older than Thursday. Broader shoulders, and a far more physical presence – the sort of controlled stillness that spoke of serious training and recent practice. Harry recognised the type immediately. He'd worked alongside enough of them over the years, although he didn't recognise this one.

'Terribly sorry,' the man said, his voice carrying the sort of educated accent that opened doors at gentlemen's clubs across London. His hand settled on Harry's upper arm with deceptive gentleness. 'Didn't see you there.'

'Monday,' Harry breathed. 'You dressed up for the occasion.'

The man's expression flickered with something that might have been amusement, or surprise that Harry was well versed on identities.

'Vanity is a vice of mine,' he replied. 'Monday's child is fair of face, after all.'

Okay then. Time to begin.

'This doesn't have to happen,' Harry said, keeping his voice low and reasonable. 'We could discuss alternatives.'

'I'm afraid the discussion phase concluded some time ago,' Mister Monday replied with what seemed like genuine regret. 'Nothing personal, you understand.'

Harry tried to step back, but Mister Monday's grip tightened. One hand maintained control while the other produced a small, needle-less syringe from his jacket pocket – the movement so smooth it might have been choreographed.

'Look here,' Harry began, glancing around desperately. 'Surely we can—'

'Some debts simply can't be negotiated,' Mister Monday interrupted gently. 'Sorry, Harold. I really am. It's new. It's quick. Be grateful for that.'

The injection happened so quickly Harry almost missed it. Mister Monday's grip loosened momentarily, just long enough for him to grab Harry's jaw, force his mouth open and squirt the syringe's contents directly onto his tongue. The entire sequence took perhaps three seconds.

By the time Harry understood what had happened, Mister Monday was already walking away, the syringe hidden in his palm as he merged with the pedestrian traffic.

Harry stood frozen on the pavement, his mind struggling to process the situation.

Poison.

The substance worked with frightening speed. His tongue went numb first, then his throat, then a spreading coldness that crept through his chest like spilled ice water. Harry's knees buckled as his training kicked in, clinical analysis overriding panic.

Neural inhibitor. Targeted paralysis. Cardiac arrest to follow within minutes. Designed to mimic natural causes with minimal trace evidence.

He'd read enough reports about this particular method over the years. He'd even been prepared for it, like the others. He never imagined he'd experience it firsthand, though.

Even as his body began to betray him, his mind remained frustratingly clear. Names and faces flashed through his consciousness – the young MI6 analyst who'd helped him trace the financial connections. The retired Special Branch officer who'd identified key personnel.

The package. Rebecca. The performance that had to be perfect. Would they get to his Rebecca? Or would they bring out their own?

His thoughts scattered like autumn leaves in a gale.

As he collapsed onto the ancient cobblestones, Harry's gaze fixed on the young couple across the street. Still taking photographs, still laughing, still beautifully unaware that they'd captured something far more significant than tourist snapshots.

Their camera would have recorded what just happened. Anyone who saw the photos would realise this wasn't simply an elderly man having an unfortunate medical episode.

Laura would find them.

Silver would find them.

His vision tunnelled, darkness creeping in from the edges. Through the gathering shadows, he could see Mister Thursday approaching with theatrical concern, playing the role of helpful bystander while combing Harry's pockets.

'Help! Someone call an ambulance!' Mister Thursday's voice carried just the right note of panic. 'I think this gentleman's had a stroke!'

Harry felt fingers slip inside his jacket, locate and remove the decoy package. The irony wasn't lost on him – they'd taken him down for something that contained nothing but newspaper clippings and blank paper.

Too late, he thought with what remained of his sense of humour. *The real intelligence is watching from the shadows.*

His final conscious thought wasn't about The Calendar or

the mission or the fifteen years that had led to this moment. It was about Rebecca, sitting in their kitchen tomorrow morning, wondering why he hadn't come home. The way she hummed while tending her roses. The bird feeder he'd installed last summer that still brought her such simple pleasure. The warmth in her eyes after twenty-seven years of marriage, even when she suspected he wasn't telling her everything.

I'm sorry, love, he thought, hoping somehow the sentiment might travel across London to find her. *But I have to leave you now. I'll explain when we meet again—*

Harry Farrell never felt the pavement rise to meet him.

Everything had gone according to plan.

MISTER THURSDAY CHECKED FOR A PULSE, MAINTAINING HIS performance for the growing crowd of concerned onlookers. He wasn't really checking – the poison was a new strain, one that Harry Farrell couldn't cheat, and after a suitable interval, he rose and backed away, loudly announcing his intention to call for emergency services while blending seamlessly into the flow of London pedestrians.

From a doorway further down the street, another figure observed the scene. The late afternoon light caught the silver head of his walking cane as his grip tightened around it. His face, partially concealed by the brim of a trilby hat, revealed nothing of his thoughts as he watched Mister Thursday's departure.

Sebastian Silver remained motionless until the first paramedics arrived, his stillness rendering him nearly invisible to the passersby hurrying about their daily business. Only when the official response began did he finally move.

After a measured pause, he turned and walked unhurriedly in the opposite direction, the soft percussion of his cane against the cobblestones lost in the growing commotion.

By the time police sirens began echoing through the narrow streets of Smithfield, Sebastian Silver had vanished entirely.

1

THE WIDOW OF QUEEN'S GATE

Laura Carlyle was rescuing her orchids when the grandfather clock in the hallway chimed eight-thirty in the morning. Its rich, familiar tones echoed through the Queen's Gate townhouse, prompting a small sigh from Laura as she set down her watering mister.

'Already?' she murmured to the delicate white blooms. 'Well then, we'll have to continue this later.'

Laura gave the orchids a final critical look – they'd been struggling since winter, stubbornly refusing to thrive despite her best efforts – before straightening. A lifetime of punctuality was a habit not easily broken, even fifteen years after James's diplomatic schedules had ceased dictating her days, and she made a mental note to check on them later before making her way to the kitchen, allowing the sunlight, streaming through the tall windows of her South Kensington home to hit her face as she descended.

The kitchen was empty, with the copper pots hanging above the centre island gleaming in the morning light. No sign yet of Aunt Celia, but this wasn't surprising – after all,

Celia considered rising before nine an absolute affront to civilised living.

Laura filled the kettle and set it to boil, enjoying the quiet moments before the household stirred to life.

She was just pouring hot water over Earl Grey leaves when she heard the front doorbell. With a glance at her watch – far too early for the usual parade of deliveries and charity collectors – Laura made her way to the entrance hall.

Through the etched glass panels, she could make out the distinctive silhouette of Eleanor Reynolds, their neighbour from three doors down.

Damnation.

Leaning back, Laura suppressed a small groan; Mrs Reynolds at this hour could only mean neighbourhood association business, most likely the ongoing battle over the proposed development at the old post office.

'Laura, darling!' Mrs Reynolds exclaimed the moment the door opened, her voice pitched at that slightly-too-loud volume that had become her signature in recent years. 'I hope I'm not calling too early, but I simply had to drop this by before the committee meeting.'

She thrust forward a large wicker basket wrapped in cellophane, containing what appeared to be an assortment of biscuits, preserves, and a bottle of something that Laura sincerely hoped was not another of Eleanor's homemade fruit liqueurs; the Christmas sloe gin still lurked menacingly at the back of a kitchen cupboard, awaiting an appropriate re-gifting opportunity.

'How thoughtful,' Laura said, summoning the polite smile that decades as a diplomat's wife had perfected. 'What's the occasion?'

'Do you need an occasion to gift friends?'

Yes, Laura thought to herself as she stepped back from the door. *Yes, you bloody well do, when the gifts looked like this.* 'Would you care to come in for tea?'

FIFTEEN MINUTES AND A DETAILED ACCOUNT OF THE neighbourhood association's latest victories later – victories that felt rather petty and both mildly classist and racist, if Laura was being brutally honest – she finally shepherded Mrs Reynolds back out the door with promises to review the development proposal documents before Friday's meeting.

'Oh, one thing,' Mrs Reynolds said at the door, a terrible attempt of a conspiratorial wink making her look like she was beginning the first stages of a sneeze. 'Who was the man at your door last night?'

Aha. Here was the reason for the call.

'What man?' Laura asked.

'Oh come on, we're both women of the world,' Mrs Reynolds smiled now, and Laura wondered if the woman even knew what that meant, as she was pretty sure the woman had never ventured past Malta, and even that was during part of a Women's Institute bus tour. 'The one in the hat, with the cane?'

Laura genuinely didn't know what Mrs Reynolds was talking about, but it didn't matter as Mrs Reynolds hadn't stopped talking.

'Fine, keep your secrets. I saw him outside the house looking up at your window last night at nine,' Mrs Reynolds now seemed to try to make some kind of knowing smile, but it was appearing as a leer, and not a good one.

'Eleanor, I promise you, I have no idea who you mean,' Laura was tiring of the games. 'What did this man look like?'

'Silver fox, like Pierce Brosnan nowadays, but dressed like he was as Bond,' Mrs Reynold's eyes lit up, and Laura almost laughed. This wasn't the first time she'd heard of Mrs Reynold's Pierce Brosnan fixation.

'Well, if Pierce Brosnan turns up in a hat and cane, I'll send him directly to your door,' she smiled. 'But I'm afraid I really must start breakfast.'

Taking the hint and reminding Laura that the notes really needed to be absorbed fully before the next meeting, Mrs Reynolds made her goodbyes and left.

'One of these days,' Laura muttered to the now-closed front door, 'I really must learn to say no.'

'You've been saying that for approximately twenty years,' came a dry voice from the staircase. 'I've yet to witness evidence of improvement.'

Laura turned to find Aunt Celia descending the stairs, already impeccably dressed in a cashmere twinset and pearls despite the early hour. At eighty, Celia Harrington remained a force of nature – tall, elegant, and possessed of the kind of bone structure that had made her the toast of London society in her youth.

Her mother's sister, she'd moved in after James died, ostensibly as a temporary arrangement, but one that had somehow stretched to fifteen years without either of them quite acknowledging the permanence.

'Eleanor was just dropping off—' Laura began.

'Another basket of inedible offerings and thinly veiled demands for your time?' Celia finished, arching one perfectly shaped eyebrow. 'That woman would have you running the entire neighbourhood if she had her way. As if you don't already sit on enough committees to qualify for sainthood.'

Laura smiled despite herself.

'Good morning to you too, Aunt Celia. Tea?'

'Please. And whatever's in that basket, I suggest we donate it to Kyle's student pantry. Young men will eat anything, even Eleanor's rock-hard shortbread. Why was she whittling on about Pierce Brosnan again?'

'Apparently he was outside the house last night, with a hat and cane.'

'We should be so lucky,' Celia smiled. 'Tell her if she sees him again, she should inform him I'm available.'

IN THE KITCHEN, LAURA BUSIED HERSELF PREPARING BREAKFAST while Celia settled at the table with the morning paper. The familiar routine had a comforting rhythm – eggs poaching, bread toasting, Celia's occasional snort of disapproval at whatever political outrage had captured the headlines.

'Your orchids are looking peaky,' Celia observed, glancing towards the row of plants on the kitchen windowsill. 'Too much water, I'd wager.'

'The white one was a gift from the Taiwanese ambassador,' Laura said, sliding perfectly poached eggs onto plates. 'I'm determined not to let it die, no matter how hard it wants to.'

'You and your rescue projects,' Celia said, but her tone held more affection than criticism. 'Speaking of which, Jennifer called while you were entertaining Eleanor.'

Laura set the plates on the table, her interest quickening.

'Oh? How is she?'

'Exhausted. Apparently, this trade delegation is even more demanding than the last. She sends her love, promises to try a video call on Sunday,' Celia paused before adding, 'she also mentioned that Kyle's father has invited him to Spain for the summer. Something about bonding with the new wife's baby.'

'Ah.' Laura absorbed this news with a small pang. She'd grown accustomed to having Kyle in the house, his boundless energy bringing a youthful vibrancy to rooms that had grown too quiet after James died. 'Did she say if Kyle's planning to go?'

'He's apparently "considering his options". Though what twenty-year-old boy would turn down a free summer in Marbella is beyond me,' Celia sniffed. 'Although that said, Rupert's new wife is a vacuous airhead who has the conversation skills of a Pomeranian, and Kyle's always been more of a cat person.'

Laura was saved from responding by the arrival of the young man in question, who wandered into the kitchen with a laptop tucked under one arm, a messenger bag over his shoulder and the perpetually harried expression of a university student with too many commitments.

'Morning, Gran. Morning, Aunt Celia,' Kyle said, kissing Laura's cheek before helping himself to toast from the rack, wisely not adding the various amounts of "greats" before the "aunt" title she required. 'Has anyone seen my economics textbook? The one with all my notes in the margins? Professor Winters wants to review my annotated bibliography before the thesis proposal, and I can't find the wretched thing anywhere.'

'Have you tried looking behind your laundry pile?' Celia suggested. 'Or perhaps under the three coffee mugs I almost liberated from your room yesterday?'

Kyle grinned, unabashed.

'I'm cultivating a fashionably dishevelled scholarly aesthetic,' he explained as if it was the most obvious thing in the world.

'Is that what they're calling it these days?' Celia remarked dryly.

Laura watched their familiar banter with a smile, even as her mind circled back to the stranger outside her house. *Did Pierce Brosnan live nearby? They had their share of celebrities in the area—*

'Earth to Gran,' Kyle's voice broke into her thoughts. 'Did you hear a word I just said?'

'I'm sorry, what was that?' Laura refocused on her grandson.

'I said Mum mentioned Dad's invitation to Spain. What do you think? Should I go?'

Laura carefully buttered her toast, buying time.

'I think it's entirely your decision, darling. Though I imagine the opportunity to know your new half-sibling might be worthwhile.'

Kyle studied her for a moment.

'You'd be alright? If I went?'

'Of course,' Laura said, smiling to cover the small lie. 'I've been thinking about taking that Viking Lines river cruise Aunt Celia's been dodging for years.'

'Heaven preserve me,' Celia muttered into her teacup.

Kyle laughed, then glanced at his watch and leapt to his feet.

'Got to dash – meeting with Winters in twenty minutes, and I need my notes.'

'Is your economics textbook the blue one with the white arrows?' Laura asked.

'Yes!' Kyle nodded eagerly. 'Have you seen it?'

'It's in your bag,' Laura pointed at the blue economics textbook with the white arrows poking out of the top.

Kyle sighed, smiled and then took a last, giant mouthful of toast.

'Don't wait up tonight – debate club might run late.'

'There's shepherd's pie in the fridge if you're hungry when you get back,' Laura told him. 'And please try not to wake Mrs Kowolski when you come in. She's been complaining about the door slamming.'

'Mrs Kowolski would complain if I floated in on a cloud,' Kyle pointed out, not inaccurately. The elderly Polish lady who occupied the basement flat had elevated tenant complaints to an art form during her residence.

After he'd gone, leaving behind a half-eaten piece of toast and the lingering scent of the ridiculously expensive cologne Jennifer had sent from Tokyo, Laura found herself staring absently into her tea.

'You're brooding,' Celia observed, setting down her cup with a decisive clink.

'I'm contemplating. There's a difference.'

'Not in your case, there isn't. You've had that same look since you found out the hydrangeas have leaf blight.'

Laura smiled despite herself.

'The hydrangeas are recovering nicely, thank you.'

'Unlike you,' Celia said, fixing Laura with her penetrating gaze. 'You're bored, Laura. Have been for months. All these committees and charities – they're just elaborate ways to fill time, not purpose.'

'Not everyone needs a grand purpose, Aunt Celia. Some of us are content with simple usefulness.'

'Rubbish,' Celia said with characteristic bluntness. 'You've spent fifteen years being a perfect widow, and what has it gotten you? A calendar full of obligations you don't care about and a house full of committees that would function perfectly well without you.'

The words stung, perhaps because they contained more truth than Laura wanted to admit. She rose to clear the breakfast dishes, more to escape Celia's too-perceptive gaze than from any real housekeeping zeal.

'James always said you were wasted as a diplomatic wife,' Celia continued, undeterred by Laura's retreat to the sink. 'Said you had the finest analytical mind he'd ever encountered. Better than half his colleagues at MI6.'

'James had a romantic view of my capabilities.' Laura rinsed a plate with more force than was necessary.

'He had an accurate view,' Celia corrected. 'And he'd be appalled to see you frittering away your talents arranging flower displays for hospital fundraisers.'

Before Laura could formulate a suitably cutting response, the doorbell rang again. She glanced at her watch – nine-thirty.

'Popular this morning, aren't we?' Celia remarked as Laura dried her hands. 'I wonder which pointless cause it is this time?'

'Probably Mrs Pollington about the charity auction,' Laura said, leaving the kitchen. 'She mentioned needing auction items when I saw her at the gallery opening.'

But when she opened the front door, it wasn't the

redoubtable Mrs Pollington who stood on her doorstep. Instead, a woman in her mid-sixties waited there, plainly dressed in a navy suit that had seen better days. She had the look of someone carrying a weight too heavy for her frame, with long black hair now peppered with silver, her hands worrying at her wedding ring as she looked up at Laura.

'Mrs Carlyle?' the woman asked, her voice tentative. 'Laura Carlyle?'

'Yes,' Laura replied, curiosity overcoming her usual caution with unexpected callers.

'My name is Rebecca Farrell,' the woman said. 'My husband, Harry, died three weeks ago, and I believe you might be able to help me.'

Laura blinked in surprise. The name meant nothing to her, and she certainly had advertised no services that might attract a recently bereaved woman seeking help.

'I'm afraid I don't—' she began, but Mrs Farrell cut her off with a quiet intensity that belied her fragile appearance.

'Please,' she said. 'Harry left instructions. He said if anything happened to him, I should come to you. He said you'd know what to do. I... I wondered if he'd sent you any packages?'

A curious sensation swept through Laura – something like a faint recognition, though she was certain she'd never met this woman before. It was as if pieces of a puzzle were being laid before her, though she couldn't yet see the picture they would form. As Laura stepped back to allow Mrs Farrell entry, she glimpsed movement across the street – a tall, silver-haired man in a pinstripe suit, watching her house with deliberate interest. He touched the brim of his trilby hat in what might have been acknowledgment before turning and continuing down the street, the silver head of his walking cane catching the morning light.

Pierce bloody Brosnan.

Laura closed the door, suddenly very aware of her racing pulse and a strange, almost forgotten feeling stirring beneath her carefully ordered existence.

For the first time in fifteen years, she felt truly awake.

2

UNEXPECTED VISITORS

LAURA LED REBECCA FARRELL INTO THE SITTING ROOM, wondering how her Tuesday had gone from executing orchids to hosting mysterious widows. The room usually put visitors at ease – antique furniture that whispered old money, modern touches that suggested actual life, Persian rugs that had survived three generations of spilled tea and family arguments.

Today, it felt like furniture arranged for a play nobody had rehearsed.

'Please, do sit,' Laura said, gesturing towards the sofa. 'Tea?'

'No, thank you.' Rebecca perched like she might need to bolt, handbag clutched as if it contained nuclear launch codes. 'I don't want to take more time than necessary.'

'Nonsense,' came Aunt Celia's voice from the doorway. 'Important matters require proper tea. It's practically constitutional law.'

Laura suppressed a smile. Celia believed Earl Grey could solve everything from diplomatic crises to existential despair.

'My aunt, Celia Harrington,' Laura explained as Celia swept in with the sort of presence that suggested she'd been born wearing pearls, a tea tray in her hands. 'She thinks she owns the house.'

'I do own half of it,' Celia corrected, settling into her throne-like armchair. 'Now then, Rebecca dear, what's this about deceased husbands and mysterious instructions? My social calendar has been dreadfully dull.'

Rebecca blinked at such directness, clearly unprepared for Celia's frontal assault approach to conversation.

'Celia doesn't believe in small talk,' Laura explained, busying herself with the tea tray. 'Considers it a waste of perfectly good conversation time.'

'I appreciate honesty,' Rebecca said, and for the first time since arriving, she looked genuinely relaxed. 'It's refreshing after dealing with officials who speak entirely in euphemisms.'

She reached into her handbag and withdrew a sealed envelope that looked like it had been handled more than a favourite prayer book. Cream paper, expensive weight, the sort that suggested someone had taken this correspondence very seriously indeed.

'Harry – my husband – left this for me,' she said, passing it to Laura. 'I was only to open it if something happened to him.'

The envelope bore careful handwriting across the front.

For Rebecca, in case of my unexpected death. With all my love, Harry.

Laura felt something cold settle in her stomach. People

didn't write notes like that unless they had an excellent reason to expect the unexpected.

Inside was a single sheet covered in a neat script that suggested years of report writing. Laura skimmed it quickly, her eyes catching on phrases that made her pulse quicken.

... not a natural death, whatever they may claim...

... trust no official channels, as some have been compromised...

... Laura Carlyle at Queen's Gate can help you find the truth...

At the bottom was a handwritten PostScript that made her breath catch.

If trouble comes, she can be trusted absolutely. James always said she saw what others missed.

Laura looked up to find Rebecca watching her anxiously, while Celia had somehow acquired the envelope and was examining it like evidence.

'Mrs Farrell – Rebecca – I'm afraid I don't understand,' Laura said carefully. 'Your husband seems to have known me quite well, yet I have absolutely no memory of ever meeting a Harry Farrell.'

'He once said you might not remember him,' Rebecca replied, her fingers finding her wedding ring and beginning the sort of unconscious twisting that spoke of anxiety. 'He mentioned you'd met only briefly, years ago, through your husband's work. But he spoke of you often, particularly these last few months when he was... troubled.'

Laura's interest sharpened. James had introduced her to hundreds of people during his diplomatic career, and she prided herself on remembering faces and names. It came with the territory when your husband's success often depended on your ability to recall that the Romanian cultural attaché was allergic to shellfish and the Belgian trade minister's wife collected miniature elephants.

'Harry was security attaché with the American diplomatic service,' Rebecca continued, lowering her voice as if someone might be listening. 'He was stationed in London for several years in the early 2000s, working in liaison between various agencies. That's when he knew James – they worked together on some sort of joint committee.'

Laura poured tea, using the familiar ritual to process this information. The early 2000s had been busy years for James, with increased security cooperation between allies and the sort of classified work that he'd never discussed at home. But a US liaison? Working between agencies?

CIA spy.

Which sounded exciting, but considering James dealt with them daily, not as much as one would think.

'You mentioned your husband died recently?' she asked, handing Rebecca a cup of perfectly prepared Earl Grey.

'Yes,' Rebecca's voice felt like it carried the precision of someone who had repeated these facts to numerous officials. 'He collapsed on the street near St. Bartholomew's Church around quarter to four in the afternoon three weeks back. The official report lists the cause of death as cardiac arrest brought on by natural causes.'

She set her cup down without taking a sip, her hands returning to that nervous wedding ring rotation.

'But you don't believe that,' Celia said, not unkindly.

'Harry was the healthiest sixty-eight-year-old man you'd ever meet,' Rebecca replied with quiet intensity. 'He walked five miles every morning, rain or shine. Had a full medical examination just two months before he died – blood pressure perfect, cholesterol levels excellent, heart strong as an ox. The doctor actually commented on his remarkable fitness.'

Laura leaned forward slightly.

'Had he been ill recently? Any symptoms that might have suggested heart problems?'

'Nothing. That's what makes this so impossible to accept,' Rebecca's voice grew stronger, as if giving voice to her doubts was helping her believe them. 'But more than that, he'd been... different lately. Worried about something. Really genuinely concerned in a way I hadn't seen since his active service days.'

'Different how?' Laura asked, genuinely curious now.

'Phone calls he'd take in his study with the door firmly locked. Papers he'd examine until all hours, spread across his desk like he was conducting some sort of investigation. I'd find him going through old address books, calling people he hadn't spoken to in years – colleagues from various postings, other retired security people,' Rebecca paused, choosing her words carefully. 'I didn't ask questions. After twenty-seven years married to someone in the intelligence community, you learn when not to pry.'

Laura nodded, understanding that particular dance all too well; the careful balance between natural curiosity and necessary discretion that came with loving someone whose work occasionally brushed against shadows.

'When did you receive this letter?' Celia asked, apparently having finished her examination of the envelope.

'I found it in our safe at home the day after he died,' Rebecca said. 'Right on top, where I couldn't miss it when I went to get his insurance papers. But there's more – something that arrived yesterday.'

She pulled out her phone and showed them an email that made Laura's blood run cold.

I have photographic evidence that Harry Farrell was

> murdered on April 15th outside St. Bartholomew's Church. The police are wrong about natural causes. £10,000 or the truth about what really happened is released. Reply to independence1776@mailnet.com to arrange secure exchange.

'Independence 1776,' Laura murmured, her diplomatic training automatically noting details. 'American Revolution. Rather heavy-handed symbolism.'

'Have you replied to this?' Celia asked, her voice sharp with concern.

Rebecca shook her head firmly.

'I went to the police first thing. They were... well, let's say they weren't particularly interested. Said it was probably someone who'd read about Harry's death in the papers and was trying to exploit a grieving widow. Standard procedure, they claimed. Happens all the time.'

'A logical conclusion,' Celia observed thoughtfully. 'Though not necessarily the correct one.'

'What exactly did the police tell you about the circumstances of Harry's death?' Laura asked.

'Heart attack. Natural causes. Case definitively closed.' Rebecca's voice carried bitter edges. 'They were remarkably efficient about it. Almost suspiciously so, if I'm being honest. The investigating officer seemed more interested in getting the paperwork completed than understanding what had actually happened.'

Before Laura could respond, Rebecca was reaching into her handbag again, producing a folded newspaper page that looked like it had been read over and over again.

'This was with his letter,' she said, handing it over. 'I don't know why he kept it.'

Laura unfolded the page and immediately groaned with recognition.

LOCAL PHILANTHROPIST SOLVES GARDEN SOCIETY MYSTERY.

Below it was a photograph of herself from some charity function, looking insufferably pleased with her own cleverness. The article described her investigation into who had sabotaged Mrs Hetherington-Smythe's prize-winning orchids at the Kensington Gardens Society's annual show, making the whole business sound far more dramatic than it had actually been. At the bottom of the clipping were two words.

They'll Know.

'Good Lord,' Celia said, reading over Laura's shoulder. 'I'd completely forgotten about that ridiculous orchid business. Though I maintain that Hetherington-Smythe had it coming – five consecutive championships does breed resentment.'

'It was hardly serious detective work,' Laura protested, checking the byline. *Keith O'Neill,* society reporter and occasional lunch companion. 'I simply mentioned my theory about growth retardants being used maliciously during the champagne reception. Keith turned it into front-page drama. And as for "they'll know", I'm afraid I really don't.'

'So, you don't regularly investigate suspicious deaths?' Rebecca asked, her face falling with disappointment. 'I'm terribly sorry to have bothered you. I thought... Harry seemed so certain...'

She began gathering her things with the defeated air of someone whose last hope had just evaporated.

'Wait,' Laura said, surprising herself with the firmness in her voice. 'I may not have "Private Detective" engraved on my business cards, but that doesn't mean I can't help you understand what happened to your husband.'

Celia shot her a sharp look, which Laura pointedly ignored.

'What exactly did Harry say about me?' Laura asked.

Rebecca paused, considering the question carefully.

'He said you were resourceful, well-connected throughout London society, and that you had a natural mind for puzzles and inconsistencies. That you wouldn't be intimidated by complicated situations involving people who preferred to operate in shadows...' she paused, then added, 'And in his note, that reference to James – that your husband believed you saw what others missed.'

The assessment was both flattering and accurate. It also sounded exactly like something James would have said about her – usually right before asking her opinion on some supposedly straightforward diplomatic problem that turned out to have seventeen layers of complexity.

'Did Harry leave anything else behind? Papers, personal effects, anything that might explain what had been worrying him?'

'The police returned his belongings after the incident,' Rebecca said. 'His wallet, house keys, mobile phone and a small notebook he always carried. Nothing seemed particularly important to them, but then they weren't looking for anything beyond confirming natural causes.'

'I'd very much like to examine those items, if you don't mind.'

'Would you really?' The relief that washed over Rebecca's face was almost painful to witness. 'They're all at my flat in

Notting Hill. Would you be willing to come around this afternoon? I could have everything laid out for you to examine properly.'

'Around two o'clock?' Laura suggested, already mentally rearranging her schedule.

'That would be perfect,' Rebecca said, rising from the sofa with renewed energy. 'I can't tell you how grateful I am that you're willing to help. I was beginning to think I was going mad.'

At this, however, she paused.

'I hate to repeat myself,' she said almost nervously, 'but nothing's arrived from him for you, right?'

Laura shook her head.

'Honestly, Mrs. Farrell, until you arrived, I'd not even heard of his name.'

'Of course,' Rebecca smiled, 'Silly of me to think he would have. It just felt...'

The comment trailed off.

Rebecca shrugged.

'I'll see you this afternoon.'

After they'd exchanged contact information and Rebecca had departed with profuse thanks and detailed directions, Celia turned to her niece with raised eyebrows.

'Well,' she said, settling back into her chair. 'This is certainly more interesting than your usual Tuesday morning routine.'

Laura picked up the newspaper clipping again, studying it with fresh eyes.

'I'd almost completely forgotten about this whole business. Keith made it sound far more dramatic than it actually was.'

'The question that interests me,' Celia said, stirring her tea thoughtfully, 'is why Harry Farrell kept it. Why connect a minor bit of garden society vandalism to something serious enough to warrant instructions in case of his death?'

'And why me specifically?' Laura added, moving to the tall windows that overlooked their small garden. 'There must be countless people in London better qualified to investigate a potentially suspicious death than a retired diplomat's wife who once solved flower sabotage.'

She stared out at the spring bulbs, her mind already working.

'James knew Harry Farrell. Intelligence connections from the early 2000s.'

'Your husband knew many people in that particular world,' Celia said carefully. 'Not all of them were as straightforward as they appeared.'

'Harry was a liaison for the US agents,' Laura muttered. 'You know what that means?'

'Yes,' Celia replied. 'It means he was a bloody spy, and not for us.'

Laura turned back to face her aunt.

'You think I should stay out of this.'

'I think intelligence matters rarely end well for civilians who get themselves involved, even very clever civilians with excellent intentions.' Celia set down her teacup with a decisive clink. 'Though I suspect that telling you to leave well enough alone would be utterly pointless at this stage.'

Laura smiled despite the gravity of the situation.

'You know me too well.'

'I've had eighty years of observing human nature, my

dear. Yours has always included an unfortunate tendency to poke at things that sensible people would leave alone.'

'I don't poke at things inappropriately,' Laura protested.

'Tanzania, 1997,' Celia replied without hesitation. 'You insisted on investigating why the ambassador's chef had been suddenly replaced, despite James practically begging you to leave it alone.'

'The poor man was being blackmailed by opposition politicians!'

'Yes, and your well-intentioned meddling nearly caused an international incident.' Celia sighed with fond exasperation. 'Though I'll admit the ambassador was extremely grateful once everything was sorted.'

Laura sat down across from her aunt, suddenly serious.

'This feels genuinely important, Aunt Celia. I can't explain exactly why, but that poor woman deserves to know the truth about what happened to her husband. And apparently Harry thought I could help provide those answers.'

Celia studied her niece with a penetrating gaze that had once reduced junior diplomatic staff to stammering apologies.

'You've been restless for months now,' she said finally. 'Increasingly bored with your committees and your charity galas and all your various worthy causes. Perhaps this is exactly what you need – a proper puzzle to solve.'

'I am not bored with charitable work,' Laura protested. 'The hospital fundraiser is vitally important.'

'My dear girl, you've reorganised those auction items three times this month. The committee members are developing anxiety disorders.'

Before Laura could mount a proper defence, the front

door opened and slammed shut, followed by thundering footsteps that could only belong to Kyle.

'Anyone home?' His voice carried the particular brand of cheerful chaos that university students brought everywhere. A moment later, he appeared in the doorway, messenger bag sliding off his shoulder. 'Professor Winters cancelled our meeting. Apparently there's a faculty emergency involving the coffee machine breakdown.'

'A crisis of epic proportions,' Celia observed with perfect deadpan delivery.

Kyle grinned unabashed and flung himself onto the sofa.

'So, what's all this then? You both look suspiciously serious. Has Mrs Pollington finally staged her long-threatened coup against the charity committee?'

'Your grandmother has decided to become a private detective,' Celia announced with barely concealed amusement.

'I have absolutely not decided to become a private detective,' Laura corrected with as much dignity as she could muster. 'I'm simply helping someone understand the circumstances of her husband's death.'

Kyle's face lit up like Christmas morning.

'Brilliant! Like Miss Marple, but with better fashion sense and functioning knees! Do we get to buy proper detective equipment? Please tell me there's going to be a magnifying glass involved.'

'There is no "we" involved in any of this,' Laura said firmly, though she couldn't suppress a smile at his enthusiasm.

'Every great detective needs a trustworthy sidekick,' Kyle declared. 'It's practically written into the genre requirements. Watson had Holmes, Hastings had Poirot...'

'You've got that backwards,' Celia pointed out. 'And you watch far too much television.'

'Netflix is highly educational,' Kyle countered, reaching for the leftover biscuits. 'I've learned loads about proper investigative techniques. Like the importance of checking alibis, following the money trail, never trusting the most obvious suspect, and always finishing the story before you get cancelled after three seasons.'

Despite herself, Laura found herself explaining the morning's events while Kyle listened with a surprisingly focused attention. When she'd finished, he sat back thoughtfully.

'Right then,' he said, brushing biscuit crumbs off his jumper. 'So, we've got a suspicious death that's been conveniently written off as natural causes, a mysterious email demanding money for photographic evidence, and a dead American intelligence officer who specifically told his wife to contact you if anything happened to him.'

He paused dramatically.

'Either that's the most massive coincidence in history, or someone knows something very important about you that you don't know about yourself yet.'

The observation was more unsettling than Laura cared to admit.

'That's exactly what I intend to find out.'

'Excellent!' Kyle said, leaping up with renewed energy. 'So, when do we start? Can I come with you to examine the evidence this afternoon? I'm genuinely brilliant at noticing important details.'

'You're brilliant at noticing when the biscuit tin needs refilling,' Celia pointed out.

'That's observational skills,' Kyle protested indignantly.

'Highly relevant to detective work. Pattern recognition, attention to environmental changes—'

'It's eating too many biscuits,' Celia said.

AFTER KYLE HAD WANDERED OFF TO PRETEND TO STUDY, LAURA found herself staring at the newspaper clipping yet again.

Why would a man she couldn't even remember meeting keep an article about her minor triumph over the garden society crime? And why would he specifically direct his widow to seek her help in the event of his death?

There was only one way to find out.

But first, she needed to understand exactly what Harry Farrell had been investigating in those last weeks of his life – and why someone might have considered it dangerous enough to kill for.

3

SEEDS OF DOUBT

REBECCA FARRELL'S FLAT IN NOTTING HILL HAD THE CAREFUL tidiness of someone who'd been preparing for visitors she'd rather not receive. The sitting room was pleasant enough – cream walls, well-worn furniture that spoke of comfort rather than fashion, and French doors leading to a small garden where someone had been taking proper care of the roses.

'Please excuse the state of things,' Rebecca said, though Laura couldn't see anything that needed excusing. 'I've been going through Harry's papers all week. The solicitors want everything organised for probate.'

'It looks lovely,' Laura assured her, settling into an armchair that had probably been chosen more for reading than impressing visitors. 'And your garden is charming.'

Rebecca's expression softened for the first time since Laura had met her.

'That was Harry's project. He said every home needed something growing – claimed it kept you connected to the seasons instead of just watching them pass by.'

Laura smiled at the sentiment.

'Sounds like something a security man would say. Always watching, always observing patterns.'

'They become part of who you are, don't they?' Rebecca moved to a cardboard box on the coffee table. 'These are Harry's personal effects. Everything the police returned, plus items from his study that seemed relevant to... well, to whatever was troubling him.'

The box contained the usual collection from a man's daily life; leather wallet, house keys, a mobile phone with a spiderweb of cracks across the screen, and a small notebook bound in soft brown leather that showed the patina of constant handling.

'The police said nothing was taken from his person,' Rebecca explained. 'Ruled out robbery straightaway.'

Laura picked up the phone first.

'This is locked with a fingerprint scanner, I assume?'

'Yes. The police claimed they couldn't access it without proper authorisation from the Home Office, you know, because of Harry's "other life" and all that.' Rebecca's tone suggested what she thought of bureaucratic hurdles. 'I didn't pursue it. If they couldn't manage it, what hope did I have?'

'Can I borrow this?' Laura made a mental note to ask Kyle about his tech-savvy friends at university; he'd introduced her once to someone who could regain entry to her iPad when she lost the password, so maybe he could help here.

'Of course,' Rebecca nodded, and Laura gained the impression she'd already expected this. The notebook drew her attention – battered leather, the sort her father had carried during his army years, though his had contained cricket scores rather than cryptic observations.

She flipped through pages of cramped handwriting.

Routine stuff mostly – appointments, bank reminders, notes about Rebecca's birthday dinner.

But then she found the odd entries.

TC expanding operations. M.W. confirms pattern shift.

New Tuesday operational – third in London Station. Previous assignment unknown. Monitor for protocol changes.

S.B. location compromised? Check alternative arrangements.

'S.B.,' Laura murmured. 'St. Bartholomew's?'

'You've found something?' Rebecca leaned forwards.

Laura indicated the entry.

'Could S.B. refer to St. Bartholomew's Church? That's where you said Harry collapsed.'

'It's possible,' Rebecca said, though she looked lost. 'Harry never mentioned the church specifically, but he'd been taking longer walks recently. Said he needed to think.'

Laura continued through the notebook, finding a series of entries that referenced days of the week in unusual contexts:

Monday relocating. Operational pause expected.

Thursday + Saturday working tandem again. Unusual pairing.

No confirmed Sunday sightings in five years. No replacement?

She looked up from the notebook.

'Did Harry ever mention anyone by the days of the week? Like calling someone "Monday" or "Tuesday"?'

'Never.' Rebecca shook her head. 'Though he did have that habit of speaking in code when he was working. Old habits from his army days, I suppose.'

Laura turned to the manila envelope from the box.

'The police report?'

'Medical examiner's findings too,' Rebecca confirmed.

Laura skimmed the documents. Odd timeline – first emergency call at three forty-five, but death estimated between three-thirty and five o'clock. Bit sloppy for a public death. Cause listed as cardiac arrest, natural causes, no mention of previous symptoms.

'Harry's family has no history of heart disease?' Laura asked.

'None. His father lived to be ninety-two. His mother is still alive at eighty-nine, sharp as a tack. Harry used to joke that he'd inherited the family's stubborn heart.'

Laura returned to the notebook, looking for the last entries. The last dated entry was from April 14th, the day before Harry died:

Meeting confirmed for tomorrow. Standard protocols in place. Package ready for transfer.

If compromise occurs, S might appear.

'Who's "S"?' Laura tapped the page.

'I've been wondering that myself,' Rebecca admitted. 'He knew several Stevens, a couple of Simons from his club. Could be a surname, I suppose.'

Laura continued examining the box's contents. Among the photographs, one made her stop – three men outside what looked like an embassy. The first was James, catching breath in her throat as she stared at his younger self, plus a sturdy man who must be Harry, and a third, slim fellow with dark hair. There was something familiar about him, though.

She turned the photo over, where written in neat handwriting was

James, Harry, and Sebastian. London 2003. The Three Musketeers ride again!

'Sebastian,' Laura whispered. 'That's our "S".'

'Who?' Rebecca asked, looking up from her own examination of Harry's wallet.

'This third man in the photo. He's identified as Sebastian.' Laura showed her the picture. 'Harry never mentioned a Sebastian to you?'

Rebecca studied the image, frowning slightly.

'No, never. Though...' she hesitated. 'There was something Harry said a few weeks before he died. About old friends you could trust in a crisis. Said some people never changed, even when everything else did.'

Laura set the photo aside carefully. Next, she found a church pamphlet tucked between the notebook's pages – St. Bartholomew the Great, with service times circled in pencil.

'Did Harry attend church regularly?'

'Not since I've known him. He was raised Catholic but hadn't been to Mass in decades. Said he'd seen too much to believe in divine intervention.'

Laura stared at the pamphlet. A document from the very

church beside where Harry had died – that couldn't be coincidence.

'Rebecca,' she said carefully, 'I'd like to visit St. Bartholomew's tomorrow. See where it happened. Would you like to come with me?'

'I...' Rebecca's composure wavered for the first time. 'I've been avoiding it. The police took me there once, just after, but I couldn't... I couldn't look at the place where he fell.'

'You don't have to come,' Laura said gently. 'But I think going there myself might help me understand what Harry was investigating.'

'No,' Rebecca said while shaking her head. 'I can't. But does this mean you'll help me?'

Rebecca's voice carried desperate hope.

Laura weighed everything – the photograph with James, cryptic notebook entries, dodgy police timeline, the mysterious "S" who might help "if needed".

'Yes,' she said finally. 'I'll help you. Though I must be clear – I'm not a detective. I'm simply... curious.'

Relief flooded Rebecca's face. 'That's all I ask.'

She hesitated, then went to a desk in the corner and returned with a sealed envelope.

'There's one more thing. This arrived yesterday morning. No postmark, no return address.'

Inside the envelope was a single sheet of heavyweight cream paper bearing a message in elegant script:

Mrs Farrell,

Your husband's affairs remain unresolved. I am endeavouring to address certain outstanding matters on his behalf. We should meet to discuss these for mutual benefit.

I will contact you again shortly.

With respectful condolences,

S

'"S" again,' Laura breathed.

'I found it pushed through my letterbox. Nobody saw who delivered it.'

'Have you received any other communications like this?'

'Just the email about the photograph.' Rebecca shook her head. 'Ten thousand pounds for evidence I can't even verify exists.'

Laura folded the note carefully.

'May I keep this? And borrow Harry's notebook?'

'Of course. Take whatever you think might help.' As Laura prepared to leave, Rebecca touched her arm gently. 'I want you to know, Harry wasn't paranoid. He was careful, methodical. If he believed he was in danger, there was a reason.'

Laura nodded.

'My husband was the same way. Some instincts you learn to trust.'

Rebecca walked Laura to the main door, but as she did so, passing a side table, Laura stopped, glancing down at a notepad. There was a note half-finished on it.

Buy milk
Feed the cat
Let Joanne know I'll be gone for a few days

'Was this Harry or you?' she asked. Rebecca looked down at the note and for a moment, Laura wondered if Rebecca had even realised the note existed, her eyes widening slightly as if revealing a secret that she wasn't supposed to have shown.

'No,' she said quickly. 'It's my writing, not Harry's. I was just... it started as a shopping list and a reminder for my next-door neighbour to look after the cat. I don't own one, but there's one that travels around a lot.'

Laura watched Rebecca as she seemed to start rambling, realising she had gone a bit too far. Rebecca took a deep breath.

'And the last part?'

'I'm going away for a few days,' Rebecca explained. 'That's all that means. I can't really stay here, but don't worry, I'll leave a mobile number for you, so if you find anything...'

Laura nodded understanding – she'd been where Rebecca was.

'Stay safe,' she said. 'I'll let you know if I find anything.'

BACK AT QUEEN'S GATE, LAURA SAT IN THE CONSERVATORY with Harry's notebook open before her. She'd spread the most intriguing items across the wicker table – the church pamphlet, the photograph, the police report, and the mysterious note from "S".'

'I hope whatever urgent business dragged you to Notting Hill was worth missing Mrs Pollington's committee meeting,' Aunt Celia said, arriving with the tea tray. 'She was positively tragic about you choosing actual life over her fundraising theatrics.'

'Mrs Pollington will survive,' Laura replied, accepting a cup of Earl Grey. 'This is from my visitor this morning –

Rebecca Farrell. There are compelling reasons to question the coroner's conclusion.'

'And those reasons have led you to transform our conservatory into an incident room?' Celia asked, settling into the opposite chair. 'How refreshingly Sherlockian of you.'

Laura gestured to the materials spread before them.

'Have a look for yourself.'

Celia picked up the police report, scanning it with a lawyer's eye.

'These medical conclusions look rather hasty.'

'Harry Farrell was in excellent health, with no family history of heart problems,' Laura confirmed.

Celia looked at the photograph.

'Good heavens, is that James? Rather dashing in his younger days.'

'Taken in 2003. That's James, that's Harry Farrell, and the third man is identified as Sebastian.'

'Sebastian,' Celia repeated thoughtfully. 'No surname?'

'Not on the photo. But there are references in Harry's notebook to someone identified only as "S". Including an entry suggesting that "S might be able to help" if something went wrong.'

'And what are these peculiar notations about days of the week?'

Laura pointed to the relevant entries.

'See here – "New Tuesday operational." And here – "Thursday and Friday working tandem again." Some kind of code, perhaps.'

'Monday's child is fair of face, Tuesday's child is full of grace,' Celia recited softly. 'The old nursery rhyme. Are you suggesting these people are using days of the week as operational names?'

'It seems fanciful, but...' Laura shrugged. 'Intelligence work often is. Either they name themselves that, or maybe Harry used these as code names for his own ease?'

'No more fanciful than a supposedly healthy man dropping dead after arranging a mysterious meeting,' Celia pointed out, examining the church pamphlet. 'St. Bartholomew the Great. Medieval, isn't it? Rather atmospheric for clandestine activities.'

'I'm planning to visit tomorrow.'

'Of course you are.' Celia studied her niece with undisguised approval. 'This is the most alive I've seen you in years. You've got that gleam back – the one you used to get when James brought home his more interesting puzzles.'

The front door slammed, announcing Kyle's return. He appeared in the conservatory doorway, took one look at the spread of evidence, and grinned.

'Brilliant! You've started a proper investigation!' He dropped his messenger bag and examined the materials with academic interest. 'Is this the evidence? Can I help organise it? Every good detective needs a system.'

'I'm not exactly a detective,' Laura protested mildly.

'Course you are. You've got suspects, motives, evidence – classic investigative work.' Kyle was already planning. 'We need a proper investigation board. Crime-show style, with photos and string. I've got coloured cards upstairs. And red wool.'

'Why on earth do you have red wool?' Celia asked with genuine curiosity.

Kyle grinned.

'Remember that Manchester United scarf you knitted for Christmas? I may have... unravelled it during exam revision. Stress response.'

'You destroyed three weeks of my work?' Celia's voice could have frozen champagne.

'I was having a crisis! Besides, I know you paid Mrs Patterson to knit it, anyway.'

'How did you...' Celia glared at Laura. 'You told him.'

'Came up in conversation.'

The doorbell interrupted their bickering. Kyle answered it, returning with a small package a minute later.

'Courier,' he announced. 'No return address.'

The package was addressed to *Mrs Laura Carlyle, Queen's Gate*. Inside was a white card.

Mrs Carlyle,

Your interest in Harry's affairs has been noted. I wish you luck.

S

'"S" again,' Celia observed. 'Your mysterious Sebastian? Maybe he wants to team up?'

'Let's be careful about speculation,' Laura replied. 'I'd like to know more about our mysterious correspondent first.'

'Sensible,' Celia agreed. 'Though your curiosity usually wins in the end.'

LATER, LAURA STOOD IN THE SPARE ROOM KYLE HAD designated their "investigation headquarters". He'd organised everything efficiently: photos pinned to a cork board, notebook entries on index cards, red wool connecting related items.

'Much better than scattered papers,' Kyle said, admiring his work. 'Now you can see the connections.'

Laura had to admit the display helped. Monday appeared far more often in Harry's notes than other days. His concern had escalated in his last weeks. He'd documented observations without ever being explicit about what he was investigating.

'Good work,' she told Kyle.

'Tomorrow we hit St. Bartholomew's,' Kyle announced. 'Can I come? I'll be helpful. Won't touch anything crucial.'

'We'll see.'

With Kyle wandering off to finish a piece for his class, Laura returned to the board. Harry had directed Rebecca to her for a reason. She intended to honour that by finding the truth – even if it led somewhere more complex than orchid sabotage at the garden society.

Tomorrow she'd visit the church where Harry died. She'd search for answers to his cryptic questions.

Tonight, though, she stood in the quiet room, looking at Kyle's web of connections, wondering what James would have made of it all.

Would he have recognised the names? Known about these day operatives?

Outside, London settled into evening. Somewhere in the city, the mysterious Sebastian was going about his business.

Harry Farrell deserved justice.

Rebecca deserved answers.

Laura would provide both.

4

CONFESSIONAL

St. Bartholomew the Great had survived Henry VIII's dissolution of the monasteries, the Great Fire, the Blitz, and countless property developers with varying degrees of architectural sensitivity. This morning it looked entirely capable of surviving one more curious widow poking about for clues.

Laura paused in the small courtyard, comparing Harry's notebook to the church pamphlet Rebecca had shown her. The building was genuinely ancient – proper Norman stone rather than the Victorian Gothic revival that passed for medieval in most of London. She'd dressed sensibly for what she'd privately begun thinking of as detective work: comfortable shoes, a jacket with decent pockets, and her pearl earrings, because one didn't abandon standards simply because one was investigating a potential murder. Though she was suspecting she looked rather too much like Miss Marple for her own comfort.

The pamphlet described the church as *"London's most magnificent surviving Norman interior,"* which was the sort of hyperbole that made Laura wonder if the author had ever actually visited London. Still, it was impressive enough, and according to the police report, Harry had collapsed just outside on Cloth Fair.

She'd walked the length of that narrow street twice this morning, noting its mix of quaint medieval remnants and aggressively modern businesses. A small bunch of withered daffodils tied to a lamppost about halfway down suggested where Harry had fallen. Very British – mark a potential crime scene with flowers and carry on with daily life.

The location offered clear views in both directions, plus easy access to the church if one needed sanctuary. James would have approved of the tactical positioning. He'd always had an eye for places that offered what he called "conversational privacy with escape options". She also took note of the varied CCTV cameras along the opposite street – *could one of these have seen the moment of Harry's death?*

Inside, the church was properly cool and atmospheric. A few tourists wandered about with that peculiar intensity of people determined to appreciate culture whether it killed them or not, so Laura drifted through the nave, letting her fingertips brush the ancient stone. She'd never been particularly religious, but old churches had a way of making you think someone was watching, where centuries of whispered prayers seemed to have seeped into the very walls.

Near the Lady Chapel, she noticed a solitary figure seated in a side pew – a distinguished gentleman in an immaculate charcoal pinstripe suit. His silver hair was perfectly styled, and despite being indoors, he wore a trilby hat at a slight angle. A walking cane with an ornate silver head rested against the pew beside him.

Laura's pulse quickened slightly. The silver-haired man both she and Mrs Reynolds had spotted outside her house –

the one she'd rather embarrassingly described as a modern-day Pierce Brosnan. Here, of all places, connected to Harry Farrell's death.

Well, that settled it. Coincidences came in pairs at most, never triplets.

He appeared utterly absorbed in contemplation, head slightly bowed, but Laura wasn't fooled for a moment. Men like that – men who reminded her of James's more interesting colleagues – were never truly unaware of their surroundings.

Weighing caution against curiosity, Laura chose the latter. She went to slide into the same pew, of course leaving a polite British distance between them, while pretending interest in the memorial plaque on the opposite wall—

'Looking for something specific, dear?'

The cheerful voice made Laura turn to find a rosy-cheeked elderly man in a volunteer sash beaming at her. His badge read "Geoffrey" in optimistic blue lettering.

'Just admiring the architecture,' Laura replied with a smile. 'First visit, I'm afraid.'

'One of London's best-kept secrets,' Geoffrey confided, as if sharing classified intelligence. 'Most people know the name from the hospital, never realising this magnificent church is tucked away here.'

'I didn't know there were two St. Bartholomews,' Laura admitted.

'Oh yes! The Lesser served the hospital, whilst the Great was for the priory,' Geoffrey warmed to his subject like a man who'd been waiting all morning for someone to ask. 'During the Reformation, this nave became a blacksmith's forge, if you can imagine. Markets, workshops, even a printing house at one point. The history in these stones!'

Laura made appropriately impressed noises, genuinely charmed by his enthusiasm.

'Has the church always welcomed visitors like this?'

'For centuries, though not always for worship,' Geoffrey gestured towards the far end of the church. 'The Prior's Chapel is worth a look – lovely fan vaulting. Though I suppose you're more interested in the quieter spots for contemplation.'

Laura thanked him warmly, making a mental note to drop something substantial in his donation box before leaving. She'd always had a soft spot for enthusiastic volunteers who actually knew their subject.

She felt a little silly moving into the pew now, and as she debated whether to do so or make her way towards the north transept, the silver-haired gentleman spoke without looking up from his apparent prayers.

'The memorial to Sir Walter Richmond is rather more impressive in the south transept,' he said conversationally, his voice a rich baritone. 'The Victorian interpretation of medieval grief is always so... enthusiastic.'

He hadn't turned to look at her, yet Laura knew with absolute certainty he was speaking to her.

'I find I'm less interested in Victorian memorials,' she replied evenly, 'than in the remarkable tendency of certain gentlemen to appear precisely where I happen to be.'

Now he turned, his grey eyes crinkling at the corners as he regarded her with undisguised interest.

'The universe rarely bothers with coincidence, Mrs Carlyle. Particularly when it comes to matters of consequence.'

'You know my name,' Laura observed. 'How refreshingly unsurprising.'

'Sebastian Silver,' he offered, extending a hand. 'And yes, we do have mutual acquaintances.'

'Harry Farrell,' Laura said, accepting the handshake. His grip was firm but not overbearing, his hand warm despite the church's chill.

'Among others,' Silver replied. He retrieved his cane and stood, adjusting his trilby with what seemed like careful precision – as if the gesture were more significant than mere habit. 'Perhaps we might walk? These pews were designed for discomfort. Medieval architects understood that physical suffering enhanced spiritual devotion.'

'You seem to have rather strong opinions about medieval architecture, Mister Silver.'

'I find historical perspective helpful when dealing with human nature,' he replied, leading her towards a less populated section of the church. His cane tapped rhythmically against the ancient stones, though he showed no signs of actually needing it for support. 'Medieval folk understood that people require both carrot and stick.'

They passed a small side chapel where a solitary candle flickered. Silver paused, studying the flame for a moment before continuing.

'You're following Harry's death,' he said matter-of-factly.

'You seem remarkably well-informed about my life,' Laura noted. 'Maybe because you've been standing outside my house?'

'Information has always been my particular currency,' Silver replied, blatantly ignoring the accusation. 'Though unlike actual money, its value fluctuates wildly depending on interpretation.'

'Like interpreting a man's death as natural causes when it wasn't?' Laura suggested.

Sebastian Silver's pace slowed slightly, his cane missing its usual rhythm for just a moment.

'Precisely.'

They had reached a small chapel tucked away from the main flow of tourists. Afternoon sunlight filtered through a stained-glass window, casting coloured shadows across the worn stone floor. Silver rested his cane against a step and turned to face her properly.

'Harry Farrell was murdered, Mrs Carlyle,' he said, his voice remaining conversational, as if discussing nothing more consequential than the weather. 'I imagine you've already reached that conclusion from what Rebecca told you.'

'I've noticed certain inconsistencies in the official account,' Laura acknowledged, observing his face.

'Inconsistencies,' Silver echoed, the word carrying a hint of amusement. 'How diplomatically phrased. James would approve.'

The casual reference to James was clearly deliberate.

'Yes, I thought it was you,' she replied, forcing herself to come across as calm as he did. 'I recognised you from the photograph with James and Harry. Though you've aged rather better than they did.'

'Time affects people differently,' Silver said, his voice gentler now. 'James was an exceptional man.'

'In many ways,' Laura agreed. 'Now, perhaps you might tell me why you've been watching my house, Mister Silver? And why you're here, in the very church connected to Harry's death?'

Sebastian Silver adjusted his trilby again – clearly a nervous habit rather than vanity.

'Direct questions. Another of James's qualities.'

'You've yet to answer any of them.'

'Fair enough.' Silver settled back, leaning onto a nearby pew, though his posture remained alert. 'I'm here because this is where things began to unravel, and because I suspected you would come here eventually. As for watching your house – a precaution, nothing more. Harry's death has stirred up a hornet's nest, and I wanted to ensure you weren't stung before we had a chance to speak.'

'Who exactly are these hornets?'

'People who prefer that certain truths remain buried,' Silver replied. 'Along with those who uncover them.'

'You're "S" from Harry's notebook,' Laura said. It wasn't a question.

Silver inclined his head slightly.

'In certain contexts, yes.'

'And what context are we in now?' Laura glanced pointedly at his trilby. 'And do you always keep your hat on in church?'

A smile transformed his face, making him look years younger and lending credence to Mrs Reynolds's Pierce Brosnan comparison.

'Old habits, Mrs Carlyle. I find I'm not quite myself without it.' He patted the trilby with obvious affection. 'As for our context – consider this a potential partnership. Harry believed you could be trusted, and that's recommendation enough for me.'

'I barely knew Harry,' Laura pointed out.

'Sometimes the briefest connections prove the most consequential,' Silver adjusted his cane, the silver head catching a ray of coloured light. 'What matters is that Harry recognised certain qualities in you – discretion, intelligence, and connections independent of official channels.'

'Official channels that might be compromised,' Laura suggested, thinking of the notebook entries.

'You've been studying his notebook thoroughly, then. Interesting. I'd worried they'd taken that. What else have you discerned?'

Laura hesitated, reluctant to reveal everything she'd pieced together, and curious who the "they" were, but then decided to continue on.

'References to days of the week as designations for people. Mentions of "TC" – an organisation of some sort, I presume.'

'The Calendar,' Silver supplied quietly, his voice dropping to a murmur though no one was nearby. 'A private intelligence network operating across multiple countries, using the days of the week as operational designations.'

The matter-of-fact confirmation was somehow more unsettling than dramatic revelation would have been.

'You're surprisingly forthcoming with someone you've just met.'

'Time is a luxury I've wasted,' Silver replied. 'I believe Harry was killed because he was building evidence that could demolish The Calendar's operations. Evidence that I've realised is now in circulation and potentially dangerous.'

'The package mentioned in his notebook,' Laura concluded.

'Precisely. Harry intended to pass critical information to a trusted source – the meeting he'd arranged for the day he died.'

'Here at St. Bartholomew's?'

'That I'm not sure,' Silver corrected. 'I do know, however, that the church was his contingency location.'

'Because the primary meeting place was compromised?' Laura realised, pieces falling into place.

'Most likely, if he'd arrived here. Which suggests someone who knew Harry's movements and security protocols.'

'Someone from this Calendar organisation?'

'Perhaps. But if it was, it'd likely be a Weekday operative,' Silver confirmed. 'Monday through Saturday, each with specific operational roles, an almost military-style hierarchical rank, according to Harry. He'd been monitoring their activities for years.'

It sounded like the plot of a particularly outlandish spy novel, yet Laura found herself believing it. Harry's meticulous notes, the cryptic day references, the careful observations recorded over months – all suggested a man documenting something very real and very dangerous.

'You act like this is news to you, too?'

'It's more a case of things I may have forgotten in the mists of time,' Silver replied, a little too casually. 'It's always better when someone can confirm half-remembered truths, don't you think?'

'Why tell me all this?' she asked, genuinely curious. 'I'm hardly qualified for intelligence work.'

Sebastian Silver looked at her carefully, his grey eyes unreadable in the chapel's dim light.

'Because Harry's final insurance policy is now in motion, and you're part of it whether you choose to be or not.'

The implications sent a distinctly unpleasant chill through Laura.

'Are you saying I'm in danger? That my family might be at risk?'

'I'm suggesting,' Silver said delicately, 'that your interest in Harry Farrell's death has been noted by people who prefer their activities to remain unscrutinised.'

'Including you? What exactly is your stake in this, Mister Silver?'

Silver straightened, his hand moving to his trilby again in that characteristic gesture.

'Let's just say I have personal reasons for wanting The Calendar's activities curtailed.'

He glanced at his watch – a vintage timepiece on a worn leather strap.

'I've taken enough of your time today, Mrs Carlyle. You'll need to contemplate your next steps.'

He reached into his jacket pocket and withdrew a small silver case, opening it to reveal a collection of eggshell-coloured business cards. The one he offered Laura bore only a stylised "S" and a mobile number engraved in elegant script.

'Should you decide to continue what Harry started, you can reach me at this number,' he said. 'Day or night.'

Laura accepted the card, surprised by its substantial weight and quality.

'And if I decide to take this matter to the police instead?'

Sebastian Silver's lips curved in a smile that didn't quite reach his eyes.

'Then I imagine we'll see Harry's convenient heart condition brought forward as a new gospel, while the police, as ever, do nothing.'

He stretched as he moved from his leaning position, retrieving his cane.

'The authorities have their place, but this situation requires a more... nuanced approach. Good day, Mrs Carlyle. I suspect we'll speak again soon.'

With a slight bow that seemed to belong to another century entirely, Sebastian Silver turned and walked away, the silver tip of his cane tapping a gentle rhythm against the ancient stones as he disappeared through a side door.

Laura remained in the small chapel, turning the business card between her fingers. Yesterday morning, her greatest concerns had been Mrs Pollington's charity auction and whether the east garden hydrangeas needed repotting, following her aunt's constant nagging. Now she sat in a medieval church with a cryptic business card, having just discussed international spy networks with a silver-haired man who wore his trilby indoors and seemed to know far more about her husband than any stranger should. A week ago, she'd have dismissed it all as preposterous. Yet something about Sebastian Silver's matter-of-fact delivery made the fantastical seem plausible.

The Calendar. Weekday operatives. Harry Farrell murdered in broad daylight on a London street.

Laura tucked the card carefully into her handbag. As she made her way back through the church, she dropped a ten-pound note into Geoffrey's donation box and smiled at the elderly volunteer's cheerful thanks.

OUTSIDE, SPRING SUNSHINE BATHED SMITHFIELD IN GOLDEN light. Tourists meandered along the cobblestones, a young mother navigated a pushchair past ancient walls, and two businessmen argued good-naturedly about a football match as they passed. Normal life continued all around her, oblivious to the shadowy currents flowing beneath its surface.

James would have found the whole situation irresistible, Laura thought with a bittersweet pang. He'd always had a weakness for puzzles and intrigues, particularly ones that couldn't be solved through official channels. Perhaps that adventurous spirit had been what drew him to her in the first place – recognising a kindred soul beneath her proper diplomatic exterior.

She paused at the lamppost with its withered daffodils, marking the spot where Harry Farrell had drawn his last breath. Whatever had happened here, whatever secrets people were willing to kill to protect, Rebecca deserved to know the truth.

Laura Carlyle straightened her shoulders and began the walk back towards the Underground, already mentally composing the list of questions she would need to answer next.

There were rather a lot of them.

5

NEW SCOTLAND YARD

'You've been remarkably busy for someone who was supposedly attending the Kensington Gardens Society meeting this morning,' Detective Chief Inspector Frank Young observed as Laura was shown into his office at New Scotland Yard.

Laura smiled, not particularly surprised that her old friend had kept tabs on her movements. 'The peonies will have to manage without my input today, I'm afraid.'

'Visiting ancient churches instead?' Frank leaned back in his chair, studying her with the mixture of amusement and concern she remembered from their younger days. 'St. Bartholomew the Great is a bit off your usual circuit, isn't it?'

'You've been having me followed, Frank?' Laura asked, raising an eyebrow.

'Nothing so dramatic,' he replied with a dismissive wave. 'Sergeant O'Malley goes there before his shift and mentioned seeing you there this morning. Pure coincidence.'

Laura wasn't entirely convinced, but she let it pass – O'Malley knew her well enough to recognise her, but it still felt convenient. She'd known Frank Young for over thirty years, first through James's work and later as a friend in her own right. They'd met at a particularly tedious embassy reception in 1998 – Frank had been a young detective constable then, assigned to security detail, whilst James was still climbing the diplomatic ladder. She remembered Frank rescuing her from a conversation with the Belgian cultural attaché about his collection of medieval doorknockers.

After James's death, Frank had been a steady, unobtrusive presence – checking in regularly, making himself available without being intrusive in her grief. He'd helped with the practical matters that suddenly seemed overwhelming: insurance forms, pension paperwork, the sort of bureaucratic details that grief made impossible to focus on. In recent years, their relationship had settled into a comfortable pattern of occasional dinners and gallery openings, with an undercurrent of potential that neither seemed eager to explore further, but this had created a kind of "older brother protector" mode in Frank, which could extend to asking his officers to watch out for her.

No. That was paranoia.

It was only paranoia if you were wrong.

'You know,' Frank said, a slight smile playing at his lips, 'James always said you were wasted as a diplomatic wife.'

'James had a romantic view of my capabilities,' Laura replied, though she felt pleased by the observation.

'Did he? I remember him telling me about that business in Prague – when you worked out that the trade minister's assistant was selling information to the competition. James was convinced the leak was coming from their own delegation until you pointed out the timing patterns.'

Laura smiled at the memory.

'That was hardly detective work. Just observation.'

'James didn't think so.' Frank's expression grew more serious. 'He also said you'd have made an excellent intelligence officer if you'd been bothered about that sort of thing.'

Laura simply smiled back in response.

'So,' Frank said, gesturing for her to sit, 'what brings you to my office on a Tuesday afternoon? Not another charity auction hoping for police participation, I hope. The Commissioner is still recovering from the Karaoke Night Incident.'

'Nothing so traumatic,' Laura assured him, taking the offered seat. 'I wanted to ask you about a death that occurred last month. Harry Farrell. American, collapsed near St. Bartholomew's Church on April 15th.'

'Why the interest?' Frank's expression shifted subtly, the affable friend retreating behind the professional detective.

'His widow came to see me yesterday. She has concerns about the official finding of natural causes.'

'And she sought you out specifically?'

'Apparently Harry mentioned me as someone who might help if anything happened to him.'

Frank's eyebrows rose.

'Did you know him well?'

'I'm not sure I knew him at all,' Laura admitted. 'Though it appears he knew James at some point.'

'Ah.'

That single syllable contained volumes of understanding. Both of them knew well that James's diplomatic work had occasionally intersected with more classified areas. Laura had never pried – partly from discretion, partly because she'd understood instinctively that some knowledge was more burden than privilege. But she'd noticed things over the years: the colleagues who visited but never stayed long, the phone calls James took in his study with the door closed, the way certain conversations stopped when she entered a room.

'James did liaison work, didn't he?' she softened. 'More than just trade negotiations and cultural exchanges.'

Frank nodded slowly.

'Your husband was good at building bridges between different... departments. The sort of person who could speak to anyone and be trusted by everyone. That's a rare skill in the intelligence world.'

'Is that how he knew Harry?'

'I'd imagine so. The 2000s were complicated times – everyone was still adjusting to new threats, nine-eleven had just happened, there were new ways of working. Men like James, and I suppose this Harry were valuable because they could navigate between official and unofficial channels,' Frank said gently. 'James protected you from a lot, Laura, but he also trusted you. I remember him saying once that you were the only person who could know what he did without trying to change him or stop him.'

The observation touched something deep inside her – a recognition of the woman she'd been before grief had narrowed her world to safe, manageable concerns.

'He said that?'

'More than once. After a few drinks, usually, when he was proud of you for something.' Frank's smile was fond. 'Like when you organised that charity event for refugees and somehow got three competing NGOs to work together. Or when you convinced the Romanian ambassador's wife to stop spreading gossip about the German delegation by appealing to her sense of historical irony.'

'I'd forgotten about that.'

'James hadn't. He said you understood people in a way

that most intelligence professionals never managed – not their weaknesses, but their motivations. Their hopes...' Frank paused, as if realising he'd laid it on a little too thick.

'And what exactly do I hope to accomplish here, Frank?' Laura asked, echoing his earlier question. She opened her handbag and withdrew the photograph of James, Harry, and Sebastian, sliding it across the desk. 'I'd like to understand why a man I barely remember would direct his widow to me after his death. And why this photograph exists showing him with James and a third man named Sebastian who just happened to approach me in St. Bartholomew's this morning.'

Frank studied the photograph, his expression thoughtful.

'This was taken when?'

'2003, according to the note on the back.'

'That would fit the timeline,' Frank murmured. 'James was doing a lot of inter-departmental work around then. As I said, post-Twin Towers, everyone was scrambling to improve information sharing between agencies. And this Sebastian – you say he approached you today?'

'Sebastian Silver,' Laura confirmed. 'Distinguished, silver-haired, carries a walking cane with a silver head. Seemed to know quite a lot about Harry's death and about me.'

Frank studied the photograph more carefully, focusing on the third man.

'You know, there is something familiar about him. The stance maybe, or the way he's positioned himself slightly apart from James and Harry. Professional habit.' He looked up at Laura. 'Did James ever mention working with freelance consultants? People who weren't officially part of any government department?'

'Occasionally. He called them "specialists." Said sometimes you needed people who could operate outside normal channels.'

'That could explain this Sebastian Silver,' Frank said. His face revealed nothing, but Laura had known him long enough to recognise the slight tension in his jaw – a tell that something had struck a chord.

'Frank,' she breathed, 'what do you know about Harry Farrell's death?'

'The official report lists cardiac arrest as the cause of death. Natural causes. No suspicious circumstances.'

'Yet you don't sound entirely convinced.'

Frank sighed, setting down his mug of coffee.

'Between us? The timeline never sat right with me. Witness statements were vague, medical examiner seemed rushed. But the American embassy made it clear they considered the matter closed, and there was pressure from above to process it quickly and move on.'

'Pressure from whom, exactly?'

'That I don't know,' Frank admitted. 'But I didn't need to ask around. You see, when certain departments ask about expediting a case, experienced officers learn not to ask too many questions.'

Laura nodded, understanding perfectly. The shadowy intersection of police work and intelligence services had been a recurring theme in James's career. And even though Frank had been a friend of James, Harry Farrell was obviously a stranger to him.

'Do you have anything concrete that contradicts the official finding?' Frank asked.

Laura hesitated, weighing how much to reveal.

'Possibly. Harry kept a notebook with entries suggesting he was investigating something called "The Calendar" –

apparently an intelligence network using days of the week as code names for operatives.'

To her surprise, Frank didn't dismiss this as fanciful. Instead, his expression grew more serious.

'Laura, I say this as someone who cares about you. Be very careful in pursuing this further. If what you're suggesting is true, you could be stepping into something far more dangerous than a widow's doubts about her husband's death.'

'You've heard of this Calendar organisation?'

'I've heard rumours,' Frank said carefully. 'Whispers about private intelligence operations that slip between the cracks of official oversight. Nothing concrete enough to investigate officially.'

'And unofficially?'

A ghost of a smile touched Frank's lips.

'There's a reason some case files never quite make it to the archives.'

Laura couldn't help but return the smile. Despite his conventional career path, Frank had always maintained a healthy scepticism about institutional infallibility.

'What about Sebastian Silver?' she asked. 'Does that name mean anything to you?'

'It might. I'd need to check some records. Laura, what exactly are you planning to do with all this?'

'I'm not entirely sure,' she admitted. 'Help Rebecca Farrell understand what happened to her husband, if I can. Beyond that...' she shrugged slightly. 'I suppose it depends on what I find.'

Frank leaned back, studying her with an expression she couldn't quite read.

'You've changed,' he said finally. 'There's something different about you today.'

'Is there?'

'You remind me of how you were when James was alive. That same spark in your eyes when you'd get hold of something interesting.' He smiled, though there was a hint of sadness in it. 'It suits you.'

Laura felt a sudden, unexpected warmth at the observation.

'Thank you, Frank.'

He nodded, then glanced at his watch.

'I'm afraid I've got a meeting in ten minutes. Budget reviews – the glamorous side of police work.'

'Of course.' Laura rose, gathering her handbag. 'Thank you for seeing me on such short notice.'

'Any time.' Frank stood as well, coming around the desk to walk her to the door. 'But listen, Laura...' he hesitated, uncharacteristically serious. 'If you're going to pursue this, be careful. And keep me informed. Please.'

The concern in his voice was genuine, and Laura felt a twinge of guilt for potentially drawing him into something complicated.

'I will.'

'This Sebastian Silver. Did he say what he wanted from you?'

'He suggested a "potential partnership". Said Harry had evidence that could destroy this Calendar group, and that the evidence is now "in circulation".'

'And did Harry's widow mention any such evidence?'

'Only that someone has contacted her claiming to have a photograph showing Harry's death wasn't natural. They want ten thousand pounds for it.'

'That sounds like simple extortion.'

'Perhaps,' Laura agreed. 'Or perhaps the photograph actually shows something significant.'

'Either way, it doesn't explain why this Sebastian character is involving himself – or involving you, for that matter.'

'No,' Laura said thoughtfully. 'That remains something of a mystery.'

Frank regarded her for a moment longer, then shook his head with a rueful smile.

'You're going to pursue this regardless of what I say, aren't you?'

'I'm merely satisfying my curiosity,' Laura replied, unable to entirely suppress a smile of her own.

'That's what I was afraid of.' Frank opened the door. 'Call me if you need anything. And Laura? Watch your back. If there's any truth to what you've told me, these aren't people who appreciate amateur investigations.'

THE WARNING FOLLOWED LAURA AS SHE MADE HER WAY OUT OF New Scotland Yard and into the bright spring afternoon.

Amateur investigation.

The phrase should have felt like a criticism, yet somehow it carried a hint of validation. Her inquiries had graduated from idle curiosity to something Frank Young, veteran detective, considered worthy of caution.

As she crossed the street, Laura felt a prickling awareness between her shoulder blades – the distinct sensation of being watched. She resisted the urge to look back, instead using the reflection in a shop window to casually scan the street behind her.

Nothing immediately suspicious caught her eye, yet the feeling persisted. Perhaps Frank's warning had simply made her paranoid. Or perhaps she was indeed taking steps into a world where surveillance was commonplace and caution a necessity rather than a precaution.

Either way, Laura faced a decision point. She could return to Queen's Gate, to her committees and her gardening and her carefully ordered existence. She could politely inform Rebecca Farrell that the matter was best left to the authorities, despite their apparent lack of interest.

Or, she could pursue the threads that had been laid before her – Harry's cryptic notebook, Sebastian Silver's warnings, the photograph showing James's connection to both men.

As she hailed a taxi, Laura realised the decision had already been made. In the past twenty-four hours, something had changed in her – a sense of purpose, a clarity of focus that had been absent for too long.

'Electronic Zone, Tottenham Court Road,' she told the driver, thinking of Raj, Kyle's tech-savvy friend who worked there. If anyone could help her access Harry's locked phone, it would be him.

As the taxi pulled away from the kerb, Laura glimpsed a black sedan pulling out to follow them. Coincidence, perhaps. Or confirmation that Frank's warning had been well-founded.

Either way, Laura thought as she settled back in her seat, *this investigation had just become considerably more interesting.*

6

ELECTRONIC EVIDENCE

Electronic Zone occupied a cramped storefront on Tottenham Court Road, wedged between a mobile phone repair shop and a café devoted to bubble tea. Garish advertisements covered the windows: gaming computers, security systems, dubious software at "unbeatable prices."

A digital pawnshop, Laura thought, as the taxi pulled away. *No sign of that black sedan from earlier. Good.*

A bell jangled as she entered. Glass cabinets lined the walls, packed with electronic devices; the centre was pure chaos – shelving units crammed with cables, adaptors, and components she couldn't identify, while the air carried solder and electronics dust, and that particular smell of heated metal and old circuits.

Behind the counter, a young man with electric-blue hair looked up from a tablet. His eyes widened when he saw Laura – her tailored coat and pearls marking her as distinctly wrong for this place.

'Can I help you?'

'I'm looking for Raj.'

'Is he in trouble?'

'No, not at all. Kyle Carlyle's his friend. I'm Kyle's grandmother.' She offered her hand. After a moment's hesitation, the other man shook it.

'Devin. Raj is out – dropping off a custom build. Back in five minutes, maybe?' He gestured towards a stained office chair by the tech bench. 'You can wait if you want.'

Laura picked her way through the electronics maze. The chair was ancient and scarily upholstered in a variety of mystery stains. She perched on the edge, not trusting whatever had created those marks.

From here she spotted two security cameras – one watching the door, another covering the counter. Modern digital systems, nothing like the antiquated setup she'd seen near St. Bartholomew's.

The church. Right. That's why she was here.

Laura pulled out Harry's mobile – cracked screen, fingerprint lock, and contents that might explain why he'd died – and stared down at it. She'd promised Rebecca she could access it, but now, facing the harsh reality of phone security, she felt less confident.

The door chimed, and a stocky young man entered, South Asian, carrying a messenger bag. He did some elaborate handshake with Devin, then spotted Laura.

'Mrs Carlyle?' he said, his London accent and surprise clear. 'Kyle said you might stop by, but I didn't expect...'

He caught himself.

Laura stood, extending her hand.

'A pensioner in a tech shop? I imagine I'm not typical.'

Raj grinned, revealing a gap between his front teeth.

'Not exactly. Kyle mentioned tech help? Something about a phone?'

Laura produced Harry's mobile.

'Fingerprint locked. I need the data.'

Raj examined it, professional interest replacing surprise.

'Not the latest iPhone, couple years old. Cracked screen's just cosmetic.' He looked up, suddenly wary. 'Is this your phone?'

'Belonged to a friend who died. His widow wants photos and contacts recovered before they wipe everything.'

Raj's expression softened.

'Sorry for your loss.' He turned the device over. 'Normally impossible without the fingerprint. Apple's security is solid – that's the point.'

'But?'

'But there might be a workaround.' He gestured towards the tech bench. 'How urgent? And how comfortable are you with... unofficial methods?'

'Very urgent. Completely comfortable.'

Raj's eyebrows shot up.

'Kyle said you were cool, but—' He shook his head, deciding not to continue the comment. 'Right. Let's see what I can do.'

He cleared space on the cluttered bench and connected the phone to a laptop. He typed quickly on the keyboard, launching programmes with unfamiliar interfaces, and a selection of code scrolled past as he sat back.

'Can't promise anything,' Raj warned. 'There's a vulnerability in this iOS version that might give us partial access. Not the full phone, but maybe some data.'

'Anything helps.'

Raj worked in silence, muttering technical terms. While he did this, Laura's attention drifted to the security cameras. They reminded her of something.

'Your shop does security systems too?'

'Hmm? Yeah, CCTV and alarms, mostly small businesses.' He stayed focused on the screen. 'Why?'

'I was near St. Bartholomew's Church yesterday, saw that one of the shops had cameras aimed at the street. How long do they typically keep footage?'

This got his attention.

'Depends. Most digital setups record over themselves every week or two, unless they archive specifically. Older systems might use physical media.'

'What if someone wanted footage from a few weeks back?'

Raj studied her.

'Might still exist, but you'd need the owner's permission. Data protection laws.' He paused. 'This isn't really about photos on a dead friend's phone, is it?'

'Not entirely.' Laura met his gaze.

Raj grinned.

'Kyle said you were getting into something interesting. Said not to ask questions, just help.' He turned back to his laptop. 'No luck with the phone yet, but maybe I can help with camera footage. Which shop?'

'Small electronics place across from St. Bartholomew's. On Cloth Fair.'

'EC Electronics. Old Nasir's place.' Raj knew it immediately. 'Been there forever, charges tourist prices. Tech community here isn't big – we all know each other from trade shows, and half the time someone's related to someone else.'

'You know the owner?'

'Sort of.' Raj tapped keys and sighed. 'Phone's going to take time. Different approach needed. Nasir might still have footage from a month ago, though. He runs an older system –

DVR-based, storing to hard drives. If he hasn't purged it manually, could still be there.'

'Would he let me see it?'

'Depends on why you want it.' Raj appraised her. 'Nasir's old-school. Doesn't do favours for strangers.'

'What if I were a potential customer? Looking at security systems for my home?'

'Might work, but he'd wonder why you came to his shop instead of somewhere closer to Kensington.'

'You know where I live?'

'Kyle talks about his gran's "massive place near Albert Hall" constantly. Plus your address isn't secret – the Carlyle Foundation is based there, right?'

'The Foundation has offices there.' Laura was impressed and slightly unnerved by how much this young man knew. Maybe her "digital footprint", as they say, was larger than she realised.

'Nasir might be more convinced if you had a professional along. Someone who could ask technical questions.'

'Someone like you?'

Raj's eyes lit up.

'I could take an early lunch. Devin can cover.'

Laura considered this, as having a technical expert would make her cover story convincing. And Raj seemed eager to help.

'When could you go?'

'Now?' Raj was already packing his messenger bag. 'The phone will take hours anyway – I've just started a brute force attempt.'

Laura didn't know what that meant, and if she was being honest, she wasn't sure if she wanted to know.

She still took the offer of help, though.

ABOUT HALF AN HOUR LATER, LAURA APPROACHED ST. Bartholomew's Church again, this time with Raj explaining facial recognition technology.

'The cutting-edge stuff can identify people even with masks on,' he said as they rounded the corner onto Cloth Fair. 'Uses gait analysis, body proportions. You think a pair of dark glasses hides your face, but the cameras literally see through the lenses.'

'Fascinating.' Laura's attention fixed on the shopfront across from the church. EC Electronics had the same cluttered look as Electronic Zone, but with faded respectability suggesting better days.

'That's Nasir's place,' Raj confirmed. 'What exactly are we looking for in this footage?'

Laura hesitated.

'A man who collapsed outside the church about a month ago. April 15th, around quarter to four.'

'The American bloke? Heart attack?'

'You heard about it?'

'Local news sites. Foreign national dies near tourist spot – gets coverage.' Raj studied her with fresh interest. 'Was he your friend? The one whose phone you're trying to unlock?'

'Yes. Harry Farrell. His widow has questions about his death.'

Raj nodded slowly.

'Like whether it was really a heart attack?'

'Precisely.'

'And you think the shop's cameras caught something the police missed?'

'Possible. The official investigation was rushed.'

Raj considered this, then shrugged.

'Let's see what we can find out.'

INSIDE EC ELECTRONICS, AN OLDER MAN SAT BEHIND THE counter, absorbed in a newspaper. He looked up as they entered, weathered face creasing in confusion.

'Yes? Can I help you?' He bore a Middle Eastern accent – Iraqi, Laura guessed.

Raj stepped forward.

'Mister Nasir? I'm Raj Patel from Electronic Zone. We met at Mandeep's wedding last year.'

Recognition dawned slowly.

'Ah, yes. The custom-build guy. What brings you here?'

'My client, Mrs Carlyle, wants to upgrade the security system at her estate, but doesn't trust the cloud,' Raj explained smoothly. 'I recommended a setup like yours – reliable, discreet, excellent image quality and storage. Thought you might show it?'

Nasir's gaze shifted to Laura, assessing her expensive coat and styled hair with a merchant's eye. Whatever calculation he made satisfied him.

'Of course. I have a professional-grade system. Very reliable. Ten years without failure.'

'Impressive,' Laura said. 'And the image quality? I understand digital systems have improved significantly, but the ones I look for seem to be of an older vintage.'

'The best. High definition, excellent in all lighting. Would you like a demonstration?'

'That would be helpful.'

Nasir led them behind the counter into a small office. A

monitor displayed four camera feeds – two showing the shop interior, one aimed at the doorway, one covering the street outside.

'Full coverage,' Nasir said proudly. 'All footage is stored automatically for sixty days on DVR drives before the system overwrites.'

'Sixty days?' Laura kept excitement from her voice. 'Exceptional capacity.'

'I upgraded storage last year. My colleagues thought it unnecessary, but I prefer thoroughness.'

'But what if I wanted to check something in particular?' Laura continued. 'Say I was worried a neighbour was deliberately allowing her dog to, well, you know, outside my door? Could I check a specific time and date?'

Nasir chuckled.

'I see why you want this now,' he said, and Laura gave a sheepish smile in response. If he wanted to think her a vapid socialite who only cared about small things, then she could reach into the "inner Pomeranian" of Rupert's new wife.

'Could I see archived footage quality? From a month ago, perhaps?'

Nasir hesitated.

'I suppose I could show a brief example. Any particular date?'

'The fifteenth?' Laura suggested casually. 'Mid-afternoon, to show performance in varying light?'

Nasir gave her an odd look but turned to the computer.

'Let me see.'

He navigated through the system whilst Laura exchanged glances with Raj, who gave a subtle encouraging nod.

'April fifteenth,' Nasir murmured, inputting the date. 'And the time?'

'Half past three to four? Maybe your outside camera, as that's what I'd have?'

Nasir entered the parameters, and the monitor switched to archived footage from the street camera. The image was clear, with St. Bartholomew's Church visible in the frame.

'How's the fast forward function?' Laura smiled. 'Say if I wanted to forward-wind past a usual dog-walking time?'

'It's a simple press of a button,' Nasir said and on the screen the footage played, showing ordinary pedestrian flow past the church. Laura leaned forward, eyes fixed on screen. At the timestamp 15:43, a familiar figure appeared – Harry Farrell, walking briskly along Cloth Fair.

She held her breath as Harry came into full view, watching him glance nervously over his shoulder. Behind him, a younger man in a black suit followed at a measured pace. Then from the left, another suited man stepped directly into Harry's path. They spoke briefly before the second man did something – but annoyingly, the camera angle was partially obscured. Harry staggered, clutched his chest, collapsed.

Thirty seconds. That's all it took.

'Oh my,' Nasir whispered. 'That's the American who died. I gave the police this footage, of course.'

He looked back at her, frowning.

'If this is some sick game—'

'Of course not,' Laura replied, mind racing. The footage clearly showed two men approaching Harry moments before his collapse. Whether it proved murder was debatable – the critical moment was partially hidden – but it contradicted the narrative of a simple heart attack.

'Mrs Carlyle?' Raj's voice broke her thoughts, concern evident. 'You all right?'

'Just surprised to witness such tragedy.' Laura gathered herself. 'Mister Nasir, I assume the police reviewed this footage thoroughly?'

Nasir shifted uncomfortably.

'They seemed satisfied. Though they didn't ask for copies, just viewed it here.'

'I see.' Laura considered carefully. 'Could I purchase a copy of this segment? It would help me evaluate the system's clarity.'

Nasir's discomfort increased visibly.

'I'm not sure that would be appropriate, given the circumstances.'

'I understand your concern, but I assure you, it's for technical evaluation only.'

'Perhaps,' Raj interjected, 'we could focus on a different segment? Something less sensitive?'

Nasir seemed relieved. 'Yes, better. Perhaps from earlier in the day?'

Laura recognised when to retreat.

'Of course. Whatever you recommend.'

As Nasir searched for innocuous footage, Laura noticed something curious – a gap in the time-stamped files. The system jumped from 15:47, just after Harry's collapse, to 16:05.

'Is it normal to have recording gaps?' she asked, pointing at the display.

Nasir frowned.

'No, unusual. The system should record continuously.'

'Could someone have deleted that segment?' Raj asked.

'Possible but it would require administrative access. I don't recall doing so.'

Laura and Raj exchanged glances, silent understanding passing between them.

'Mister Nasir,' Laura said carefully, 'when you showed police the footage, did they see the entire sequence, including what happened after that poor man collapsed?'

Nasir's expression grew troubled. 'I believe so. Yes, I'm certain I showed them everything I had.'

'Which apparently wasn't everything that happened,' Raj observed quietly.

The shop bell chimed – a customer. Nasir looked relieved at the interruption.

'Excuse me, I must attend to that. Omar!' No response. 'My assistant must be on break. Please, continue examining the system. I'll return shortly.'

As soon as he'd left, Raj turned to Laura.

'Someone deleted the footage showing what happened after your friend collapsed.'

'Yes, and I'd like to know who. And why.'

Raj glanced at the unattended computer.

'I might be able to recover it. These systems rarely delete data properly, just often remove it from the index.'

'How long would that take?'

'Longer than we have before he comes back. But I could return another time, maybe when he's not about? Omar owes me a favour; I got him a sick graphics chip last week.'

'Let's hold that as backup. For now, I want to find other witnesses to Harry's death. Did you notice the young couple who appeared before he collapsed?'

'Vaguely. They were taking photos?'

'Yes, and I'd like to find them.' Laura said. 'The camera showed they had come out of this shop before Harry collapsed. They might have been customers.'

Raj's eyes lit up.

'And shops keep transaction records. Credit card receipts, sales logs...'

'Exactly.'

When Nasir returned, apologising for the delay, Laura had refined her approach.

'Mister Nasir, your system is impressive,' she said warmly. 'But before deciding, I'd like to understand your customer experience. For example, the young couple in your shop just before that unfortunate incident – how did you handle customers who might have witnessed something traumatic?'

Nasir looked confused.

'I'm not sure I understand.'

'Professional ethics,' Raj supplied helpfully. 'Mrs Carlyle's estate hosts high-profile visitors. Discretion is paramount.'

'Ah, of course.' Nasir nodded, and Laura wondered if he'd taken the time out of the office to look her up, as there was no surprise to this comment. 'Well, in that case, I wasn't present. My assistant, Omar, handled their transaction. Tourists, I believe. The man was American. Bought a digital camera memory card.'

'Cash or credit?'

'Credit, I believe. All transactions are logged in the system.'

Laura feigned sudden recollection.

'Oh, that reminds me – my assistant mentioned a technical question about your point-of-sale integration with the security system. How does that work?'

As Nasir launched into a detailed explanation, directing his attention mainly to Raj, Laura casually glanced at the monitor still displaying the security footage interface. The timestamp from mid-April was visible, and beside it on the desktop, a small icon was labelled "Transaction Log".

Catching Raj's eye, she subtly showed the screen. He nodded almost imperceptibly before asking Nasir increasingly technical questions that drew him into a passionate discussion about system architecture.

Laura used the distraction to move closer to the computer. After a quick glance to confirm Nasir's attention remained diverted, she clicked the transaction log icon. A new, smaller window opened, displaying a spreadsheet of sales data, organised by date and time.

She quickly located April 15th and scanned down to the relevant timeframe. There – at 15:32, a transaction for a "SanDisk 64GB SD Card" paid for with a Visa card by one REVERE, DAVID.

Laura committed the name and the last four numbers of the card to memory just as Nasir turned back.

'Mrs Carlyle, would you prefer the four-camera or six-camera package for your building?' he asked, clearly trying to steer the conversation back to a potential sale.

'I'll need to consult with my security advisor before deciding,' Laura replied smoothly. 'Raj has given me much to consider. Thank you for your time and the demonstration, Mister Nasir. Most illuminating.'

OUTSIDE, AS THEY WALKED BACK TOWARDS THE UNDERGROUND station, Raj could barely contain his excitement.

'That was fully like spies! Did you get what you needed?'

'David Revere,' Laura confirmed. 'Paid by credit card at 15:32, just before Harry Farrell's death.'

'And I'm guessing your next step is to find this David Revere?'

'Precisely.' Laura smiled at the young man. 'You were remarkably helpful in there, Raj. Thank you.'

Raj waved away her thanks.

'Most fun I've had in ages. Kyle always said his gran was cool, but I thought he was exaggerating.'

As they reached the station, Laura paused.

'Would you let me know if you make progress with Harry's phone?'

'Of course. Though it might take time – these brute force attempts aren't quick.'

'I understand. And Raj—' Laura hesitated, then continued, 'Perhaps we could keep this between ourselves for now? I'd rather Kyle didn't worry.'

Raj's expression turned serious.

'Of course, Mrs Carlyle. Client confidentiality and all that.'

They parted ways, Raj returning to his shop whilst Laura descended into the underground, her mind already turning to her next step. She needed to identify David Revere more specifically and locate him – which meant another visit to Frank Young. As she waited for the train, she found herself checking the platform more carefully than usual, alert for anyone showing an undue interest in her movements.

Revere. The name might not have meant much these days, but it was an important name nevertheless; after all, it had been Paul Revere, a silversmith from Boston who had, according to the epic poem by Henry Wadsworth Longfellow, been the sole rider who alerted the colonies that "the British were coming", which led to the American War of Independence.

Independence1776@mailnet.com

Could David Revere be honouring his namesake in an email address that tried to blackmail Rebecca Farrell?

The morning's adventure had confirmed what Sebastian Silver had told her – Harry Farrell hadn't died of natural causes. Someone had killed him, and someone else had gone to considerable trouble to obscure the evidence. The question now was what had Harry discovered that made him dangerous enough to eliminate, and why had he directed his widow to Laura Carlyle, of all people, for help?

7

THE PHOTOGRAPH

'David Revere,' Frank Young said, squinting at his computer screen. 'Twenty-six years old, lives in Wharf Apartments, by the Thames in Battersea. No criminal record, not even a parking ticket.'

He glanced up at Laura with that familiar mix of exasperation and fondness she'd known for decades.

'Though given what you've told me, I suspect his worst crime might be questionable taste in photo locations.'

Laura smiled, cradling her coffee cup. The Portuguese bakery round the corner from the station had been Frank's weakness for as long as she'd known him – as well as several of Whitehall's finest – and the pastéis de nata she'd brought had vanished within moments of her arrival.

Some things never changed.

'You're making light of it, but I can tell you're concerned.'

Frank sighed, his chair creaking as he leaned back. The office was standard police issue – functional furniture, filing cabinets, and the inevitable stack of papers that seemed to breed overnight – but Frank had made it his own. To the side was a Manchester United mug, even though he didn't support them. Beside that were photos of his nieces and nephews and a potted plant that had survived years of neglect through sheer bloody-mindedness, much like its owner.

'Concerned doesn't begin to cover it. You've gone from charity galas to investigating possible murders in a week.' His expression softened. 'Though I'll admit, this version of Laura Carlyle feels more... authentic than the one I've seen these past years.'

'What do you mean?' Laura looked up sharply.

'Come on, Laura. You were always sharp as a tack, always three steps ahead of everyone else in the room. James knew it. I knew it. Then after he died, it was like you packed that part of yourself away.' He gestured vaguely. 'All those committees – they kept you busy but never challenged you.'

Laura bristled slightly at the comment.

'I was grieving.'

'For fifteen years?'

'Grief doesn't have an expiration date, Frank.'

'No, but it shouldn't become a permanent address either.'

Silence fell between them, weighted with decades of shared history.

Frank broke it first, scribbling David Revere's address on a Post-it note.

'I'm only doing this so you scratch this bloody itch you have, yeah?' he said as he finished writing. 'Promise me something, though. Whatever you find, bring it to me first. Not this Sebastian Silver, not Rebecca Farrell. Me.'

'I promise,' Laura replied, knowing even as she said it that circumstances might not allow her to keep that promise.

From Frank's expression, he knew it too.

'Will you be at the Harrington Gallery opening next week?'

The question caught her off-guard – a sudden return to their normal social rhythm.

'I'd planned to, yes.'

'Good.' A smile warmed his face. 'We can catch up properly. Without mysterious deaths looming over us.'

'I'd like that.'

OUTSIDE, SPRING SUNSHINE GAVE LONDON'S EDGES A GOLDEN quality. Laura took a moment to breathe it in, aware that her world had shifted in ways she was only beginning to understand. As she hailed a taxi and gave the Battersea address, Laura noticed a familiar black sedan across the street.

The coincidence had moved beyond unsettling into absurd territory.

She made a mental note of the partial plate she could see; the rest obscured by the car in front.

LK21

She didn't know what she was going to do with it, but it felt productive, either way.

THE JOURNEY TOOK FORTY MINUTES IN MID-AFTERNOON traffic, and as the taxi wound through streets beginning to bloom with spring flowers, Laura used the time to plan her approach. Arriving unannounced at a stranger's home required finesse, particularly when fishing for information about potential murder.

David Revere's building was one of those glass and steel developments that had sprouted along the Thames – modern, pristine, characterless. They all had sleek names like *The Riverview* or *The Monarch*, attempting to evoke luxury whilst disguising their essential sameness. This one was *The Wharf*, which at least had geographical accuracy.

The security door was propped open with a folded leaflet, a common sight in London buildings where convenience routinely trumped security – the chances were someone had popped down to the location where the bins were, and really didn't want to argue their way back in. Laura took the elevator to the fourth floor, where the corridor smelled of new carpet and last night's cooking.

Flat 29 was at the corridor's end. Laura adjusted her jacket, checked her reflection, and knocked firmly. She didn't have any form of official ID, just a business card from the Carlyle Foundation. She hoped it'd be enough.

A young woman answered – late twenties, or maybe a young-looking thirties, with that carefully cultivated "effortless" appearance Laura recognised from her daughter, one that often took considerable effort to achieve. Strawberry-blonde hair artfully tousled, minimal makeup applied to appear natural.

'Yes?' A slight Eastern European accent, consciously softened.

'Good morning. I'm Laura Carlyle from the St. Bartholomew's Neighbourhood Safety Initiative' Laura said with a smile, showing the card briefly, too briefly to read clearly, before placing it back in her pocket. I'm looking for David Revere. Are you his wife?'

The young woman's expression shifted subtly – wariness entering her eyes like a cat spotting movement.

'No, I'm Louise Richards. David Revere is my partner. He's inside. What's this about?'

'We're interviewing with people who frequently visit the Smithfield area,' Laura explained, injecting her voice with the tone she used in persuading reluctant donors. 'There have been several incidents recently, and we're gathering information to improve safety measures.'

Louise hesitated, weighing options.

'We don't visit that often. Just occasionally.'

She went to close the door, but Laura leaned closer.

'Your perspective would still be valuable. Won't take more than a couple of minutes.'

Louise's hand tightened on the door.

'Who did you say you were with again?'

Before Laura could respond, a male voice called from inside.

'Who is it, Lou?'

'Someone from a safety group. About Smithfield.'

A young man appeared behind Louise – tall, with boyish good looks suggesting rugby captaincy and easy university popularity. Brown hair flopped over one eye, probably styled each morning but appearing carelessly dishevelled.

'Smithfield?' His brow furrowed. 'What's happened?'

'Nothing specific,' Laura assured him. 'We're being proactive after a few concerning incidents. I understand you and Ms Richards were near St. Bartholomew's Church recently? The day an elderly man had a heart attack?'

'And how would you know that?'

'No idea,' Laura lied with a smile. 'I'm just a doorknocker.'

David's expression cleared.

'Well, that was ages ago. Weeks, at least. Terrible thing – we saw him collapse from across the street.'

'Perhaps I could come in? I have a few questions about what you might have observed.'

David stepped back, gesturing Laura inside despite Louise's visible reluctance.

'Sure, why not? We were just having coffee.'

THE FLAT WAS PURE YOUNG-PROFESSIONALS-IN-LONDON: IKEA furniture arranged to appear expensive, framed travel posters, obligatory houseplants in various states of neglect, books arranged more for spine colour than content. Tidy enough, but with the particular clutter suggesting regular quick cleans when expecting company – mail shoved in drawers, random items tucked behind cushions.

'Nice place,' Laura observed as David led her to a small dining table by the window. The view was mostly of a car park, but a sliver of the Thames was visible if one leaned at the right angle.

'Thanks. We've only been here six months. Still getting things sorted. Coffee? Just made a fresh pot.'

'That would be lovely.'

As David busied himself in the kitchenette, Louise remained standing, arms folded. Everything about her body language screamed caution, whilst David seemed entirely at ease.

'So, you're interviewing everyone who was in Smithfield that day?' Louise asked, voice quietly sceptical.

'Not everyone. We're focusing on those present during

specific incidents. Your names came up in connection with the American gentleman who collapsed.'

'We didn't really see anything,' Louise said quickly. 'We were across the street when it happened.'

'That's helpful information. Even negative observations can help establish timelines.'

David returned with coffee in mismatched mugs – one bearing Imperial College's logo, the other declaring its owner a *Coffee Queen.* He set them down with a friendly smile that crinkled his eyes.

'Here you go. So, what exactly do you want to know?'

'I'm curious if you noticed anything unusual before the incident occurred.'

David and Louise exchanged a quick glance. There was something there – a shared secret or mutual understanding.

'Not really,' David said, running a hand through his already-tousled hair. 'Normal afternoon. We'd just bought a new memory card for my camera from that electronics shop across from the church.'

'Oh, you're photographers?' Laura seized the opening, sipping at the coffee.

'Amateur,' Louise clarified, her voice softening as conversation turned to safer territory. 'David's more into it than I am.'

'I've been getting into urban street photography,' David explained with genuine enthusiasm. 'Trying to capture those everyday London moments that tourists miss. That's why I couldn't wait to take a shot – the church has amazing architecture, and the light was perfect that day.'

Laura nodded encouragingly.

'Did you take any photos around the time the gentleman collapsed? Maybe saw how people reacted, all of that?'

Another glance between them, more pronounced. Something unspoken passed between the young couple.

'A few,' David admitted. 'Nothing of the actual... you know. We weren't that close when it happened.'

'I'd be very interested in seeing them. They might help establish what was happening in the area just before the incident.'

'What's your name again?' David asked.

'Laura.'

'I'm not sure...' Louise began, but David was already rising.

'No problem. They're on my laptop. Give me a sec.'

As David disappeared into what Laura presumed was a bedroom, silence fell. Louise remained standing, fingers drumming silently against her arm.

'How long have you lived in London?' Laura asked, attempting to bridge the awkward gap.

'Ten years. I came to university and stayed.'

'It has a way of keeping hold of people. I came for a six-month posting with my husband over thirty years ago. Somehow we never left.'

Something in her casual mention of those decades seemed to remind Louise of the age difference, and her posture softened slightly.

'You're not really from a neighbourhood safety group, are you?'

'Does it matter?' Laura met her gaze steadily.

Before Louise could answer, David returned with a sleek silver laptop.

'Found them! I've got everything organised by date.'

He placed the computer on the table, opening a photo editing programme displaying thumbnail grids.

'Here we go – April fifteenth.'

Most were architectural shots of the church or close-ups of interesting details – weathered stone, ornate carvings, light through stained glass. Then came a series of Louise posing in front of the church, smiling with the self-conscious expression of someone not entirely comfortable being photographed.

'These are lovely. You have a good eye for composition.'

'Thanks,' David replied, visibly pleased. 'I've been thinking about taking a proper course.'

'May I?' Laura indicated she'd like to look through the photos herself.

David nodded, sliding the laptop towards her.

'Go ahead. I've been playing with black and white treatments for some of them – I think they work better for architectural details.'

Laura clicked through slowly, listening with half an ear as David enthusiastically explained his photographic process. Most showed nothing beyond what David had displayed. Then she reached the series taken of Louise standing on the kerb across from the church.

In the background of the third image, partially obscured but unmistakable, were Harry Farrell and a well-dressed man in a dark suit. They appeared to be in conversation, with the man's hand reaching towards Harry's face.

The timestamp read 15:43:27.

Laura kept her expression neutral as she continued through the sequence. The next photo, taken seconds later, showed Louise in the same position, but in the background, Harry was staggering backward, his expression shocked.

'This is exactly the kind of documentation that's helpful.

Do you mind if I email these to myself? For the committee's records?'

David seemed about to agree when Louise stepped forward, placing a hand on his arm.

'I'm not comfortable with that. Those are personal photos, and we didn't consent to be part of any study or investigation.'

'I understand your concern, but these images could be quite important for understanding what happened that day.'

'Why?' Louise challenged, her accent now distinctly stronger. 'The man had a heart attack. What's to understand?'

Laura looked between them, weighing options. Direct confrontation seemed unwise, but she needed those photos.

'The truth is,' she said, deciding on a calculated risk, 'the gentleman who died was Harry Farrell, an American citizen. His family has raised concerns about the circumstances of his death, and I'm helping them gather information. I'm working with Mister Farrell's widow.'

David looked between them, confusion clear.

'Wait, so you lied to get in here? What's this really about, Mrs... Carlyle, was it?'

'It's about determining whether Harry Farrell died of natural causes or whether something else happened to him. And your photographs suggest the latter.'

'I think you should leave,' Louise said firmly, though Laura noticed a flicker of something else beneath her anger – *fear, perhaps?*

'In a moment. But first—' she quickly selected the two key photos and before either could object, airdropped them to her iPhone. '—these may be evidence in a criminal investigation. I suggest you preserve them carefully.'

David looked between Louise and Laura, clearly unsettled.

'Criminal investigation? You think someone killed that guy?'

'I think it's a possibility worth exploring,' Laura replied, rising from her chair. 'Thank you for your time and the coffee.'

'This is ridiculous,' Louise declared, colour rising in her cheeks. 'David, call security.'

'Lou, calm down—'

'Don't tell me to calm down!' Louise's accent grew stronger with agitation. 'First you take those stupid photos without thinking, then you show them to some stranger who lies about why she's here—'

'You've got no proof of anything,' David turned to Laura, though he made no move towards a phone. 'They were just random photos.'

'Were they random, David?' Louise turned on him. 'You said you wanted to photograph that church specifically. You said the light would be perfect at that exact time.'

David's face flushed.

'I did say that, but—'

'But nothing. You dragged me there for your photography project, and now we're involved in God knows what!'

Laura paused at the door, struck by the tension crackling between them. Whatever was happening here went deeper than her visit.

'I'm sorry for the deception, but this is genuinely important.'

'Give me your real contact information,' David said suddenly, ignoring Louise's sharp look. 'In case... in case we remember anything else.'

Despite Louise's visible alarm, he handed Laura his phone. She entered her name and number, then returned it.

'Thank you. And please be careful. Don't discuss this with anyone else.'

'We won't be discussing it with anyone,' Louise said coldly, 'because we're not getting involved.'

'Lou—'

'No, David. I mean it.' Louise stormed off now, leaving David with Laura. 'Whatever this is, we're staying out of it.'

Sighing, David looked back at Laura.

'You work for Mrs Farrell?' he asked.

'Yes.'

David leaned in.

'Well, you tell them I'm still waiting for a response,' he said softly. 'And in a week the price goes up.'

As the door to the apartment closed in her face, she heard the beginning of what promised to be a heated discussion, but Laura wasn't listening, still considering the last line.

David was the blackmailer.

Now outside the building, Laura paused to check her phone, confirming the photos had arrived. They weren't definitive proof of murder – no smoking gun or visible syringe – but they clearly showed Harry in distress immediately after interacting with the strange, suited individual.

Her phone buzzed. A text from an unknown number:

> Your timing is remarkable, Mrs Carlyle. Though not quite remarkable enough. We should talk. The Blackfriar pub, Queen Victoria Street. Twenty minutes. - S

Laura looked around. No sign of Sebastian Silver or his distinctive trilby. *How did he know where she was?*

She started to walk off, but then a thought halted her, a line from David Revere.

'What's this really about, Mrs Carlyle?'

David hadn't been there when she gave her name to Louise – *how did he know her surname?*

Maybe he'd been closer than she thought when she arrived, she decided. Either way, she had the photos, and now they could move on.

THE BLACKFRIAR WAS PURE VICTORIAN ATMOSPHERE – DARK wood, etched glass, the sort of pub that had survived the Blitz and property developers through sheer stubbornness. Laura found Sebastian Silver at a corner table, beside a barely touched pint. He looked up as she approached.

'Mrs Carlyle. Please, sit.'

'How did you know where I was?'

'I make it my business to know.' Silver gestured to the chair across from him. 'Tea? The coffee here is appalling, but they do a decent cup of tea.'

Laura sat, handbag clutched tightly.

'What did you mean about my timing?'

'You've stirred up a hornet's nest, I'm afraid. The Calendar has taken notice of your activities. They're not pleased.'

'And you know this how?'

'Because I've been watching them watch you.' Silver's expression was serious. 'They followed you to young Mister Revere's flat. They know about the photographs.'

'Sedan? Starts with *LS21*?'

'That's the one.'

Laura felt ice in her veins.

'Are David and Louise in danger?'

'I believe they are, but not just from your actions.'

'You mean the fact David is a blackmailer?'

Silver's eyebrow raised at the revelation, and Laura wondered if this was new information to him.

'Quite possibly. Which is why we need to discuss terms of partnership rather urgently.'

Before Laura could respond, her phone buzzed. A text from an unknown number.

> Had a row with Louise about all this. She's left. Tell them the price is now £15k.

Laura frowned, showing Silver the message.

'She's left him. And he thinks I'm able to get Rebecca to up the blackmail cost.'

'When?' Silver's expression grew troubled.

'Just now, apparently,' Laura replied. 'You think they're in danger?'

'I think a young man on his own, with photographic evidence of a murder, who's been trying to gain financial reward from it has just become extremely vulnerable.' Silver's voice carried new urgency. 'We need to check on him.'

Laura was reading the message again.

'He keeps saying "them",' she whispered. 'He said it at the door, too. He must mean Rebecca, I said I was working for her, but surely he would have said "her" instead?'

'That seems the most likely explanation,' Silver gave a smile, but it felt fake, like Silver didn't believe the suggestion.

They moved through the pub's afternoon crowd, Silver's cane tapping a rhythm against worn floorboards. Outside, he hailed a black cab, and during the journey, Laura tried David's number repeatedly.

No answer.

Eventually, the building she'd been at less than an hour earlier came into view, looking perfectly normal in the afternoon sunlight.

The glass doors stood unlocked, no longer propped open with a flyer, but simply left open. Laura couldn't explain it, but she knew without a doubt that something was wrong here.

They took the elevator to the fourth floor; they were silent, but so was the corridor once they arrived. Too silent. Laura caught a faint smell she couldn't identify – something chemical, cleaning-related.

'David?' Laura called as they approached David and Louise's apartment. The door was slightly ajar.

Silver stepped in front of her, pushing the door open with his cane.

'Stay behind me.'

The living room had been systematically searched. Drawers pulled out, cushions sliced open, papers scattered, and David's laptop, last seen on the kitchen counter an hour earlier, was gone.

They found him in the bedroom.

He lay beside the bed, eyes closed, looking almost peaceful. No blood spatter, no signs of struggle. It was almost as if he'd suffered a heart attack… just like Harry Farrell.

Laura pressed a hand to her mouth.

'Oh God. David.'

Silver knelt beside the body, careful not to disturb anything, sniffing the mouth.

'I can't smell anything, but I'd wager it's the same poison that killed Harry. You were here an hour back, and he texted you twenty-five minutes ago, so we just missed whatever happened here.' He looked up grimly. 'They came for the photos, like you did.'

'They killed him.'

'They killed him because he'd seen them. Spoken to you, perhaps. Become a liability.' Silver's voice was quiet. 'Louise's leaving may have saved her life.'

Laura stared at David's still form, killed for taking photographs in the wrong place at the wrong time. The cold fury and guilt that had sustained her through the months after James's death began to build again.

'This is my fault. If I hadn't come here—'

'If you hadn't come here, this would have happened anyway. Your visit didn't create the danger, Laura. It simply revealed it.'

They left the apartment, Silver using his handkerchief to wipe the door handle. In the elevator, Laura absorbed what had happened.

'We have to call the police.'

'We will. Anonymously.' Sebastian Silver's expression was grim. 'But first, we need to get those photos somewhere safe. And we need to understand exactly what Harry discovered that made The Calendar willing to kill for it.'

As they left the building, Laura felt something fundamental shift inside her. David Revere was dead because she'd involved him in her investigation. The charity committees and garden parties belonged to a different woman now.

The Calendar had made this personal.

'What Harry discovered. It's time I knew exactly what that was.'

Silver nodded.

'Yes. Because understanding what killed Harry Farrell may be the only way to prevent more deaths like David's.'

He called for a taxi, but as he did so, Laura stared at him, a realisation running through her.

How had he known the address to come to? When they left the pub, he'd instantly grabbed a passing black cab and sent it to the correct address, but she hadn't told him it, and she'd only gained the address herself an hour earlier.

Even if he'd followed the men who'd followed her, he'd returned to the pub too soon to see the address.

Sebastian Silver had known where David Revere had lived.

And he hadn't told her.

What else was he keeping from her? And how much could she really trust him?

8

IMPROVISED INVESTIGATION

The anonymous call to the police took thirty seconds. Silver used a pay phone outside a newsagent's, his voice muffled by a handkerchief as he reported a "disturbance" at David's address. Nothing more.

'How long before they find him?' Laura asked as they climbed back into the taxi.

'An hour, perhaps two. Depends how seriously they take anonymous tips.' Silver gave the driver Laura's address, then settled back against the worn leather seat. 'Are you prepared to explain this to your family?'

Laura considered the question. *How did one casually mention that a young man was dead because of her investigation? That her comfortable world had shifted into something far more dangerous?*

'I'm not sure I have a choice any more.'

The taxi wound north across the Thames and then through South Kensington's elegant streets. Everything looked the same, but everything felt very different.

'Mrs Carlyle,' Silver said quietly as they turned onto

Queen's Gate. 'There's something you should know about your street.'

Laura followed his gaze and saw that a dark-blue van was parked opposite her house, two men sitting in the front seats. They weren't reading newspapers or chatting – just sitting, watching.

'Calendar?' she asked.

'Almost certainly.' Silver's hand moved to his trilby – that gesture Laura now recognised meant serious thinking of some kind, in the same way that some people twirled their hair, or a pen over their knuckles. 'They're being rather obvious about it, which suggests they want you to notice.'

'Intimidation?'

'Or assessment.' Silver leaned forward to speak to the driver. 'Could you go round the block twice more? Take your time.'

As they repeatedly circled Queen's Gate, Silver pointed out two more watchers – a man reading a book on a bench who stared above it and never turned a page, and a woman walking a dog who'd covered the same fifty yards three times.

'They're not trying to be subtle.'

'No. Which means they're either supremely confident or supremely stupid.' Silver adjusted his trilby. 'In my experience, people like this tend towards the former.'

The taxi pulled up outside Laura's house, and Silver paid the driver whilst scanning the street.

'Walk normally to your front door. Don't look at the watchers. I'll be right behind you.'

Laura did so, deciding not to ask Silver about the other address until they were safe. Her key was in the lock when she heard Silver's voice, carrying clearly in the afternoon air.

'Excuse me, gentlemen. I believe you're lost.'

She turned to see him approaching the van, cane in one hand, the other straightening his trilby with deliberate precision. The men in the van looked startled – clearly they hadn't expected to be confronted by him.

'Private street, you see,' Silver continued conversationally. 'Residents only. I'm sure you understand.'

One man got out of the van – tall, well-built, and wearing the sort of dark suit that said government or security services.

'We're not causing any trouble, mate.'

'Oh, I'm sure you're not.' Silver's voice carried the particular tone Laura recognised from diplomatic receptions – polite, pleasant, and absolutely implacable. 'Still, I think you'll find this isn't quite the area you're looking for.'

The man's hand moved inside his jacket.

Sebastian Silver's cane moved faster.

The silver base of the walking stick touched the man's wrist, and the effect was immediate; the man convulsed as if he'd grabbed a live wire, stumbling backward with a sharp cry.

'Terribly sorry,' Silver said mildly. 'Static electricity. Dreadful problem with these old canes.'

The second man was getting out of the van now, but Silver had already stepped back, positioning himself between the watchers and Laura's front door.

'I'd suggest moving along before I'm forced to demonstrate other fascinating properties of antique walking accessories.'

The men exchanged glances. After a moment's hesitation, they got back in their van and drove away. Silver watched them go, then turned to Laura with a perfectly normal smile.

'Shall we go in? I believe I could murder a cup of tea.'

Laura found her voice.

'Your walking cane...'

'Family heirloom. Great-grandfather was quite the inventor. Useful hobby in his line of work.'

THEY WERE BARELY THROUGH THE FRONT DOOR WHEN AUNT Celia appeared from the sitting room, took one look at Laura's face, and immediately shifted into crisis mode.

'Brandy or tea?'

'Tea, please. And perhaps you could ask Kyle to join us? It's time for proper introductions.'

Celia's gaze fixed on Silver.

'You must be the mysterious gentleman with the trilby hat. Mrs Reynolds has been beside herself with curiosity.'

'Sebastian Silver.' He offered a slight bow. 'At your service, madam.'

'Celia Harrington. Laura's considerably more sensible aunt.' Celia's tone could have etched glass. 'I suppose you're responsible for the fact that my niece looks like she's seen a ghost?'

'I'm afraid the responsibility is somewhat shared.'

Kyle bounded down the stairs at that moment, stopped dead when he saw Silver, and stared.

'Kyle,' Laura said carefully, 'this is Sebastian Silver. The gentleman I mentioned.'

'Right.' Kyle was still staring. 'The one Mrs Reynolds thought was Pierce Brosnan.'

'I'm flattered by the comparison,' Silver replied.

Kyle's gaze dropped to the walking cane.

'That's... quite an interesting cane.'

'Family heirloom. Great-uncle's.'

'I thought you said it was your great-grandfather's?' Laura asked, frowning.

'He invented it, but gifted it to his brother,' Silver said without breaking a stride, but Laura couldn't shake the thought that this was a lie. Wherever Silver got the specialised cane from, he wasn't telling anyone anytime soon.

'Okay then,' she said, deciding to change the subject. 'We need tea, biscuits and possibly some sherry for what we need to tell you.'

IN THE SITTING ROOM, WITH PROPER TEA SERVED IN PROPER CHINA and a small sherry beside it, Laura found herself explaining the day's events. She kept the details general – David had been killed; The Calendar was responsible; the danger was escalating.

'Killed?' Kyle's excitement faded instantly. 'You mean actually murdered?'

'I'm afraid so. That is, there were no wounds, but it bore a distinct similarity to Harry Farrell.'

Celia set down her teacup.

'And this Calendar organisation is now watching our house because...?'

'Because your niece has become rather inconveniently effective at uncovering their secrets,' Silver replied.

'I see.' Celia studied Silver with a penetrating gaze that had once reduced ambassadors to nervous stammering whenever they met her at events. 'And your role in all this, Mister Silver?'

'I'm trying to prevent anyone else from being killed. Including your family.'

'How reassuring.' Celia's tone suggested she found it anything but. 'And your qualifications for this protective role?'

Silver smiled, and for a moment Laura glimpsed something harder beneath the charming exterior.

'I used to work for people very much like The Calendar. Before circumstances changed.'

'Circumstances?' Celia pounced on the vagueness.

'Differences of opinion regarding methodology.'

Kyle leaned forward.

'So, you really are a spy?'

'Was. Retired, you might say.'

Before anyone could ask more questions though, the doorbell rang. Kyle jumped up.

'I'll get it.'

'No!' Laura and Silver spoke simultaneously.

'I'll go,' Silver continued, rising and reaching for his cane. 'Kyle, perhaps you could show me the way whilst maybe staying well behind me?'

They left the room, and Laura looked at Celia.

'He's dead because of me,' she whispered, knocking back the sherry and motioning for another.

'Poppycock,' Aunt Celia muttered, shaking her head as she sat back. 'That man was likely heading in that direction before you turned up. What if he was the blackmailer? That doesn't sound like the sort of man who walks in polite society, and with a name like Revere, he wouldn't have been unaware of his name's heritage.'

'Tarquin Russell walked in polite society and he was blackmailing half of Chelsea,' Laura countered.

'Tarquin Russell is a rogue and a ne'er do well, and is best left out of conversations,' Celia coldly replied. 'That said, he threw a good bash.'

'Well, it's irrelevant as I believe you're right, and David *is* the blackmailer,' Laura sighed. 'Before he died, when he realised I worked for Rebecca, he said the price would go up if it wasn't paid. Which is "blackmailer" talk if ever I heard it. Of course, with him being dead now, I—'

They paused their conversation as Silver and Kyle returned a moment later, with a motorcycle courier, holding a small package.

'Mrs Laura Carlyle?' he asked, confused at the security.

Laura nodded and signed for the package whilst Silver examined the courier. Only after the man had left did Silver nod approval.

'Legitimate delivery service. Though I'd suggest being more cautious about unexpected packages in future.'

The package contained nothing more than some printed flyers for an upcoming fete Laura had agreed to assist with. Silver examined the box carefully before deciding he was happy with the authenticity.

'What happens if we have a delivery and you're not here to save us from junk mail?' Celia asked, perhaps a little too bitingly.

'I've arranged several contingencies for such a situation,' Silver replied, taking it as a serious question. 'Including the possibility that I might need to disappear again quickly.'

'Disappear?' Celia's voice was sharp.

'I don't generally stay in one place long. It's safer for everyone concerned.'

'Including us?' Celia challenged. 'How convenient for you to arrange communications from a safe distance whilst we deal with the consequences of Laura's investigation.'

Silver had the grace to look uncomfortable.

'That wasn't my intention.'

'Wasn't it? You've been watching my niece, making decisions about her safety, all whilst maintaining your own comfortable distance. Mister Silver, exactly how long have you been watching her?'

'Only since she became involved in this business. Though I knew of her through James, of course.'

'And you didn't think to introduce yourself properly? Instead of lurking about like some sort of Victorian villain?'

Silver looked slightly embarrassed.

'I was hoping to resolve matters quietly. Without involving civilians.'

Celia's eyes flashed dangerously.

'Civilians?' Her voice could have frozen champagne. 'Mister Silver, I spent forty years in diplomatic service. I've been shot at in three different countries and negotiated with people who made Machiavelli look like a choirboy. Exactly which part of that qualifies me as a civilian?'

Sebastian Silver blinked.

'I... apologise. That was presumptuous.'

'Indeed, it was.' Celia's tone was ice cold. 'Perhaps you meant inexperienced amateurs? Or helpless bystanders?'

'Aunt Celia—' Laura began.

'No, Laura. This gentleman has been deciding about our family's safety without consulting us. I'd like to understand his reasoning.'

Silver adjusted his trilby.

'You're quite right. I should have approached you directly from the beginning.'

Laura examined Silver again; there was something off

here. Silver's smile was slightly strained as he tried to move on.

'Now, perhaps we should discuss immediate precautions? Those gentlemen outside, alongside the dog walker and the book reader may have left, but they'll be back.'

'What sort of precautions?' Celia's eyebrows rose.

'Simple things. Don't answer the door to unexpected visitors. Vary your routines. Check for followers when you go out. If you spot surveillance, call me immediately and go to the nearest public place.'

'And where exactly will you be when we call?' Celia asked pointedly.

'I have a place in East London. Secure communications, proper equipment,' Silver replied. 'I can be here within thirty minutes if needed.'

'How reassuring,' Celia said dryly. 'Meanwhile, we remain here as sitting ducks. Rather convenient arrangement.'

Silver looked uncomfortable now.

'Mrs Harrington, I understand your concerns—'

'What about the investigation?' Laura asked, changing the subject. 'We still need to understand what Harry found. Sebastian, what exactly did Harry discover that made him so dangerous?'

Sebastian placed his trilby carefully on the side table. For a moment, he looked older, wearier than his usual composed self.

'The Calendar isn't just a private intelligence service, Laura. They're a clearing house for the worst kinds of operations. Assassinations, blackmail, industrial espionage. But more than that – they've been infiltrating legitimate intelligence services for years.'

'Infiltrating how?'

'Recruiting sources, placing operatives, corrupting officials. They know things they shouldn't know. Have access they shouldn't have.'

Laura absorbed this.

'And Harry found proof?'

'Harry found a network of corruption stretching from London to Washington to Moscow. People in positions of trust selling secrets to the highest bidder, and I believe a long-lost list of Calendar sleeper agents, unused for decades,' Silver's voice was quiet. 'He was going to expose it all.'

'Including you?'

Sebastian Silver met her gaze steadily.

'I left the security services years ago, Laura. But yes, my name would have been in Harry's files.'

'Is that why you're helping me? Guilt?'

'Partly. But also because Harry was right. The Calendar needs to be stopped. The man who I believe killed Harry? He goes by the name "Mister Monday", and I want nothing more than to see him behind bars, paying for his crimes.'

Laura was about to continue when she heard a car door slamming outside – not the gentle thunk of a taxi, but the decisive bang of someone who'd driven themselves whilst thoroughly annoyed. She moved to the sitting-room window and immediately spotted Frank Young's battered Vauxhall parked at an aggressive angle to the kerb.

'Ah, botheration,' she muttered, looking back to Silver. 'DCI Frank Young is—'

But Sebastian Silver had vanished so completely she might have imagined him entirely.

'Rather like the Cheshire Cat,' Celia observed, looking

over to the living room door, 'though considerably less helpful in terms of explaining himself. Shall I go make some more tea for our new guest?'

'It depends if he's here to arrest me or not,' Laura sighed.

9

OFFICIAL CONSEQUENCES

The doorbell rang with the particular aggressive rhythm of someone who intended to keep pressing until the door opened, possibly until next Tuesday.

'Frank!' Laura said, opening the door with what she hoped was appropriate surprise. 'What a lovely—'

'Don't.' His voice could have cut glass. 'Just don't, Laura.'

He stood on her doorstep looking like a police-recruiting poster entitled *"What Not To Aspire To"*, with a rumpled mackintosh, stubble, and the sort of expression that suggested he'd been drinking station coffee and questioning his life choices in equal measure.

'Tea?' she offered, because when in doubt, one reverted to the basics.

'This isn't a social call.'

'I gathered *that* from your expression.'

Frank pushed past her into the hall with considerably less courtesy than usual. Laura closed the door and followed him to the sitting room, where Aunt Celia was pointedly ignoring the drama whilst Kyle had developed sudden academic enthusiasm for his economics textbook.

'Evening, Frank,' Celia said without looking up. 'You appear murderous. Seven across: "Detective's nightmare." Nine letters.'

'Amateurs,' Frank replied. 'And yes, I am murderous.'

'Doesn't fit. Not enough letters.'

'Try "*meddling* bloody amateurs".'

Kyle snorted. Frank's glare back however suggested his patience for family humour had expired sometime around Vauxhall Bridge.

'Kyle, perhaps you could give us privacy?' Laura suggested.

'Can't I stay? This sounds properly dramatic.'

'Kyle.' Celia's voice carried the authority of age and position. 'Your grandmother is about to receive a professional dressing-down. It's not entertainment.'

Kyle gathered his books with obvious reluctance.

'Are you in actual trouble, Gran?'

'That depends.'

'What sort of trouble?'

'The expensive sort, I expect.'

After Kyle's footsteps had faded upstairs, Frank turned to Laura with an expression that belonged in interview rooms.

'David Revere is dead.'

'Oh.' Laura kept her voice steady. 'What happened?'

'No idea. Looks like his heart gave out, but his positioning feels like someone moving him post-mortem. Usually, when you have a heart attack, you don't politely lay back on your bed in a position of comfort. There was no struggle, but the apartment was ransacked afterwards. And according to our forensics team, someone else had been there recently. Someone who drank from his coffee mug.'

The Imperial College mug. Laura's pulse quickened.

'That's terrible. He seemed such a pleasant young man.'

'Cut the diplomatic nonsense, Laura,' Frank snapped. 'I gave you his address this morning. By afternoon he's dead. Care to explain the connection?'

Before Laura could attempt an explanation, however, Aunt Celia set down her pen with a decisive snap.

'Detective Chief Inspector Young,' she said, frost forming on every syllable, 'I've known you for nearly twenty years. Whilst I understand you're upset; I won't have you interrogating my niece as if she were some common criminal.'

Frank deflated slightly.

'You're right. Sorry, Laura. But a man is dead, in a similar way to a second man you're investigating – whether I like it or not – and I feel responsible.'

'Why would you be responsible?'

'Because I gave you information thinking you were indulging a harmless curiosity. I never imagined you'd track the poor lad down and get him killed.'

The accusation hit like ice water. Laura sank into her chair.

'You think I caused his death.'

'I think you wandered into something dangerous and dragged an innocent person with you.' Frank's anger was cooling into something worse – disappointment. 'What were you thinking?'

'I was thinking Rebecca Farrell deserved answers about her husband's murder.'

'*Alleged* murder, Laura. And now David Revere is dead because of it.'

'That's quite enough.' Celia's tone could have preserved meat. 'Detective Chief Inspector, my niece didn't kill that young man. If he's dead, it's because of what he witnessed, not because Laura spoke to him.'

'She had no business approaching him.'

'And you had no business providing his details if you considered the matter dangerous.'

Frank opened his mouth, then closed it. Celia had identified the flaw in his argument with surgical precision.

'The boy was already in danger,' she continued. 'Laura simply discovered it. If anyone bears responsibility for his death, it's whoever killed him, not the person seeking truth.'

Frank stared at a point above Laura's head.

'What did David tell you?'

Laura set her teacup down carefully.

'That he and his girlfriend had photographed the area near St. Bartholomew's Church when Harry Farrell died. They'd bought camera equipment from the electronics shop and were testing it.'

'And?'

'The photographs showed Harry in apparent distress after speaking with an unknown man. It contradicted the heart attack theory.'

'Did David give you copies?'

Laura hesitated. *The images were on her phone.*

'He showed them to me. I saw what appeared to be Harry Farrell in some sort of confrontation.'

'But no copies.'

'No.'

The lie came surprisingly easily. A month ago, she'd have been incapable of deceiving Frank about anything more serious than surprise parties, but now...

Now she was becoming more like Sebastian Silver, it seemed.

'Laura.' His voice carried the weight of their history. 'I need a straight answer. When exactly did you visit David Revere?'

The sitting room fell silent except for the grandfather clock's measured ticking.

'This afternoon,' Laura said finally. 'Around half-past two.'

'Anyone else there?'

'His girlfriend, Louise. Though she seemed uncomfortable with my questions.'

'Uncomfortable how?'

'Nervous. Protective. She didn't want David showing me photographs.'

'Where is she now?'

'David mentioned in a text afterwards she'd gone to visit her mother. He seemed upset about it.'

Frank's expression darkened.

'Laura, can I see that text?'

Laura nodded, showing the text, but making sure Frank couldn't take hold of the phone, in case he wanted a deeper search. He read it, nodded to himself and then looked up.

'Laura, there's no Louise Richards at that address. Neighbours say they never saw a girlfriend – just David living alone. And I don't think that's his number – the one I was given ended with seven-eight. That doesn't.'

Laura blinked.

'That's impossible. I spoke to her. She answered the door.'

'Well then, whoever she was, she's vanished completely. Along with any trace of having lived there.'

The implications settled around them like a fifties London fog.

If Louise hadn't been David's girlfriend, what had she been? Could she have been his killer?

'Frank,' Laura said carefully, 'what did the crime scene tell you?'

'I didn't see it, but the SOCO report – that's "scene of crime officer"—'

'Please,' Celia muttered sarcastically, returning to her crossword. 'Tell us what well-known acronyms mean.'

'The SOCOs told me it looked like a non-suspicious death, something we wouldn't usually continue with, if it wasn't for the positioning of the body. And the fact the apartment was systematically searched – not burglary, but someone seeking specific items.'

'The photographs.'

'Most likely. His laptop was taken, along with any storage devices, if he had any to start with.' Frank's smile held no warmth. 'Whoever did this was thorough enough to clean most surfaces. Except for spots they missed.'

'Coffee mugs?'

'Among other things.'

Laura understood. Her fingerprints were at the scene, and Frank was choosing not to pursue that fact. For now.

Or had the mug been left deliberately to muddy the waters? If so, did they know Laura had been there?

'What happens next?' Celia asked.

'Next, we investigate properly whilst *civilians* stay clear.' Frank's gaze fixed on Laura. 'I mean it. This isn't intellectual curiosity any more. Somehow, someone killed David Revere in cold blood, making sure the method couldn't be traced. They won't hesitate with anyone else who interferes.'

'Including me?'

'Especially you. You're asking questions they don't want answered.'

Before Laura could respond, Kyle's voice drifted downstairs.

'Gran? Someone's at the back door.'

All three adults froze. The back door led to the garden, accessible only through the mews. Casual visitors didn't use that entrance.

Frank's hand moved to his jacket, removing an extendable baton.

'Expecting anyone?'

'No.'

'Kyle!' Frank called upstairs. 'Stay exactly where you are. Don't approach any doors.'

Ignoring the command, Celia rose.

'I'll check the kitchen window.'

She moved towards the back of the house whilst Frank gestured for Laura to remain seated. Laura waited, and after several minutes, Celia returned.

'Delivery man,' she announced. 'Flowers for Mrs Reynolds next door. Couldn't make anyone hear at the front.'

Frank relaxed marginally, placing the baton away.

'Still. Be careful of unexpected visitors. If you notice anything off, call me immediately.'

'We will.'

Frank gathered his mackintosh. At the door, he paused.

'Laura, I need you to promise something.'

'What?'

'Promise you'll let the police handle this. Whatever happened to Harry Farrell, whatever David Revere witnessed and died for – it's too dangerous for amateurs.'

Laura met his gaze.

'I promise I'll be careful.'

'That's not what I asked.'

'It's what I'm offering.'

Frank sighed.

'James always said you were too stubborn for your own good.'

'James married me anyway.'

'James was a diplomat. He understood strategic compromise.' Frank's expression softened. 'Be safe, Laura. I couldn't bear losing you too.'

After his car had departed with another aggressive door slam, Laura sat in the quiet sitting room whilst Celia resumed her crossword and Kyle reappeared.

'So,' he said, settling on the sofa with barely contained excitement, 'how much trouble are we in?'

'Considerable,' Celia replied without looking up.

'Expensive trouble or dangerous trouble?'

'Does it matter?' Laura asked. 'We're committed now.'

'What do you mean?'

Before she could answer, Silver's voice drifted from the conservatory.

'She means, dear boy, that retreat is no longer possible.'

They turned to find him in the doorway, trilby perfectly positioned, walking cane at a casual angle. He might have materialised from thin air.

'How long have you been there?' Laura demanded.

'Long enough to hear Detective Chief Inspector Young's warnings about amateur investigation.'

'You were eavesdropping.'

'I was gathering intelligence. There's a distinction.'

Kyle stared at Silver with frank admiration.

'How did you get back in?'

'Who said I left?'

'What did you make of Frank's report?' Laura asked, deciding to change the subject from Kyle becoming Sebastian Silver's next acolyte.

'Illuminating. The systematic search confirms The Calendar took David's death seriously. They wanted those photographs.'

'But didn't find them.'

'Perhaps not. They found the laptop, which he showed you the photos on, but if he was the blackmailer, he would have had something hidden elsewhere. It seems David was cleverer than anticipated.'

Laura leaned forward.

'Meaning?'

Silver paused, considering his words.

'David Revere understood photography, Laura. Digital storage, backup systems. The Calendar found his laptop and memory cards, but that doesn't mean they found everything.'

'You think he hid copies?'

'I think a young man who'd accidentally photographed a murder, especially one who might have turned towards blackmail might have taken precautions.'

Kyle's eyes lit up.

'Cloud storage! Everyone backs up automatically now. Google Photos, iCloud – his phone probably uploaded everything the moment he took it.'

Silver nodded approvingly.

'Precisely. Though accessing cloud accounts requires passwords The Calendar didn't have time to extract.'

'We don't have them either,' Laura pointed out.

'No. But we know where David lived. And young people often record passwords in predictable places,' Sebastian finished.

'Or password managers on their phones.'

'Which we don't have, but which might still be on the scene.'

Laura stared at him.

'You're suggesting we search his apartment.'

'I'm suggesting we conduct a more thorough examination than The Calendar managed. They sought physical storage and had bare minutes to work through. We'd seek information and have all the time we need if we did it tonight.'

'The apartment's a crime scene. It'll be sealed.'

'Police seals are fragile things. Easily broken, often accidentally.'

'Silver, that's breaking and entering.'

'It's evidence preservation. We'd be recovering material the police might overlook.'

Laura went to ask another question, but finally, the one that had sat in the back of her mind for the last hour burst out of her lips.

'Mister Silver, exactly how do you know where David Revere lived?'

The question hung in the air. Silver's hand moved towards his trilby.

'Harry mentioned him.'

'Harry mentioned a young man by the Thames specifically?'

'Harry was investigating The Calendar's network. David's name appeared in his research.'

'Come on, that's impossible,' Laura said, but as she spoke

she felt something cold settle in her stomach. 'What aren't you telling me?'

'Nothing relevant to—'

'*Everything is relevant now!*' Laura's voice carried more force than intended. 'David is dead. Frank thinks I'm responsible. So please, explain exactly how you knew David Revere well enough to direct a taxi to his building without consulting an address, when he was just some guy taking a *sodding photo!*'

Silver looked genuinely uncomfortable.

'Harry believed David might be connected to The Calendar. A consultant or informant.'

'Connected how?'

'The photographs weren't accidental, Laura. I watched them outside the shop, and they were waiting for Harry to appear before taking the shots, positioned perfectly to capture Harry's death. Too perfect for coincidence. Proof of death, perhaps. Maybe cataloguing how the agents of The Calendar did it.'

The sitting room fell silent except for the clock's ticking. Laura processed the implications whilst Celia observed Silver, as if realising finally the full danger of the man.

'You thought David was working for Harry's killers.'

'It seemed possible. Harry's intelligence suggested someone was monitoring his movements. David's presence at the scene, with camera equipment, at the precise moment...'

'So, when I found David, you assumed I'd located a Calendar operative.'

'Yes...' Silver paused. 'I saw Harry's death,' he eventually muttered. 'I was there. Not watching Harry, I'd been following David and Louise. It was pure chance I saw Harry. I was going to warn him, but then I saw Mister Monday, and it all happened so fast.'

Laura stared at Silver, and for the first time since meeting him, she actually felt he was being genuine. There was no bravado, no "ex-Superspy" going on here. Just a man who saw a friend die, and potentially lost something personal in the process.

She leaned back, processing this revelation.

Silver had been playing a deeper game – not just helping her investigate but pursuing his own agenda.

'David died because you suspected him.'

'David died because The Calendar couldn't risk witnesses. Whether I suspected him or not.'

Silver removed his trilby entirely, running fingers through silver hair.

'I bear responsibility for his death.'

'We both do.'

'Perhaps. But that's reason enough to ensure his death wasn't meaningless.'

Kyle looked between them, excitement warring with confusion.

'So, are we searching his flat?'

Celia sighed.

'Kyle, darling, "we" are not going anywhere. If anyone is foolish enough to break into a crime scene, it certainly won't include university students.'

'But—'

'No arguments. This is dangerous enough without involving twenty-year-olds who should be studying.'

Laura studied Silver's face, trying to read the man beneath the charming exterior. Without his trilby, he seemed diminished somehow. More human, perhaps, but also more vulnerable.

'If we do this,' she said carefully, 'I want complete honesty. No more strategic omissions.'

'Agreed.'

'And if we find evidence, we share it with Frank. Regardless of how it affects your personal vendetta.'

Silver hesitated, then nodded.

'Agreed.'

'When?'

'Tonight. Crime scenes are monitored less closely after the initial investigation.'

Laura looked around the sitting room – at Celia's concerned expression, Kyle's barely contained excitement, Silver replacing his trilby with careful precision. A few days ago, her greatest concern had been charity auction logistics.

Now she was planning to break into a crime scene with a man whose identity remained largely mysterious.

'All right,' she said finally. 'But we do this carefully, quietly, with proper exit strategies.'

Silver's smile returned, transforming his face back into something dangerously charming.

'My dear Laura, I wouldn't have it any other way.'

10

BREAKING AND ENTERING

LAURA HAD NEVER REALISED HOW MANY ETIQUETTE considerations were involved in basic criminality. It was nearly eleven o'clock at night now, and she'd spent the better part of two hours discovering that one simply didn't break into high-class expensive apartments in London without considerable advance planning.

'Are you absolutely certain this is necessary?' she asked Silver for what might have been the fourth time as they sat in his surprisingly comfortable black Mercedes outside David's building. She'd expected an Aston Martin when he'd gone to fetch it, commenting about how *it was far easier to taxi around London, but right now it was a necessity,* but it was comfy and the seats were heated. 'Couldn't we simply ring Frank and suggest the police conduct a more thorough search?'

'And tell him what, precisely? That we suspect David hid evidence based on Kyle's theories about password storage?'

Laura straightened her dark wool coat. If one was going to commit one's first burglary, one ought to dress appropriately.

'When you phrase it like that, it does sound rather flimsy.'

'Besides,' Silver added, consulting his pocket watch, 'Detective Chief Inspector Young made his position quite clear. He wants you nowhere near this investigation.'

'Frank's position is entirely sensible from a professional standpoint.'

'And entirely unhelpful from a practical one.'

Laura looked up at the building. Most windows were dark now, though she could see the blue flicker of late-night television behind a few curtains and blinds. According to Silver, the police had finished hours ago.

'How exactly do we know the authorities have departed?'

'Because I've been monitoring their communications since this afternoon.' Silver tapped what appeared to be an ordinary mobile phone. 'Crime scene team departed at seven-thirty. Building security does rounds every two hours.'

Laura stared at him.

'You have police monitoring equipment?'

'Among other useful devices. The benefits of a misspent youth.'

'I thought you claimed to be in intelligence work.'

'As I said. Misspent youth.'

Despite everything, Laura found herself smiling. There was something oddly reassuring about Silver's matter-of-fact approach to lawbreaking, as if burglary were simply another social engagement requiring proper preparation.

'Remind me again why we couldn't do this during daylight hours?'

'Because, my dear Laura, afternoon burglary suggests desperation. Evening burglary suggests planning. There's a distinction.'

'I'm not sure the magistrates would appreciate the nuance.'

'The magistrates won't be involved unless we're spectacularly incompetent.'

Laura hoped Silver's confidence was justified. She'd never committed a crime more serious than exceeding diplomatic parking privileges, and those hardly counted given ambassadorial immunity.

'Right then,' Silver said, gathering a small leather case from the back seat. 'Shall we?'

'What's in the case?'

'Tools of the trade. Lock picks, mostly, though David's building security appears somewhat optimistic rather than effective.'

Laura followed him towards the entrance, trying to project the casual confidence of someone who lived there. The effort was rather undermined, however, by her tendency to glance about like a tourist expecting pickpockets.

'Laura,' Silver said gently as they reached the glass doors, 'you're walking as if you expect immediate arrest. Try to appear more... residential.'

'I don't know how to appear residential whilst committing breaking and entering.'

'Think of it as visiting a friend who's temporarily unable to answer the door.'

'A friend who's been murdered?'

'A minor detail,' Silver said, producing what appeared to be a credit card from his wallet. 'The principle remains sound.'

He slid the card along the door frame. The lock clicked open with embarrassing simplicity.

'That seems rather inadequate security for a modern building,' Laura observed.

'Most security exists to deter honest people. Dishonest

people have always found alternatives. And this card might be more than it seems.'

They entered the lobby, and Laura stared at the building directory as if it contained state secrets rather than simply apartment numbers and surnames.

'You realise,' she said as they waited for the elevator, 'that Aunt Celia is going to ask pointed questions about what happened this evening.'

'And what will you tell her?'

'That depends on how successfully this venture concludes. If we're arrested, I suspect she'll deduce the truth from the morning papers.'

The elevator arrived with a soft *ding* that echoed like thunder in the quiet building.

'Fourth floor,' Silver murmured as the doors closed.

'I remember the address,' Laura replied, though she was grateful for his steadying presence. The lift seemed determined to announce its arrival to the entire building.

THE CORRIDOR WAS DIMLY LIT BY EMERGENCY LIGHTING, casting shadows that made Laura's imagination work rather harder than necessary. David's door looked perfectly ordinary, though she could see faint marks where police tape had been attached and removed.

'How exactly do we gain entry?' Laura whispered.

'We ask politely,' Silver replied, producing his lock picks.

Watching him work was oddly fascinating. His movements were quick and sure, suggesting considerable experience, and within seconds, it felt, the lock surrendered with barely a sound.

'You're disturbingly competent at that.'

'Thank you. I do try to maintain useful skills.'

Silver pushed the door open carefully, listening for sounds from within. The apartment was dark, silent, and carried a faint chemical smell of police forensics work.

'After you,' he said with a slight bow.

'Oh no. This was your idea. You go first.'

Silver stepped inside, leaving Laura to follow. She closed the door behind them, then immediately wondered if that had been wise. *Were they now trapped, or was she being overly dramatic?*

'Torch?' Silver offered, producing a small LED light.

'Shouldn't we use the normal lights?'

'And advertise our presence to the entire building? Laura, you have considerable scope for improvement in basic criminality.'

The torch beam revealed the sitting room much as she'd left it that afternoon, though considerably more dishevelled after the police examination. Cushions had been restacked carelessly, drawers left partially open, books returned to shelves in entirely the wrong order.

'Where precisely are we supposed to begin?' Laura asked.

'Think like a young man hiding important information quickly. Someone with security services training, perhaps.'

'I don't have that sort of training. I—'

'You met enough people through your husband who did,' Silver interrupted. 'I'm sure you'll do fine. Where would you place something requiring both security and accessibility?'

Laura considered this whilst Silver moved towards the bookshelf.

'Somewhere obvious enough that I wouldn't forget it, but subtle enough to escape casual discovery.'

'Precisely.'

Laura surveyed the sitting room with fresh eyes. Whoever had gone through the apartment – either the killer, the police, or a mixture of both – had clearly been thorough; every drawer was emptied, every cushion overturned, every book examined for hidden materials.

But they'd been seeking physical evidence of the crime, not digital storage solutions, or hidden drawers.

Silver was pulling volumes from the shelf.

'Most people employ variations of meaningful dates, names, or phrases,' he explained. 'Often recorded in seemingly innocent locations.'

'Such as?'

'Address books, calendar margins, inside book covers...' Silver paused, holding up a photography manual. 'Technical guides, for instance.'

'Or their phones.'

'Yes, but first, we don't have the phone, and second, if Mister Revere is more than the average person, he might not keep things on something that could be pickpocketed. He might be more analogue.'

Laura moved to the kitchen area, where the Imperial College mug had been removed, maybe for forensic testing, but everything else was untouched.

'Silver,' she called softly. 'Come look at this.'

She was staring at the microwave, which struck her as oddly positioned. It sat on the counter beside the refrigerator, but at an angle that seemed impractical for a small kitchen.

'Curious placement,' Silver mused. 'Most people position microwaves for convenient access. This one's rather awkwardly situated.'

Laura opened the microwave door. Inside was completely

clean – not just tidy, but pristine. No food stains, no lingering odours, no signs it had ever been used for cooking. This could simply have meant that David was someone who cleaned up after himself, but in the corner was a strip of plastic; the covering of the plate that spun around lazily when you turned it on.

But the microwave wasn't new.

Could the plate have been bought recently? But why leave the plastic on it?

'This microwave has never heated so much as a cup of tea,' she observed.

Silver nodded absently, already looking at the microwave's back panel.

'Laura, you've struck gold, as they say. This is interesting.'

'What?'

'There's a cable running from the back of this microwave into the counter. That's not standard installation.'

Laura crouched down to look. Sure enough, a thin black cable disappeared into what appeared to be solid counter surface.

'Grounding wire?' she asked.

'Have you ever seen a microwave that needs grounding?' Silver added, tapping the front panel, turning it on. 'And look at the timer display.'

The microwave showed in green digital numbers a pre-set time.

29:36:00

'Twenty-nine hours and thirty-six minutes,' Laura read. 'That's rather a long time to cook anything.'

Silver was quiet for a moment; his brow furrowed in concentration.

'Laura, what's twenty-nine hours and thirty-six minutes in total minutes?'

'I haven't the faintest idea. Why?'

'Because twenty-nine times sixty is... one thousand seven hundred and forty... Plus thirty-six makes... '

'One thousand seven hundred and seventy-six,' Laura finished, understanding immediately. 'The American year of Independence. Look at you, Mister Math genius!'

Silver looked slightly embarrassed at the off-hand compliment.

'I'm rather good with numbers.'

'That's more than just "good with numbers". That's quite impressive mental arithmetic.'

'Just a knack, really.' He cleared his throat.

'The email was *Independence1776*,' Laura added. 'And David's surname was Revere, so maybe the number is the code?'

'Excellent deduction,' Silver smiled. 'Shall we see if this timer setting does anything useful?'

Silver deleted the number and typed in a new timer number.

17:76

This done, he pressed the start button on the microwave. With the fact that there was no "76" on a clock, Laura expected little, but instead of beginning to heat, or even beeping an incorrect time, instead it gave a soft electronic chime.

And they heard mechanical whirring from inside the counter.

'The cable,' Laura said, understanding. 'It's connected to something.'

They both crouched down, and Silver found a small section of the counter's base panel that was now not quite flush with the rest. When he pressed it, a narrow drawer slid open.

'Clever,' he murmured. 'Hidden in plain sight.'

The concealed drawer contained items that made Laura's pulse quicken. Photocopies of passports – at least four of them, all bearing Louise's photograph but different names and nationalities, next to stacks of foreign currency, a small digital storage device and a manila envelope marked *INSURANCE*.

'Well,' Silver said, his voice carefully neutral. 'This is enlightening.'

Laura picked up the first passport photocopy. "Louise Richards" looked back at her from Polish documentation. The second showed the same face as "Irena Romanovitch" with Russian credentials. A third identified her as "Luisa Romano" from Italy.

'She wasn't David's girlfriend,' Laura whispered.

'No. I rather suspect she was sent to watch him.'

'Do you think he knew?'

Silver was looking at the digital storage device.

'Louise – or whatever her real name might be – was almost certainly intelligence. The question is which service. For David to have these hidden away though? It shows he knew about her, as she likely knew about him.'

'This hidden drawer couldn't have been hers?'

'Firstly, I don't think she would have known this even

existed. Or, maybe she didn't care. Your friend said there was no proof of a girlfriend here, so if she was removing all traces and she'd known of this, the photocopies and the money would be gone, I'm afraid.' Silver shook his head. 'She didn't know. And maybe David knew more than he let on, too.'

Laura opened the manila envelope. Inside were printouts of emails, bank transfer records, and surveillance photographs.

'These emails are printed copies of messages sent to David – from someone called "Sunday". Look at this.'

She handed him an email dated three weeks earlier:

From: Sunday
Subject has been asking questions about backup procedures. Recommend immediate assessment of security protocols.

'And this bank statement,' Laura continued. 'The deposits to David's account are from something called "Meridian Photography Services" but look at the reference numbers. They're all identical. Nobody does that, as the accounts department would have a heart attack.'

Silver looked over her shoulder at the documents.

'And this?'

He pointed to a series of printed surveillance photographs showing Harry at various London locations.

'It seems Mister Revere was monitoring Harry's every movement before he died,' Laura realised. 'But why?'

'Because David Revere wasn't an innocent bystander,' Silver said quietly. 'Look at the deposit amounts. A thousand pounds weekly for three months. That's serious money for a budding photographer.'

'Payment for what, though?'

'For watching St. Bartholomew's Church as well as other places, perhaps. For being positioned perfectly to photograph anything significant that happened.' Silver's expression was grim. 'David was surveillance, Laura. Paid surveillance.'

'But then why was Louise—'

'Surveilling the surveillance, maybe? Making sure David was doing his job properly or perhaps ensuring he didn't understand what he was really documenting. Until something made him realise he could make financial gain from this.

Laura gathered the documents carefully.

'So, Harry Farrell died whilst being monitored by at least two different intelligence operations.'

'It appears so. David photographing for one group, Louise monitoring David for another. Maybe MI5 watching CIA, or worse.'

'Do you think he knew?'

'I'd say so,' Silver nodded at the drawer. 'This is old school CIA. Meridian is a CIA slush fund too, if I remember right, but that's from a good few years back.'

'And now David's dead and Louise has vanished.'

'Along with whatever David might have known about who hired him and why.'

Before Laura could respond, they heard the unmistakable sound of the elevator arriving in the corridor. Both froze, listening to footsteps approaching along the hallway.

The footsteps paused outside David's door. Laura held her breath, acutely aware that they were standing in a murder scene with stolen intelligence materials spread across the kitchen counter.

After what felt like several geological ages but was probably only moments, the footsteps continued.

'Right,' Silver said quietly. 'Time to depart.'

Laura hastily gathered the passport photocopies, money and documents whilst Silver pocketed the digital storage device and after resetting the safe, they moved towards the front door with considerably more speed than dignity.

'Have we collected everything?' Laura whispered.

'Everything relevant. The authorities can have the rest.'

'What about passwords?'

Silver thought for a moment.

'You know,' he said eventually, 'I really think they may have been on his phone.'

Before Laura could say anything else Silver cracked the door, listening for corridor sounds. After a moment, he gestured for Laura to follow. They moved towards the stairwell rather than risk the elevator announcing their presence.

'Stairs are quieter,' Silver explained as they began their descent.

'Also more exhausting,' Laura pointed out.

'The sacrifices we make for justice.'

They reached the ground floor without drama, and Silver checked the lobby before leading Laura towards the exit.

'Walk normally,' he advised. 'We're visitors returning home now from a pleasant evening with friends.'

'At nearly midnight?'

'Dinner party. Excellent wine, fascinating conversation, lost track of time entirely.'

Despite everything, Laura smiled.

'You've clearly done this before.'

'Once or twice.'

They were approaching the main doors when Silver paused.

'Actually, let me check the rear exit first. Sometimes security patrol the front entrance, and I need to make sure we left nothing damning.'

He disappeared towards the back of the building, leaving Laura standing alone in the lobby. She found herself staring at the building directory again, trying to appear casual whilst wondering how long one should wait for someone who'd vanished to check exit routes.

In front of her, the main doors opened, and three men in dark suits entered the building's lobby, moving with the sort of purposeful stride that suggested they weren't here for social calls. Laura's stomach dropped.

These were definitely not residents returning from dinner parties.

The lead man was tall, well-built, and had the sort of controlled stillness that Laura recognised from her husband's more interesting colleagues. His companions were younger and flanked him with military precision.

'Good evening,' the leader said pleasantly, spotting Laura immediately. 'Or perhaps I should say good morning, given the hour.'

'Good evening,' Laura replied, falling back on diplomatic training. *When in doubt, be polite.*

'Lovely night for a walk,' he continued conversationally.

'Yes, quite pleasant.'

'Indeed. Though perhaps not the best night for visiting places you shouldn't be.'

Laura felt ice settle in her stomach.

They knew.

'I'm afraid I don't follow.'

'Monday's child is fair of face,' the man said, his tone remaining conversational. 'Tuesday's child is full of grace.'

'Wednesday's child is full of woe,' one of his companions continued.

'Thursday's child has far to go,' finished the third.

Laura had absolutely no idea what they were talking about, but the nursery rhyme delivery was deeply unsettling.

'How charming,' she said, forcing a smile. 'Are you practising for a children's performance?'

The leader smiled coldly, and Laura realised she'd seen him before, in a photo outside St. Bartholomew's Church.

Mister Monday.

'Friday's child is loving and giving, Saturday's child works hard for his living.'

Before Laura could ask what this had to do with anything, the man's hand moved inside his jacket, producing what appeared to be a small syringe.

Laura did the only sensible thing.

She ran.

11

CAR PARKING

She didn't know where she was going, but the building's rear exit seemed like a reasonable destination. Behind her, she could hear footsteps in pursuit. Only one pair, though – it looked like Mister Monday and one of the two men had likely decided only one of them was needed here, the sort of casual confidence that made Laura's teeth clench.

The rear door led to a set of stairs heading into the building's underground car park, which seemed like excellent cover, until she realised she had no idea where Silver had gone or that his car was parked outside the bloody apartment complex. The concrete steps were lit by harsh fluorescent lighting that made everything feel like a theatrical set – which, given the circumstances, seemed rather appropriate.

'Mrs Carlyle,' her chaser called pleasantly from the entrance. 'There's no need for dramatics. We simply want to chat.'

It wasn't the voice of the leader, and in fact it sounded young, maybe not much older than Kyle. The casual tone made it worse somehow – as if pursuing sixty-two-year-old women through underground car parks was simply part of his evening routine. Laura ducked behind a concrete pillar, her heart hammering against her ribs like a trapped bird. She was wearing sensible shoes, a woollen coat that had seen better decades, and being pursued by what appeared to be professional assassins.

This was definitely not covered in any diplomatic protocol manual.

James would have found the whole situation absurd right until he'd started planning seventeen different ways to extract them both safely.

'Come now,' the man continued, his voice echoing in the car park with that peculiar acoustic quality of underground spaces. 'We know you visited David's flat. We're pretty sure you probably found, or removed certain items. We'd simply like them back, maybe any information you might have about Harry Farrell.'

Laura looked around desperately; all around her were concrete pillars painted in that shade of institutional beige that suggested the architect had given up on life. There were parked cars that ranged from sensible family hatchbacks to the sort of expensive sports cars that suggested some residents had more money than sense, all lit by fluorescent lighting that made everything look slightly unreal, as if she'd wandered into a particularly mundane nightmare.

Not exactly a wealth of defensive options. Though Aunt Celia had always insisted that desperate situations called for creative solutions – a philosophy that had apparently served her well during forty years of diplomatic service in some of the world's more challenging locations.

The footsteps were getting closer. Measured, unhurried.

The sort of pace that suggested this young man was entirely confident in the outcome of their encounter.

Laura did the only thing she could think of. She opened her handbag – the sensible large leather *Aspinals of London* one that James had bought her for their twentieth anniversary and which had accompanied her to diplomatic functions across three continents – pulled out her keys, and when the young, suited man rounded the pillar, she swung the bag at his head with all the force she could muster.

The bag connected with a satisfying thunk, the sound echoing off the concrete walls like applause. Years of carrying essential diplomatic wife supplies meant the large handbag had considerable weight, including a purse, diary, reading glasses, emergency sewing kit, travel-sized umbrella, and a small torch that Celia insisted all sensible women carried – as well as the items taken from the apartment.

The man staggered, more surprised than hurt, giving Laura enough time to dart towards a nearby car – a dark-blue BMW. She put it between them, the metal warm under her palm from the car's recently used engine.

'That was remarkably undignified, Mrs Carlyle,' the man said, rubbing his temple with the air of someone providing constructive criticism. His accent was educated, possibly Cambridge, which somehow made the entire situation more irritating.

'Yes, well, I've had a very trying evening,' she shouted back, surprised by how steady her voice sounded. 'Being chased by people with syringes wasn't exactly on my social calendar.'

'I imagine so. Though it's about to become considerably more trying.' He reached into his jacket, like Mister Monday had upstairs, producing another syringe with the sort of efficiency that suggested this wasn't his first time threatening elderly ladies in car parks.

Laura was wondering if she could reach the exit – it seemed impossibly far away now – placing the keys between her knuckles as she did so; if she punched with these, they'd do considerable damage. She'd spent three years learning self-defence a few years before James died, partly on Celia's insistence, partly because diplomatic wives in dangerous postings learned to be practical about personal safety. The instructor had been Israeli, former military, and someone who'd spent considerable time convincing people to reconsider their life choices.

He'd taught her that elegance was less important than effectiveness, and that surprise was worth more than strength.

'Most attackers,' he'd said in his gravelly accent, 'expect ladies like you to faint or cry for help. They don't expect you to fight dirty.'

When the man rounded the car, confident in his approach, Laura stepped inside his reach and drove her knee upward with all the force she could muster, targeting the spot her instructor had described as *"universally effective, regardless of the gentleman's background or training."*

The man doubled over with a very undignified wheeze.

'Basic anatomy, I'm afraid,' Laura said conversationally, stepping back as he struggled to breathe. 'Diplomatic wives learn many useful skills. You'd be surprised what passes for essential knowledge in certain postings.'

The man tried to straighten, still clutching his stomach and making the sort of sounds that suggested her instructor's lessons had been thoroughly absorbed. Laura slammed down with her fist, a vicious punch catching him along the cheek, the keys leaving a distinctive welt as both the man and his syringe clattered to the concrete.

'You know,' she said, slightly out of breath but oddly exhilarated, stamping down hard on it, hearing it shatter under her shoe, 'I'd rather assumed I'd never need to use any of that training. James always insisted it was just a precaution.'

The adrenaline was making her hands shake, but not unpleasantly. There was something deeply satisfying about applying practical skills in appropriate circumstances.

However, the man rose again, slowly, clutching his bleeding cheek and reaching for something else in his jacket – apparently he came well-equipped for various contingencies – when Silver's voice carried across the car park with the sort of crisp authority that made everyone stop what they were doing.

'I wouldn't if I were you.'

Both Laura and the man turned to find Silver approaching, his walking cane held casually in both hands but somehow suggesting that it was considerably more than a mobility aid. His trilby was positioned at exactly the right angle, and despite everything they'd been through this evening, he looked as if he'd just stepped out of his club.

'Well, well,' the man said, genuine surprise replacing his previous professional confidence. 'This is unexpected.'

'Life's full of surprises,' Silver replied, his tone conversational but with an undertone that suggested the conversation was unlikely to go the young man's way.

'Indeed it is. We were told you were dead.'

'Greatly exaggerated, I'm afraid.' Silver's cane moved suddenly – not like a walking stick, but like a weapon wielded by someone who'd spent considerable time learning exactly how to use it effectively.

The silver base struck the man's shoulder with a sharp crack. The man staggered but didn't fall. Instead, he laughed – the sort of laugh that suggested he knew something the rest of them didn't.

'One charge, old man. That's all those antique toys carry, and you've not recharged since the last use.'

'You're quite right,' Silver agreed pleasantly, twisting his cane. Laura heard a soft click as he did so, the sound precise and mechanical. When he pulled at the top, a thin blade slid out from the wooden shaft with a whisper that suggested excellent craftsmanship. 'Fortunately, I believe in redundancy plans.'

The man's expression changed rapidly from confident amusement to professional concern.

'That's not regulation issue.'

'No,' Silver said, advancing with the sword held with the casual competence of someone who'd learned to use it properly. 'It's considerably older than that. But you're too young to know that, aren't you? Maybe a Saturday, perhaps? New recruits and all that?'

The man looked at the blade, then at Silver's determined expression, and seemed to recalculate his options rapidly. Whatever he saw in Silver's face apparently convinced him that retreat was the better part of valour.

'Look,' he said, backing away with his hands raised, 'I'm a Friday. Not even a senior Friday. So, maybe we can discuss this like civilised people?'

'Splendid idea,' Silver agreed pleasantly, though his grip on the sword-cane didn't relax. 'Though I think you'll find the discussion rather one-sided.'

He punctuated this by flipping the sword cane in his hand with a theatrical flourish, and then quickly slamming the hilt into the man's head with precisely the right amount of force. The young man stumbled backwards, tripped over his own feet with perfect comedic timing, and then slammed the back of his skull into the concrete floor with a sound that made Laura wince.

'Gravity,' Silver observed, sliding the blade back into his cane with a satisfied click. 'Remarkably effective weapon when properly applied. Time to leave, I think.'

'Is he...?' Laura gestured at the unconscious figure, who was lying in the sort of position that suggested he'd be waking up with more than just wounded pride.

'Sleeping. He'll wake with a headache and wounded pride, nothing more. Though I suspect his colleagues will be rather less sympathetic about his failure than his physical condition.'

'And the others?'

'I may have delayed them on my way down here.' Silver was hurrying towards the exit, and a familiar Mercedes that sat waiting with the sort of convenient timing that suggested considerable forethought. 'Though not for long.'

As if to emphasise his point, the distant sound of sirens began echoing through the London night, growing stronger by the moment.

'Police?' Laura asked as Silver opened the car door for her with old-fashioned courtesy.

'Possibly. Or more of their colleagues.' Silver started the engine, which turned over with the smooth purr of expensive German engineering. 'Either way, I'd prefer not to explain our presence here.'

They drove out of the car park just as blue lights began

reflecting off the building's windows, painting the concrete walls in shifting patterns of emergency services blue. Laura looked back to see police cars arriving at the main entrance.

'Rather convenient timing,' she observed.

'Yes. Though I suspect that wasn't a coincidence.'

'What do you mean?'

Silver was quiet for a moment, focusing on the traffic with the sort of careful attention that suggested he was thinking about more than just navigation.

'Someone called the police, Laura. Someone who knew we'd need help.'

'Who?'

Silver adjusted his trilby with one hand whilst steering with the other, the gesture automatic and somehow reassuring.

'That,' he said, 'is an excellent question. Another is how my car arrived where it needed to be.'

'You mean you didn't drive it there?' Laura's eyes widened as the implications struck her. 'I assumed that's what you'd run off to do.'

'I'm afraid not,' Silver shook his head, his expression troubled. 'I was only checking doors. Someone else decided we might need a quick getaway from the car park. Which very much assumes they knew we'd be heading to the car park.'

'But how did they drive without the keys?'

Silver reddened slightly.

'I admit I might have left them in the ignition,' he admitted.

Laura stared at him – it felt off to make such an amateur mistake here. What was Silver truly hiding? Did he know someone would need to drive the car? Or was this for a quick getaway?

As they drove through quiet streets towards Queen's Gate, Laura thought about what had just happened. She'd been chased by armed men, defended herself with a handbag and a keyring, and had almost witnessed a sword fight. The adrenaline was fading, leaving her feeling oddly hollow and strangely proud.

'Silver,' she said finally.

'Yes?'

'When that man said you were supposed to be dead...'

'Yes?'

'That wasn't the first time you'd heard someone say that to you, was it?'

Silver's hand moved to his trilby again, but this time he stopped himself before completing the gesture.

'No,' he said quietly. 'It wasn't.'

'And those men knew you.'

'They knew someone they thought I was, yes.'

Laura looked at him in the car's dim light, seeing not the charming gentleman who'd been helping her investigation, but someone far more complex and potentially dangerous. Someone who carried sword-canes and knew exactly how to use them.

'Who are you really, Sebastian Silver?'

'That,' he said, turning onto Queen's Gate where the familiar streetlights promised warmth and safety and explanations over tea, 'is the question I've been trying to answer for fifteen years.'

12

MOCKINGBIRD

LAURA WOKE TO THE SMELL OF PROPER BACON. SUNLIGHT streamed through her bedroom curtains with the sort of cheerful persistence that suggested London was having one of its rare, good weather days.

She was reaching for her dressing gown when Aunt Celia appeared in the doorway, already immaculately dressed despite the early hour and carrying a cup of tea like a peace offering.

'Good morning, dear,' Celia said, settling into the reading chair by the window. 'Sleep well?'

'Surprisingly well, actually,' Laura replied, accepting the tea gratefully. 'You're up early. It's barely eight o'clock.'

'Difficult to sleep when one's niece arrives home at half-past twelve in the morning looking like she's been wrestling with London itself.'

Laura sat up properly, wincing slightly as muscles she'd forgotten she possessed reminded her of the previous evening's adventures.

'We encountered some complications.'

'Complications involving what appeared to be concrete dust, and a torn hem?'

'You could say that.'

Celia raised an eyebrow. 'I could say many things, Laura. In particular how a now vintage *Aspinals of London* handbag looks like it was on the Dunkirk beaches. I'd prefer to hear the actual story first.'

Before Laura could attempt an explanation that wouldn't sound completely mad, Kyle's voice echoed up the stairs with the particular enthusiasm that suggested he'd discovered something either fascinating or potentially explosive.

'Gran! There's post for you! Fancy post! Really fancy!'

'Anonymous correspondence at breakfast time,' Celia observed with the tone of someone who'd spent decades navigating diplomatic intrigue. 'How delightfully mysterious. Though I do hope it's not another charity committee attempting to recruit you for something involving the arrangement of flowers, realising this is the only way to get your attention these days.'

Laura pulled on her dressing gown and followed Celia downstairs, where Kyle was standing in the kitchen examining a cream envelope as if it might contain state secrets.

'Someone slipped it under the door,' he said, handing it over. 'Feels expensive. Like wedding invitation expensive.'

The envelope bore Laura's name in elegant script. Inside was a single sheet of matching paper:

Mrs Carlyle,

Recent events suggest we have mutual interests. David Revere was under our protection, though he didn't know it.

His death represents a significant escalation in activities we've been monitoring.

I believe Sebastian Silver has been honest with you about some things, but not others. The man you knew as Harry Farrell left materials that may interest you. The newspaper clipping he kept wasn't about your garden investigation – look at the byline.

Ask about Mockingbird.

Watch your back. The people who killed David won't hesitate to expand their target list.

The one who wouldn't let you enter.

'Well,' Aunt Celia said, reading over Laura's shoulder with the focused attention she usually reserved for particularly challenging crossword clues, 'that's refreshingly direct. No beating about the bush with pleasantries.'

Kyle peered at the letter with frank curiosity.

'Who's the one who wouldn't let you enter?'

'Probably the woman who called herself Louise,' Laura suggested.

'Louise? The nervous girlfriend who turned out not to be a girlfriend at all?'

'The same.' Laura looked at the handwriting – confident, educated, nothing like the young woman who'd answered David's door. 'Though clearly she's rather more than she appeared.'

'She mentions looking at the byline,' Celia observed, settling back with her tea. 'Presumably from that newspaper clipping Harry kept about your orchid triumph. Keith O'Neill wrote that piece, didn't he? Rather dramatic treatment of what was essentially neighbourhood gossip about plant sabotage, purely to make you good, so you'd likely go to dinner with him.'

'Celia, he's gay.'

'I didn't say sleep with him, dear. I said dinner,' Celia smiled. 'Maybe this Harry was trying to point towards him?'

Sighing, Laura nodded slowly.

'Keith might know something. Or at least be able to help us understand what we discovered last night.'

'Ah yes,' Celia said, settling at the kitchen table with her own tea and the morning crossword. 'About last night. I'm still waiting for that explanation.'

Laura poured herself cereal and considered how to explain the previous evening without sounding like she'd lost her mind entirely.

'We searched David's apartment,' Laura continued matter-of-factly, as if discussing her weekly shopping arrangements. 'Broke in, found evidence that David was likely CIA, but was also being paid to monitor Harry at various events and locations, such as St. Bartholomew's Church, whilst Louise was apparently monitoring David. Rather like those Russian dolls that nest inside each other.'

'Surveillance watching surveillance,' Celia mused, not looking up from her crossword. 'How wonderfully recursive. Fifteen across: "Spies watching spies." Starts with M.'

'Matryoshka?' Kyle suggested.

'Too many letters. Think simpler.'

'Mirrors?'

'It'll do for the moment.' Celia pencilled it in. 'So, David wasn't the innocent photography amateur he appeared to be?'

'Far from it. He was receiving regular payments through something called Meridian Photography Services. Thousand pounds a week for months. And Louise had enough false passports to supply a small theatre company. Russian, Polish, Italian – all with her photograph but different identities.'

'Multiple nationalities suggests serious intelligence work,' Celia observed. 'You remember what the briefings were like. MI5, MI6, or possibly something more exotic. Though given the quality of her performance as a nervous girlfriend, I'd lean towards British training. We've always been rather good at that sort of thing.'

'It gets more interesting. We were leaving when three men in suits appeared. They knew Silver.'

Kyle leaned forward eagerly.

'What happened? Did you fight them?'

'I hit one with my handbag, and might have... well, punched him, too. Drew blood.'

'How?'

'I... um... might have used keys as a "knuckleduster", I believe the term's called.'

'Gran.' The awe in Kyle's tone was unmistakable.

'Anyway, that's all I did, while Silver made them leave using that walking stick of his.'

'The electric one?'

'Among other capabilities, yes. Turns out it's also a sword.'

Celia looked up from her crossword.

'Of course it is. Because apparently we're living in a spy novel now.'

'How do you feel about all this?' Kyle asked, clearly fascinated by his grandmother's transformation into some sort of senior citizen action hero.

'Oddly energised,' Laura admitted. 'Though also concerned about what we've stumbled into.'

'Both perfectly reasonable responses,' Celia replied. 'And Mister Silver? How did he handle things?'

'Like someone trying very hard to remember something he'd rather forget.'

Before Celia could pursue this observation, the doorbell rang. Kyle went to answer it, and a few minutes later he returned with Silver himself. He looked as impeccable as always, but Laura noticed a slight tension around his eyes.

'Good morning, ladies. Kyle allowed me in on the condition I allow him to play with my cane. I'm unsure if this is some kind of teenage euphemism or something.' Silver nodded to both of them. 'I trust everyone recovered from our eventful evening?'

'Define recovered,' Celia replied dryly. 'Laura appears to have developed new muscles overnight, and you've become one of the *Three Musketeers*.'

Silver looked genuinely concerned as he looked at Laura.

'Are you injured?'

'Just stiff. Nothing serious.' Laura showed him Louise's letter. 'Though this arrived this morning.'

Silver read it carefully, his frown deepening.

'Mockingbird.'

'You know the name?'

'I...' Silver paused, looking genuinely puzzled. 'It's familiar. But I can't place why.'

Kyle watched this exchange with the intensity of someone watching a particularly good television drama.

'Is it a code name?'

'Possibly.' Silver looked troubled at his inability to pinpoint the name. 'The note mentions that Harry kept a newspaper clipping. Do you still have it?'

Laura retrieved the clipping from her handbag. The headline about her orchid investigation seemed rather ridiculous now, but the byline was clear:

Keith O'Neill, Society Reporter.

'Keith wrote the piece about my garden society triumph,' Laura said. 'If Harry kept it...'

'He might have been trying to point you towards your friend without explaining so loudly that everyone realised,' Silver finished. 'As the writing says at the bottom – "they'll know". Maybe the clipping wasn't leading to you but leading you to Keith.'

'*They know* could be *Keith knows*,' Laura nodded. 'Surely Rebecca would have known this, though? It would have saved a lot of tedious running around.'

'You would have thought so. Still, it's worth investigating,' Silver said, glancing at Celia. 'If your aunt allows you out to play.'

Celia glanced up from the crossword for a moment, fixed Silver with an ice cold glare, and then returned to the paper.

'I thought I'd go see Keith this morning,' Laura replied. 'If Harry left anything with him, I need to know what it contains.'

'I'll come with you,' Silver said immediately.

'Actually,' Laura said carefully, 'I think I should go alone.'

'Is that wise?' Silver looked surprised.

'Keith's an old friend. He'll be more open if it's just me asking casual questions...' Laura paused. 'Besides, those men last night clearly knew you. Your presence might make him nervous.'

Silver considered this.

'You may be right.'

'I'll take Kyle,' Laura added. 'University students are excellent camouflage.'

'Research project?' Kyle brightened considerably.

'Exactly.'

'And what should Mister Silver do whilst you're conducting journalism?' Celia set down her crossword pen.

'Perhaps examine those materials we found more thoroughly,' Laura suggested. 'That digital storage device might tell us something useful.'

Silver nodded, though he still looked uncomfortable with the separation.

'Very well. But please be careful, Laura. If the letter writer is correct about escalating situations...'

'It's broad daylight, and Keith's hardly a dangerous character. What could possibly go wrong?'

'You could be murdered outside a medieval church, for a start,' Celia observed, returning to her crossword.

An hour later, Laura and Kyle were walking through Fleet Street towards *The Herald* building, one of the last papers based anywhere near the legendary address, and even then it was just an editorial office – the printers were out past Wapping.

Kyle carried his usual messenger bag, looking like any

other student heading to the library, whilst Laura had dressed in the sort of understated elegance that suggested connections without being flashy about it.

So, basically, her normal attire.

'Nervous?' Kyle asked as they approached the building.

'Oddly, no,' Laura smiled. 'I'm beginning to enjoy this investigative business.'

'Even after last night's excitement?'

'Especially after last night. For the first time in years, I feel like I'm doing something that matters rather than just arranging flowers for hospital fundraisers.'

The Herald's reception area was pure faded grandeur – marble columns that had seen better decades, brass fittings that needed polishing, and the lingering aroma of cigarettes from back when smoking indoors was still legal. Laura gave her name to the receptionist, a young man who looked barely old enough to read newspapers properly.

'Keith O'Neill? Yeah, he's in. Third floor, editorial. Lift's broken, so you'll need the stairs, I'm afraid.'

'Thank you.'

Three flights of increasingly worn-carpeted stairs later, they emerged into a newsroom that hummed with the particular energy of people chasing deadlines. Reporters hunched over computers, mobile phones rang constantly, and the air carried that mixture of coffee, paper, and mild panic that seemed to define newspaper offices everywhere.

Keith O'Neill sat at a desk near the windows, looking exactly as Laura remembered – rumpled shirt, reading glasses sliding down his nose, surrounded by papers that could have represented either brilliant organisation or complete chaos.

'Laura!' He stood as she approached, his face lighting up.

'What brings you to my humble corner? Don't tell me the garden society has uncovered another conspiracy involving prize-winning roses and international espionage.'

'Nothing quite so dramatic, I hope.' Laura smiled. 'Keith, this is my grandson Kyle.'

'University?'

'Yes. Economics.'

'Excellent. Always good to meet the next generation.' Keith gestured to chairs beside his desk. 'So, what brings you both here? Research project?'

Laura settled herself carefully.

'Actually, I wanted to ask about a mutual acquaintance, a chap called Harry Farrell. American.'

At the name Keith's whole demeanour changed.

'Oh,' he said. 'The man on the street.'

'You sound familiar with it,' Laura said. 'How familiar, Keith?'

'Why are you asking, Laura?'

As a reply, Laura pulled out the clipping, passing it across.

'Because he wrote that on this before he died,' she said.

Keith opened the clipping and read the two words slowly.

They'll Know.

'Okay, yes, I met him,' he mumbled. 'Few weeks back. He said he knew you through your husband's work. Diplomatic circles, that sort of thing. Read my piece, learnt we were friends.'

Kyle leaned forward.

'What did he want exactly?'

Keith lowered his voice slightly.

'Said he was researching something from years ago. Something involving your family, Laura. Asked if I'd be willing to hold on to some materials – research he'd been doing.'

'What sort of materials?' Laura tried to keep her expression neutral.

'Newspaper clippings, old photographs, that sort of thing. Said if anything happened to him, I should give them to someone I trusted,' Keith smiled sadly. 'Specifically, he said I should give them to a familiar face if they asked. A week or two later, he's dead. What exactly have you gotten into, Laura?'

Kyle looked between them.

'Did you take the materials?' he asked.

'I did. Though I'll admit, I thought the old boy might be paranoid. Research into old diplomatic functions, society pages from almost twenty years ago – it all seemed rather harmless.'

'And now?' Laura asked quietly.

Keith's expression grew sombre.

'Now Harry Farrell's dead, and you're here asking questions. Makes a journalist wonder if perhaps his research wasn't quite as harmless as it seemed.'

He opened his desk drawer and withdrew a manila envelope. Laura accepted it with hands that trembled slightly.

'What's in here?'

'See for yourself. Though I'll warn you, if Harry was right to be worried, you're looking at something that got him killed.'

Laura opened the envelope carefully. Inside were newspaper clippings, society pages, and several photographs – all dating from around twenty years ago, maybe a couple of years less. Most featured James at various diplomatic functions and charity events. But as she examined them more closely, her breath caught.

In the background of several photos, barely noticeable unless you were looking for him, was a familiar figure. A younger man, his hair dark, but the trilby hat was a dead giveaway as he watched from the edges of the frame.

'Keith,' she whispered, holding up one photograph. 'Do you recognise anyone in these pictures besides James?'

Keith adjusted his glasses and peered at the photo.

'Your husband, obviously. Some other diplomatic types I vaguely recognise. Why?'

Laura pointed to the background figure.

'This man. In the trilby.'

Keith squinted.

'Bloke in the hat? Can't say I do. Bit blurry, isn't he? Could be anyone.'

But Laura knew better. It was Sebastian Silver, twenty years younger but unmistakably the same man, looking exactly as he had in the "Three Musketeers" photo.

'Laura?' Keith asked, noting her expression. 'What is it?'

'I think,' she said slowly, studying the photographs with new understanding, 'Harry Farrell knew a great deal more about my family's history than he let on.'

There was a crash to the side that made all three jump, but it was merely a reporter moving too quickly and knocking a box file onto the floor. Regaining their composure, they settled back down.

'Keith,' she said finally, 'may I take these?'

'They're yours. If I'm right, Harry left them specifically for you…' Keith paused. 'Laura, be careful. If Harry was right about this conspiracy, then you're walking into something considerably more dangerous than garden society politics. They seem to have an interest in you and your late husband.'

'I understand.'

'Do you? Because the last person who apparently tried to investigate them ended up dead on a London street.'

'There's one more thing,' Laura placed the clippings back into the envelope. 'Does the name Mockingbird mean anything?'

'Harry mentioned someone called Mockingbird. Said if anything happened to him, Mockingbird would make contact with the right people.'

'Did he say who Mockingbird was?'

'No. But he seemed to think this person would know how to find you when the time was right.'

A young man with thick-rimmed glasses and pen-stained fingers leaned through the doorframe at this moment, pausing the conversation.

'Photos are up for the afternoon edition,' he said. 'If you want them enhanced, I'll need to move soon.'

'Thanks, Jason,' Keith said, looking back at Laura. 'Look, if there's anything else I can help with...'

Laura paused, her hand moving instinctively to her phone.

The photographs from David's camera – she'd been so focused on Harry's materials that she'd almost forgotten about them.

'Actually, there is something else. I have photographs from the day Harry died. Digital images that might show what actually happened. Could you enhance them?'

'What sort of photographs?'

'A young man was taking pictures near St. Bartholomew's Church that afternoon. His girlfriend was posing in front of the building, but Harry and another man are visible in the background.'

Laura pulled up the images on her phone, her fingers trembling slightly as she scrolled to the crucial shots.

'Here. This was taken just moments before Harry collapsed.'

Keith studied the screen, squinting at the small display, zooming in with his fingers.

'I can see figures, but they're too pixelated and compressed to make out details. Let me get these onto Jason's workstation – he handles our photo editing.'

They moved to a computer across the editorial floor, where the same young man with thick-rimmed glasses and pen-stained fingers looked up from a layout he was working on.

'Jason, mate,' Keith said. 'Emergency photo enhancement job. Can you help us out?'

Jason pushed his glasses up his nose and examined Laura's phone.

'What have we got then?'

'Possible crime scene photographs,' Keith explained. 'Background figures we need to bring into focus.'

'Right.' Jason began transferring the images to his workstation. 'Right, well, for a start you're lucky these are RAW files. No compression artefacts to work around – the camera saved everything. Most phones these days compress automatically, but this looks like someone knew what they were doing.'

'What difference does that make?' Kyle leaned forward with interest.

'Huge difference,' Jason replied, warming to his subject as

the images loaded onto his monitor. 'JPEG compression throws away data to make smaller files. When you try to enhance a compressed image, you're basically guessing what information was lost. But RAW files? They keep everything the sensor captured, even when compressed to a smaller screen.'

Laura watched, fascinated despite her anxiety, as Jason began working with professional software she'd never seen before.

'See here?' Jason pointed to the background figures. 'All that detail's still there, just waiting to be brought out. Bit like a darkroom, really, except I can push these pixels harder than any chemical process ever could.'

He adjusted levels and sharpening algorithms before eventually stepping back from the monitor.

'There. Much better resolution. Keith, what exactly are we looking for?'

'The interaction between these two men,' Keith replied quietly. 'Just before one of them died.'

Laura watched, mesmerised, as Jason continued refining the image. The blurry figures in the background resolved into recognisable shapes. Harry's face became clearer first, his expression showing obvious distress.

'We can use AI to enhance but I'd rather not,' Jason explained. 'You can't prove what's real and what's hallucinated.'

'I don't think you need to, as that's definitely Harry,' she confirmed, her voice barely above a whisper.

Jason continued working, isolating the second figure. The well-dressed man came into focus – tall, confident, positioned very close to Harry.

Mister Monday.

'Look at his hand,' Keith said quietly, Jason now zooming in further.

Laura leaned forwards, her breath catching. The man's right hand was extended towards Harry's face, and in it was something small and tubular that caught the afternoon light.

'Oh my God,' she whispered.

'What is it, Gran?' Kyle asked, concern clear in his voice.

'A syringe.' The word came out as barely a breath. Laura's mind flashed back to the lobby the night before and Mister Monday, to the identical small syringe he'd produced with such casual efficiency. 'It's a syringe.'

The room seemed to tilt around her. She gripped the edge of the desk, her knuckles white.

That could have been her in this photograph. Would have been her, if Sebastian hadn't appeared when he did.

'Laura?' Keith's voice seemed to come from very far away. 'Are you all right?'

She couldn't answer immediately. The enhanced photograph showed Harry's last moments with terrible clarity – the shock in his expression, the calculated precision of his killer, the casual nature of murder disguised as a medical emergency.

Keith was already printing the enhanced photographs in silence, and when he handed her the crisp, clear images, Laura stared at documentary evidence of premeditated murder.

'This isn't just proof that Harry was killed,' she breathed. 'This is proof of how they operate. How they've probably killed others.'

'Laura,' Keith said gently, 'you need to take this to the police. This is evidence of an assassination.'

She nodded, though part of her wondered if the police

would understand the full scope of what they were dealing with. Looking at the photograph, she could see Mister Monday's face clearly now – professional, calm, utterly without conscience.

'Yes,' she said, carefully folding the photographs. 'Though I suspect this is only the beginning of what we're going to uncover.'

'Well, whatever happens, when this is all sorted, we get exclusivity on these,' Keith said, the editor side returning. 'After all, we did the donkey work here.'

'Agreed,' Laura smiled, patting Keith on the shoulder. 'And when this is all sorted? Dinner's on me.'

As they walked back through Fleet Street, Kyle couldn't contain his curiosity any longer.

'Gran, who was that man in the photographs? You looked like you'd seen a ghost.'

Laura clutched the envelope tighter.

'Someone I thought I'd only just met. But apparently, he's been part of my life much longer than I realised.'

'The man with the trilby? Sebastian?'

'It appears so. Which means either Sebastian Silver has been watching my family for almost twenty years, or...'

She paused, the implications settling in her mind.

'Or whatever happened fifteen years ago, around the time of your grandfather's death, involved Sebastian directly.'

'That's a bit scary, isn't it?'

'Terrifying,' Laura agreed. 'But also illuminating. Harry wasn't just investigating The Calendar organisation. He was investigating my family's connection to it.'

As they reached the main road, Laura looked over her shoulder, wondering if Sebastian Silver was watching them even now. And if he was, whether it was for their protection or for reasons far more complex and potentially dangerous.

The envelope in her hands felt heavier than it should, weighted with fifteen years of questions she'd never thought to ask.

13

CRIME SCENE INVEST-I-GATION

Laura sat in her conservatory, staring at the enhanced photographs spread across the wicker table alongside Harry's newspaper clippings. The images were damning – clear evidence of Harry's murder, with the syringe visible in Mister Monday's hand as he approached his victim.

She picked up the phone, then set it down again.

How exactly did one ask a charming gentleman whether he had been following her for years? Particularly when that gentleman had saved her life and seemed genuinely committed to finding Harry's killer?

The grandfather clock in the hallway chimed half-past twelve, and Laura realised she'd been sitting here for nearly an hour, trying to work up the courage for a conversation that might change everything.

'You're brooding again,' came Aunt Celia's voice from the doorway.

'I'm contemplating,' Laura replied, gathering the photographs into a neat stack.

'Poppycock. You've had that same look since you discovered someone had been watering your orchids with tap water.'

'I was right to be irritated, thank you.'

Celia settled into the opposite chair, eyeing the evidence spread across the table.

'This is rather damning, isn't it? This has to be obvious proof that Harry Farrell was murdered.'

'Yes, though I'm wondering if we can trust the source of our information.'

'The photos?'

'The man.'

'Mister Silver?' Celia's eyebrows rose. 'What's brought on this sudden scepticism?'

Before Laura could explain about Harry's clippings, her mobile rang with Frank's name appearing on the screen.

'Afternoon, Frank. Please tell me this is a social call.'

'Laura.' His voice sounded like he'd been chewing gravel since dawn. 'I need you to come look at something. And bring your mysterious friend with the fancy walking stick.'

Laura's pulse quickened. 'What's happened?'

'We found a body this morning. Brian Waterstone, twenty-six, shot twice around two in the morning. Spotless work...' Frank paused. 'He was carrying detailed surveillance notes about your daily routine.'

The conservatory seemed to grow silent.

'Surveillance notes about me?'

'Three days' worth. Times, locations, shopping habits – someone's been documenting your every movement, Laura. And now that someone is very dead.'

Celia leaned forward, abandoning all pretence of working on her crossword.

'Should I recognise the name Brian Waterstone?' Laura asked down the phone.

'You tell me. Laura, what were you doing at David Revere's building last night?'

Laura blinked. 'I'm sorry?'

'We have evidence placing you in the building lobby and car park late yesterday evening. A couple of hours before Brian was killed.'

'How do you—' Laura caught herself, mind racing. 'I don't understand.'

'It doesn't take much detective work, Laura. So, what were you doing there?'

Laura's mouth went dry. She couldn't exactly explain they'd broken in to search a murder victim's flat.

'I... we went back to look for Louise.'

'Louise Richards, who doesn't exist?'

'I thought she might return. To collect her things. She'd left so suddenly after David was killed, and I wondered if she might know something more about what happened.'

'At midnight?'

'Not midnight. Earlier. Perhaps... oh, I can't remember. I thought if she was avoiding the police, she might come back late when no one was watching.'

'And did you find this mysterious Louise?'

'No. The building was quiet. We waited in the lobby for a while, then left.'

'The lobby and the car park?'

Laura hesitated.

'We... checked the car park in case she was avoiding the main entrance.'

'I see. And how long did this Louise-hunting expedition last?'

'Not long. Twenty minutes, perhaps.'

Frank's silence stretched uncomfortably. Laura could feel Celia watching her with sharp interest.

'Laura,' Frank said finally, his voice carrying the patience of someone who'd heard thousands of unsatisfactory explanations. 'That's a touching story about looking for a woman who may not exist. But I think we both know you weren't there hunting for mysterious girlfriends at twelve o'clock at night. For a start, you're not mentioning what you *did* in the car park. Especially with Brian Waterhouse, who was there at the time.'

Laura felt the room spinning. She'd always considered herself a woman of the world, but now with news of more death...

'All right,' Laura said, recognising defeat, sitting back, taking a deep breath to calm her nerves. 'Perhaps I should explain properly when we meet.'

'That would be wise. Bring chum in the trilby, too. Rotherhithe. Forty-seven Albion Street. And Laura? Don't be late.'

After ending the call, Laura looked at Celia, who had set down her pen entirely.

'Well,' Celia said, 'that was dreadful. You sounded like you were making it up as you went along. Which of course, you were, but you should never actually sound as if you are.'

'It was the best I could manage on short notice.'

'James would have done better. Though I suppose it's rather difficult to explain midnight burglary without sounding like a criminal.'

'We weren't burgling. We were investigating.'

'With lock picks, in the middle of the night.' Celia's tone was perfectly dry. 'Simple mistake to make.'

Laura sent a message to Silver.

Frank wants to meet. Crime scene in Rotherhithe. 47 Albion Street. Can you come?

The reply came within moments:

Of course. What's happened?

Someone was watching me. Now they're dead. Brian Waterhouse. Do you know the name?

There was a pause and then in quick succession

He was Mister Friday.

I'll be right there.

'You know, for a dead man, he certainly answers his texts quickly,' Celia observed, setting down Harry's organisational chart. 'You're worried about trusting him.'

'Shouldn't I be? According to Harry Farrell's research, Sebastian Silver disappeared years ago.'

'And last night people who wanted to kill you said he was dead, according to you this morning,' Celia replied cooly. 'Yet here he is, very much alive and remarkably well-informed about murder investigations. People in the intelligence world have been known to arrange their own deaths for various reasons. The question is whether his reasons align with your interests or oppose them.'

She was paused from continuing, however, when Kyle's voice echoed down from upstairs, accompanied by what sounded like furniture being moved around.

'What's he doing up there?' Laura asked.

'Reorganising his investigation board. Apparently your evening's discoveries require "proper criminal enterprise organisation".' Celia smiled. 'He's having the time of his life with all this.'

'Someone should enjoy themselves, I suppose.'

'Laura.' Celia's voice grew more serious. 'You've been different these past few days. More like the woman you were when James was alive – engaged, purposeful, alive in a way you haven't been for years. James always said you were wasted as a diplomatic wife.'

'James had a romantic view of my capabilities.'

'James had an accurate view,' Celia corrected firmly.

Kyle thundered down the stairs at that moment, messenger bag over his shoulder and looking pleased with himself.

'Raj just texted. He's finished with Harry's phone!'

'What did he find?' Laura asked.

'Claims it's mainly a video file and an image, but he's not touching either without a lawyer or the police present – his exact words.' Kyle waved his mobile. 'Can we go see? Please?'

Laura gathered the photographs and Harry's files.

'We'll collect the phone data after we meet Frank at a crime scene.'

'Crime scene?' Kyle's eyes lit up. 'Someone *else* is dead?'

'Yes, and before you get excited, this one was apparently watching me for days before someone executed him.'

'Executed?' Kyle's voice cracked slightly. '*Actually* executed?'

'Shot twice around two in the morning. Very professional work.' It was Celia's turn to answer now, apparently taking pleasure in watching Kyle become more squeamish by the second.

'That's...' Kyle swallowed. 'That's not quite as exciting as it sounds, is it?'

'No, darling,' Celia said gently. 'It really isn't.'

LAURA STOOD OUTSIDE THE NARROW TERRACED HOUSE IN Rotherhithe and took a slow, rotating look around the area. It felt like the sort of street where neighbours minded their own business and didn't ask awkward questions about late-night disturbances. The house itself was unremarkable – a red-brick front that needed repointing, white window frames showing years of London weather, and to the front, a small garden where someone had once been optimistic about roses.

Crime scene tape fluttered whilst forensics officers moved methodically in and out with evidence bags and photography equipment, while a small crowd of neighbours lingered at an appropriate distance, drawn by morbid curiosity, whilst uniformed officers maintained the perimeter. Laura looked to her side, where Kyle waited nervously.

'Say nothing,' she ordered. 'I don't want anything said that can damn either of us here.'

Kyle went to speak, and Laura knew she'd overstated the seriousness there.

'Okay, yes, I know I'm the one who did the thing we're likely in trouble for, but I just want you looked after.'

Kyle nodded, a small, relieved smile on the edges of his mouth.

Before Laura could continue, however, Frank emerged

from the front door looking like he'd been dealing with unpleasant surprises all day and sustained by nothing more than police station coffee; his usual cheerful demeanour had been replaced by the mask he wore when dealing with the unpleasant realities of human nature.

'Laura.' He approached. 'I have to say, I'm getting rather tired of calling you to murder scenes.'

'This is only the second one,' Laura pointed out.

'That's two more than most respectable widows manage in their entire lives.' Frank consulted his notebook. 'But that was a trick question, wasn't it?'

Laura grimaced. Although she *had* been to another crime scene – that of David's murder – that'd been on her own cognisance, and not on a call from Frank.

'I think Gran assumed you meant the garden show,' Kyle stepped in quickly. 'You know, when Keith did the piece on her.'

Frank went to reply, thought better of it, and returned to his notes.

'I see you brought your grandson,' he muttered. 'I'll save him the crime scene photos, as he's only what, twelve?'

Kyle said nothing, which actually impressed Laura; usually he'd "clap back" with something – as he liked to call it – but perhaps this time he was wise enough to know a solid rebuttal could cause an arrest.

'Brian Waterstone, twenty-six, officially unemployed for the past eight months but somehow affording the rent on this place plus a rather nice BMW parked round the corner,' Frank read from the pad.

'Expensive lifestyle for someone without income,' Kyle observed.

'Very expensive. Two bullets to the back of the head

sometime around two in the morning, execution style. Clean work – no forced entry, no struggle, no defensive wounds to the hands – although he has a scratched up cheek.'

Laura desperately wanted to ask more on that but decided for the moment she knew better. If Kyle could shut up, so could she.

'Whoever killed Brian, he knew them well enough to let them into his house,' Frank finished.

Laura shivered despite her warm coat.

'And the surveillance notes?'

'Comprehensive. Three days' worth of detailed observations.' Frank flipped through pages. 'Your address, daily routine, shopping preferences, which coffee shop you visit, what time you leave the house, which route you take to the Underground. He knew you prefer Earl Grey over English Breakfast, that you shop at Waitrose rather than Tesco, and that you take the Northern line when you could perfectly well take the Piccadilly, that you met a man in a trilby in St. Bartholomew's.'

The violation of privacy made Laura's skin crawl.

'Someone paid him to document my every movement?'

'Paid him well, judging by his lifestyle. But here's the interesting part—'

Frank paused as Sebastian Silver's voice carried from down the street.

'Mrs Carlyle! Detective Inspector Young, I presume?'

Even in this shabby neighbourhood, Silver looked like he was heading to a diplomatic reception rather than a crime scene. His charcoal suit was perfectly tailored, trilby set at precisely the right angle, walking stick clearly serving purposes beyond mere support.

'Mister Silver.' Frank turned, taking in Silver's immaculate appearance. 'You'd be the helpful gentleman I've been hearing about.'

'Sebastian Silver.' He offered his hand with a slight bow. 'Delighted to meet you properly, Detective In—'

'Detective *Chief* Inspector.'

'Didn't I just say that?'

'No, you said Detective Inspector.'

'And a Detective Chief Inspector isn't a Detective Inspector, if a little more senior?'

'A rank title needs the full title.'

'Ah,' Silver smiled. 'In that case, let me introduce myself. Lord Sebastian Silver of Glencoe, Reverend Minister, Doctor of Divinity, Knight of the Sovereign Order of the Temple of Jerusalem, Archdruid of the Universal Life Church, Esquire.'

'Those are made up!' Frank exploded.

'All titles are made up, as they were once created from nothing,' Silver waved an accusatory finger. 'But I guarantee my titles are all genuine, and I have the online certificates to prove so.'

Kyle watched this introduction, clearly enjoying the formal politeness that barely concealed underlying tensions.

'And you knew Harry Farrell how, exactly?' Frank asked, deciding to ignore this, notebook poised.

'Old friends from years past. His death was rather unexpected, though not entirely surprising given the circumstances.'

'What circumstances? According to our medical examiner, Harry Farrell died of natural causes.'

Silver's expression remained pleasantly neutral, but Laura caught something flickering behind his grey eyes.

'Medical examiners are skilled professionals, naturally,

but they occasionally miss subtleties that become apparent with closer examination.'

'What sort of subtleties?'

'The sort that require analysis to detect properly.'

Laura watched this exchange. Silver was being his usual charming self, deflecting questions, yet Frank's instincts were clearly engaged. She could almost see him filing away Silver's responses for later analysis.

'You know, things like enhanced photography—' she started, but then winced, knowing what'd happen next.

'Enhanced photography?' Frank repeated. 'What enhanced photography?'

'Perhaps Mrs Carlyle could explain,' Silver said smoothly, deferring to Laura whilst simultaneously avoiding direct answers about his own knowledge. 'She barred me from attending that meeting, so I cannot provide you with full assistance.'

Laura pulled the enhanced photographs from her handbag as she stared at Silver.

Was he genuinely assisting Frank here, or was he throwing her under a bus because she'd dared go somewhere without him?

'These were taken near St. Bartholomew's Church on the day Harry died. When enhanced by professionals, they show rather more than natural causes.'

Frank studied the images, his expression growing serious.

'This shows someone intercepting Harry Farrell?'

'Moments before his collapse. Clear documentation of premeditated murder.'

'Well, I'm not too sure of that,' Frank muttered. 'I see some kind of tube in the hand, but it could be anything, and we found no needle marks in the tongue.'

'Did you check the roof of the mouth?' Silver enquired pleasantly.

'And where exactly did you have these enhanced?' Once more, Frank was ignoring the man with the trilby hat.

'*The Herald*. Keith O'Neill provided technical assistance.' Laura could see Frank's expression beginning to darken. 'Before you say anything, we didn't know what we'd find. You weren't exactly encouraging when I mentioned Harry's death might not be natural.'

Frank looked between them, his jaw tightening.

'Let me see if I understand this correctly. You took potential evidence in a murder case to a *newspaper* before bringing it to the police?'

'To be fair,' Silver interjected smoothly, 'Mrs Carlyle had no reason to believe the authorities would take the matter seriously, given the determination of natural causes and the apparent lack of interest in investigating further, and she had no actual proof of it being a murder, because of the size and resolution of the image. Ask yourself this, Frank. Can I call you Frank? Much easier than that mouthful of a title. If she'd come to you with the photos, *Frank* – would you have believed her?'

'Of course,' Frank's tone was so cold, it could have preserved meat. 'And I suppose this was your idea, *Sebastian*?'

'Not at all. Although, if I had been part of the discussion, I would have suggested that enhancement could reveal details invisible to casual observation.'

'How thoughtful. And your background in photographic analysis comes from where, exactly?'

Silver's smile became more enigmatic.

'Varied experience, Larry – Lawrence - Detective Chief Inspector. Advisory roles, risk assessment, that sort of thing.'

'Risk assessment for whom?'

'Various clients over the years. Confidentiality agreements, I'm afraid.'

Frank made several notes whilst studying Silver.

'You seem remarkably knowledgeable about investigative techniques for someone with a consulting background.'

'I read extensively. Crime novels, forensic textbooks, police procedural manuals. Fascinating field of study.'

'Crime novels,' Frank repeated flatly.

'Among other sources, yes. Pattern recognition applies across multiple disciplines.'

'Including murder investigations?'

'Including human behaviour under extreme circumstances, certainly.'

Laura studied Sebastian Silver more carefully during this exchange. His responses were smooth and charming, yet somehow unsatisfying – like getting perfectly polite service that left you wondering what the server was really thinking. And remembering Mister Friday – was that really the dead man upstairs – suggesting Sebastian Silver was supposed to be dead made his evasiveness even more troubling.

'Mister Silver,' Frank continued, 'you mentioned that Harry's death wasn't entirely surprising. What did you mean by that?'

Silver paused, his hand moving instinctively towards his trilby before apparently thinking better of the gesture.

'Harry had been asking questions recently. Questions about old cases, former colleagues, matters that some people prefer to leave undisturbed.'

'What sort of questions?'

'The sort that tends to make dangerous people nervous.'

'And you know this how?'

'Harry mentioned his concerns during our last conversation. He seemed to believe he'd uncovered something significant about past operations, though he was rather vague about specifics.'

'When was this last conversation?'

'Several days before his death. He was planning to meet someone, though he didn't say whom.'

Frank made more notes, clearly filing away every detail.

'And where exactly do you live, Mr Silver?'

'East London, though I move around rather frequently for security reasons.'

'Security reasons?'

'Old habits from my consulting work. One learns to vary routines when dealing with sensitive matters.'

Kyle leaned forward, unable to help himself.

'What sort of sensitive matters?'

'The sort that occasionally result in people being shot twice in the head,' Sebastian replied matter-of-factly, gesturing towards the house.

Before Frank could pursue this line of questioning further, commotion from inside the house caught their attention. A forensics officer appeared in the doorway, holding an evidence bag.

'Detective Chief Inspector? You'll want to see this.'

Frank glanced at Laura and Sebastian.

'Wait here. Both of you.'

He vanished into the house, leaving Laura and Sebastian standing together on the pavement whilst uniformed officers maintained a discreet but obvious watch over them.

'Well, this is all going rather swimmingly,' Silver smiled, looking from Laura to Kyle. 'Don't you think so?'

'What I think is that Frank has us on CCTV last night,' Laura muttered.

'The car park? Yes, I hadn't expected to go that route, so hadn't altered the footage in advance.'

'How did you alter the footage?' Kyle asked.

'Oh, in the most analogue way,' Silver smiled. 'I hit the cameras with my cane earlier so they all faced the wrong direction. I simply forgot the car park, as we parked out front.'

He paused.

'Of course, someone dropped the car off down there, so maybe they wanted us to be caught on camera.'

'Well, Frank has us likely on CCTV, and with the man who's dead in that house,' Laura straightened. 'Young man, scratched up cheek? Mister Friday? They'll work it out, Sebastian. They'll realise I was the last to see him, and now he's dead. I'll be in prison within hours.'

'My dear Laura,' Silver placed a hand on her shoulder. 'That's not what's going to happen.'

'No?' Laura felt a sliver of hope, regardless of whether she now believed this man or not.

'Of course not,' Silver smiled. 'I was there too, remember? So, it won't be just you in prison, will it? It'll be both of us. A trouble shared—'

'Is a trouble bloody doubled,' Laura muttered, shaking her head.

14

FOUND FOOTAGE

The minutes stretched on as Frank Young stayed in the house, and Laura actually wondered whether he was now hiding from the trilby-hatted man with the cane.

'Sebastian,' Laura said quietly, 'Frank's going to ask much more detailed questions about your background. Are you prepared for that level of scrutiny?'

'Detective Chief Inspector Young strikes me as a thoroughly competent officer,' Silver shrugged. 'I imagine his questions will be quite penetrating indeed.'

'That's not really an answer.'

'No,' Silver agreed, adjusting his trilby. 'I suppose it isn't.'

Kyle looked between them.

'There's something you're not telling us, isn't there? About who you really are?'

Silver smiled, though it didn't quite reach his eyes.

'Young Kyle, if I told you everything about who I really am, you'd either not believe me or you'd be considerably more frightened than you are now.'

'Try me,' Kyle challenged.

'Perhaps another time, when we're not standing outside a crime scene being watched by suspicious police officers.'

Frank emerged from the house, his expression even more serious than before and carrying an evidence bag containing what appeared to be documents.

'Right. Change of plans. We're all going back to the station for a proper conversation.' He fixed Laura with a penetrating stare. 'Among other things, forensics reckon someone got our victim with keys or something sharp across the cheek. Care to comment on that?'

Laura sighed.

'That would be me, I'm afraid. Yesterday evening – or was it early this morning – in David Revere's car park. I never know the etiquette of the midnight hour when describing actions.'

Frank seemed unsurprised by this.

'You knew,' Laura nodded to herself. 'CCTV?'

'Many of the cameras had been assaulted, but a couple showed you,' Frank replied.

'The lobby and the car park,' Kyle said. 'That's why you mentioned them.'

'Actually, we didn't have the lobby,' Frank admitted. 'But the car park CCTV revealed you emerging from the stairs, so we knew you were coming from there.'

He looked back at Laura now.

'Would you like to tell me your side before I tell you what we saw?'

Laura glanced at Silver, but before he could say anything, she nodded, looking back.

'As I said on the phone, we went to see if Louise was back,' she lied. 'When we found nothing, we left, but as we did so, we found ourselves intercepted by three men.'

'What did they look like?'

'Black suited, ties,' Laura continued. 'The leader looked very much like the man in the photo with Harry, especially after it was enhanced. I was in fear for my life, and I ran.'

'And where were you during this?' Frank glared at Silver, who had the good grace to redden at the accusation.

'I hadn't seen them,' he said simply. 'I was checking the rear entrance. By the time I found them, Laura and the youngest had already run off.'

'So, you took on two of them, with what, your cane?' Frank asked but then smiled. 'Or was it with the sword inside it? That's an illegal weapon.'

Silver paused, staring down at his walking cane.

'I can assure you, Detective Chief Inspector Young, I did defend myself with the cane, but there's no sword. Have a look.'

He passed the cane across, and Frank took it, pulled at the top and then, with a bark of success, he twisted the handle off.

'Oh dear,' Silver muttered. 'You found my bad little secret.'

Frank triumphantly pulled the handle free – to reveal no blade, but instead a slim, test tube-shaped hip flask.

'My joints,' Silver smiled. 'Purely medicinal.'

Frank nodded but then passed the silver top of the cane to a forensics officer, tossing the other part back at Silver as he glared at Laura.

'So, why did you run?' he asked.

'Three strangers, at night—'

'Facts, Laura! The CCTV shows you hitting him with a handbag and slashing him across the cheek!'

'Fine. He was trying to inject me with something, and I defended myself.'

'Inject you with what?'

'Small syringe, very similar to what we discovered in the enhanced photographs of Harry's death,' Laura explained. 'I assumed it contained whatever substance they used to kill Harry, and I really didn't want to taste it.'

'So, Brian Waterstone attempted to murder you using the same method that killed Harry Farrell?'

'It certainly appeared that way. You've yet to show me a photo of the man.'

Frank nodded, opened his phone and scrolled to one of the least-blood covered images of the victim's face.

'Him?'

Laura stared down at the image of the very dead, very young man.

'Mrs Carlyle, there's no need for dramatics. We simply want to chat. Come now, we know you visited David's flat. We're pretty sure you removed certain items. We'd simply like them back.'

'That's him,' she whispered.

'In fairness, Mrs Carlyle only defended herself,' Silver added. 'When I arrived, he stated his name was "Mister Friday", decided prudence was the best form of action, but tripped and fell.'

Frank looked between them.

'And then a couple of hours later someone kills him? Right. We're definitely having that extended conversation. Both of you, in my office, detailed statements, everything you know about Harry Farrell, David Revere, and whatever organisation is killing people with syringes.'

'Can I come too?' Kyle asked hopefully. 'I've never been interviewed by the police.'

'Kyle,' Laura said firmly, 'this isn't a social outing.'

'But I helped with the investigation! I organised the evidence board, I found the tech expert, I've been helpful!'

'You're a child,' Frank corrected. 'Which means you get to wait outside whilst the adults discuss murder and international conspiracies.'

'I'm twenty.'

'You're still a child to me.'

'Well, you've changed a lot in my eyes, "Uncle Frank". And I've been very mature about all this.'

Sebastian looked amused at this family dynamic.

'Perhaps Kyle could assist with reviewing Harry's phone data while we speak with Detective Chief Inspector Young. Educational opportunity, you might say.'

'What phone data?' Frank asked, clearly recognising that his investigation had just gained another unexpected dimension.

'Harry Farrell's mobile,' Laura admitted, knowing this conversation was about to become even more complicated. 'We thought it might contain useful information about his investigation.'

'You thought you'd conduct your own forensic analysis of evidence from a potential crime scene?'

'No, because you yourself told me that officially Harry died of natural causes, remember?' Laura pointed out.

'Laura, that's called tampering with evidence regardless of determinations.'

'Can't be tampering if it wasn't evidence to begin with,' Kyle added helpfully.

Frank stared at Kyle.

'Are all the Carlyles this casual about legal technicalities?'

'It runs in the family,' Kyle said cheerfully. 'Though Gran's definitely the most dangerous one.'

'I'm standing right here,' Laura protested.

'Which is why I'm being diplomatic about it.'

'Look,' Silver replied, holding a hand up for peace. 'Mrs Carlyle was hired by Harry's widow to look into his death, one already decided as a heart attack. You didn't believe her claims, purely humouring her, so if she conducted her own investigation, you cannot be angry at this. You had the phone; you could have done this. You could have found the photographer. You could have investigated. But you didn't. You passed them back to the widow.'

'No, we didn't.'

Silver went to reply but stopped.

'Sorry, what?'

'We never gave her husband's things back to her,' Frank replied. 'They disappeared before they could be passed on. I found this out yesterday.'

'But Rebecca gave them to me,' Laura said, confused.

'Oh, I'm sure they got to her, but officially, we have no chain of evidence that shows Rebecca Farrell signed for them,' Frank argued. 'Likely an overenthusiastic uniformed officer.'

'Well, it was classed as a heart attack at the time,' Silver replied casually. 'But now, Mrs Carlyle is offering to share this with you. Surely this makes her a consultant rather than a rival? A partner rather than a suspect?'

Frank considered this development, whilst weighing the benefits of gathering all evidence against the administrative nightmare of explaining why he was working with civilian hackers and amateur detectives.

'Right. We'll collect the phone data first, then back to the station for comprehensive statements from everyone involved,' he said. 'Apart from you, Mister Silver.'

'Me?' Silver cleared his throat diplomatically. 'Surely I should be there too?'

'Oh, you will be, and we will have those words, but I'd like to speak to you alone.'

Laura said nothing. She, too, wanted her own time to interrogate Sebastian Silver.

'Fine. Although there's something you should consider about Brian's execution.'

'Which is?'

'Who executed him,' Silver shrugged. 'If it's his superiors for doing a poor job, this is off-brand for The Calendar.'

'The Calendar being this super-secret spy group, right?'

'Yes. But if they did kill him, there's something wrong in the hierarchy. The Calendar doesn't shoot, they poison, as we've now seen twice. Alternatively, if he was killed by a double cross, maybe a traitor, then when his employer realises he's failed to report in on schedule, they'll likely accelerate their operational timeline.'

'Meaning what exactly?'

'Meaning direct action rather than continued surveillance. Mrs Carlyle has progressed from being monitored to being targeted, as seen last night. The next attempt won't involve careful observation and planning.'

'You're saying she's in immediate danger?'

'I'm saying whoever ordered Brian's execution won't hesitate to expand their target list to include anyone who might compromise their operation.' Silver's usual charm was replaced by something harder, more serious. 'In my experience, organisations like this prefer to eliminate problems permanently rather than manage them indefinitely.'

Frank looked at Laura.

'Right then. You're all staying exactly where I can see you until we figure out what sort of organisation we're dealing with and how to stop them from killing anyone else.'

'Are we under protective custody?' Kyle asked.

'You're under "stop asking stupid questions and do exactly what I tell you" custody,' Frank replied without humour, glancing back as the forensics officer passed him back the top of the cane, which he then continued to return to Silver. 'Apart from our man in the hat. He can leave right now.'

'Even better,' Silver glanced at the top of the cane, grimacing as he screwed the two pieces back together. 'You dusted for prints? You could have just asked for a clean set, you know.'

Laura was surprised by the decision, but Frank looked as if he had his reasons. As they prepared to leave the crime scene, Laura found herself studying Sebastian Silver more carefully.

'Give me a moment, and I'll join you,' she said.

Frank went to argue, but then nodded, his face tight, and walked off with Kyle.

'Sebastian,' she said quietly. 'We need to talk. Properly. About Harry's investigation and what he discovered about you.'

Silver's expression grew more serious, his usual charm replaced by something that might have been genuine concern.

'I wondered when you'd ask about that.'

'You knew Harry was investigating you?'

'Harry was investigating everyone connected to The Calendar, including people who supposedly died years ago.'

'And did you? Die, I mean?'

Sebastian Silver adjusted his trilby, once more as a nervous habit rather than vanity.

'That's rather a complicated question.'

'Most questions about death are fairly straightforward.'

'Not when you're dealing with people who specialise in making problems disappear permanently.'

'He has photos of you and James.'

'I never shied from admitting I knew your husband, Mrs Carlyle.'

'Are you on the side of the Angels?' Laura asked, unsure as to the answer.

'You should go with Frank,' Silver patted her on the shoulder. 'We'll talk later, and I'll explain everything.'

As Frank's car pulled away from the kerb, taking them towards whatever revelations Harry's phone might contain, Laura realised her investigation had developed far beyond a widow's doubts about her husband's death. She was now dealing with killers, organised surveillance, and a partner whose very existence seemed to be questionable.

The question was whether Sebastian Silver was her greatest ally in uncovering the truth, or the most dangerous person she'd ever trusted with her life.

And where would he go now he was left alone at a crime scene?

15

FIRE ALARM

Raj looked up from a circuit board as Laura, Kyle and Frank entered Electronic Zone, his face brightening.

'Mrs Carlyle! Perfect timing – I've got everything ready...'

He trailed off as he realised he didn't know one of the three newcomers. In response, Frank surveyed the shop, clearly wondering what he'd gotten himself into.

'Detective Chief Inspector Young,' he said, showing his warrant card. 'I understand you've been helping with data recovery?'

Raj's enthusiasm dimmed slightly.

'Er, yeah. Kyle asked me to help his gran recover some data from her friend's phone. Nothing illegal about that, right?'

'Depends on how you got the phone to open,' Frank replied. 'What exactly did you find?'

Raj glanced at Laura, who nodded.

'Well, most was still encrypted, and it took me a while, but I got into one of the file structures.' He gestured towards his workstation. 'Want the full tour?'

'Start with the interesting bits,' Frank said, checking his watch.

'Right, well, your friend Harry was seriously paranoid. Two years' worth of messages, contacts from all over Europe and America, meeting schedules, financial records.' Raj opened several files on his laptop, currently connected through an app to the phone. 'This bloke was documenting everything.'

The screen showed conversations between Harry and various contacts, identified only by initials or code names. Most were routine intelligence chatter, but several caught Laura's attention.

'There,' she pointed. 'S.S. – that appears repeatedly.'

'Yeah, loads of messages about someone with those initials over the past few months.' Raj scrolled through the conversations. 'Harry was definitely keeping tabs on whoever this is.'

Frank leaned forward.

'What sort of surveillance?'

'Meeting locations, behavioural observations. Look at this one from three weeks ago.'

Raj opened a message thread:

S.S. remains consistent with established patterns. Memory gaps are still clear during casual conversation. Subject appears genuinely confused when pressed about past experiences. Recommend continued caution.

'Who's he talking to?'

'No idea,' Raj shrugged. 'Encrypted. The number doesn't even show. This isn't something you download off the Apple Store, though.'

'Memory gaps?' Kyle read over their shoulders.

'Gets weirder,' Raj continued, opening another file. 'Look at these financial records.'

The screen showed bank transfers, payment schedules flowing between multiple accounts and countries.

'Your mysterious S.S been receiving regular payments. Monthly deposits, same amount each time, for over a year.'

'From whom?' Laura asked.

'Government health services, looks like. Perhaps pension payments, plus some from something called the Public Sector Pensions Authority, and GCHQ. This S.S. person gets care allowances – two grand monthly from official sources.'

'For what?' Kyle asked.

'No idea. But someone's been funding whoever this is for ages.' Raj was clearly enjoying his role as digital detective. 'And there's more. Harry had meeting schedules, surveillance notes, even some audio recordings.'

'Audio recordings?' Laura asked.

'Phone calls, mostly. Some face-to-face meetings' Raj clicked through several files. 'Want to hear one?'

'Yes,' Frank said immediately.

Raj selected a file dated two weeks before Harry's death. A familiar voice filled the shop, though it sounded different – uncertain, almost confused.

'I keep having these dreams, Harry. Or memories, I'm not sure which. Fragments of things that feel familiar but I can't quite grasp.'

'Tell me about them,' Harry's voice replied.

'Men in dark suits. Operations that seem real but make no sense. And this persistent feeling that I'm supposed to be somewhere else, doing something else entirely.'

'Have you considered that these might not be dreams, Phillip?'

'That's absurd. I'm hardly the sort of person who'd be involved in anything... well, anything like what these fragments suggest.'

Raj stopped the recording. The shop fell silent except for the hum of electronics.

'That sounded like Sebastian,' Kyle said quietly. 'But he called him Phillip?'

'Sounded like someone pretending to be confused,' Frank observed, making notes. 'Or someone genuinely losing his grip on reality.'

'There's more,' Raj said, opening another file. 'Harry was tracking multiple people. Look at this contact list.'

The screen filled with names, numbers, locations – all coded, but clearly part of a larger network. Some entries were marked with days of the week.

'Monday, Tuesday, Wednesday,' Laura read aloud. 'Like The Calendar organisation Sebastian mentioned.'

'And here's the really interesting bit,' Raj continued. 'Harry had a video file that was buried pretty deep. Encrypted, hidden in the system directories. Took me ages to find it.'

'A video?' Laura leaned forward.

'Yeah, looks like he recorded it himself. The night before he died, according to the timestamp. He probably intended to send it on, but... well, you know.'

Frank moved closer to the screen.

'Play it.'

Harry's phone sat connected to Raj's laptop. Raj navigated through the recovered files until he found what he was looking for.

'Here we go.'

The laptop filled with Harry Farrell's face, looking tired

but determined. He was sitting in what appeared to be his study, books and papers visible in the background.

'If you're watching this, then my concerns were justified, and I'm most likely dead.'

Kyle tensed beside her. Frank was paying complete attention now.

'Rebecca, if this reaches you first, give it to Laura Carlyle immediately. She has the skills to understand what I've discovered, and the connections to act on it.'

On the screen, Harry paused, seeming to gather his thoughts.

'I've been investigating a private intelligence network that calls itself The Calendar. They use days of the week as operational designations – Monday through Saturday for active operatives, with Sunday reserved for something else entirely.'

'Just like Sebastian mentioned.' Kyle nodded.

'The Calendar has been infiltrating legitimate intelligence services across Europe and America. They've placed operatives in positions where they can access classified information, manipulate operations and eliminate threats to their organisation.'

Laura was taking mental notes, but something in Harry's expression suggested the actual revelation was coming.

'But here's what makes them truly dangerous – they had a leader once, someone who knew all their operations, all their secrets, all their methods. This person was eliminated years ago, but I have evidence suggesting—'

A piercing electronic wail suddenly filled the shop.

Fire alarm.

Not just Electronic Zone's system – the sound was coming from throughout the building, joined by alarms from neighbouring businesses.

'Bloody hell,' Raj muttered, looking around in confusion. 'That's the whole block.'

'Everyone out!' Frank said, immediately switching into professional mode. 'Fire regulations – no exceptions.'

'But the video—' Laura protested.

'Will be here when we get back,' Frank said firmly. 'Move!'

They joined the stream of people evacuating onto Tottenham Court Road. The entire block was emptying – shop workers carrying laptops and handbags, confused customers clutching half-finished coffee cups, office staff from the floors above streaming down stairwells whilst fire engines approached with sirens wailing.

The street filled with that particular London mixture of resigned annoyance and mild excitement that accompanied any disruption to routine, and Laura watched the familiar chaos of an unplanned evacuation, noting the woman in expensive shoes carefully navigating around puddles whilst balancing her mobile phone conversation, and two students from the nearby university treating the disruption as an impromptu social gathering. A business manager, who'd clearly been in an important meeting stood on the kerb in his shirtsleeves, still clutching a presentation folder and looking genuinely annoyed. A young mother managed a toddler who seemed to think the oncoming fire engines were the most exciting thing he'd ever seen.

'Probably a false alarm,' Kyle observed, watching firefighters deploy. 'Happens all the time in university buildings. Someone burns toast in a staff kitchen, and the whole place empties.'

Frank was speaking into his radio, coordinating with other officers in the area whilst keeping an eye on the crowd. Laura noticed his professional habits – automatically positioning himself where he could see both the building and potential escape routes, cataloguing faces, noting anyone who seemed out of place.

She'd found herself doing the same thing, scanning faces in the growing crowd.

Most people looked exactly as they should – mildly irritated Londoners dealing with an unexpected inconvenience.

Then she saw *him.*

Standing near the bus stop across the street, watching the evacuation with more interest than seemed warranted, was one man from the van that had been parked outside her house. The same broad build, the same dark suit, the same professional stillness that had made him so obvious when Silver had confronted him.

Laura's pulse quickened.

Had he triggered the fire alarm? Was this some sort of cover for something else?

She nudged Kyle and gestured discreetly towards the bus stop.

'That man – do you recognise him?'

'Should I?' Kyle squinted across the street.

'He was watching our house. In the van with his colleague.'

But even as Laura watched, the man checked his watch, looked once more at the building, then turned and walked away with the casual stride of someone whose business was finished; just another bystander leaving after the excitement died down.

'Probably a coincidence,' Kyle said, though he didn't sound entirely convinced. 'Lots of people work around here.'

'Excuse me, Mrs Carlyle?'

Laura turned to find the young woman from David's flat

approaching through the crowd. But she looked completely different now – confident, professional, nothing like the nervous girlfriend who'd answered the door. Gone was the carefully tousled hair and minimal makeup; this woman had presence, authority.

'Louise,' Laura said, recognising her despite the transformation.

'We need to talk,' Louise said quietly, glancing at Frank and Kyle who were still watching the fire brigade. 'Privately.'

She guided Laura a few steps away from the others, moving quietly.

'Sebastian Silver isn't who you think he is,' Louise said without preamble, her voice low but urgent.

'What do you mean?'

'I mean be very careful about trusting him. He's not what he appears to be.' Louise glanced towards where Kyle and Frank stood. 'This isn't about one identity, Mrs Carlyle, it's about many, all hidden and long forgotten. I'm not warning you off – just promise me you'll be cautious. Don't let yourself become too dependent on his help.'

'Why? What's wrong with him?'

'Nothing's wrong with him exactly. But he's... complicated. More complicated than you realise.'

The fire chief was calling for people to return to buildings. The emergency was over – apparently someone had left food cooking unattended on the third floor.

Louise checked her watch.

'I have to go. But please be careful.' She looked directly at Laura. 'And don't trust everything you think you know about the people around you.'

'David,' Laura quickly blurted out. 'You know he had photocopies of your passports hidden, right?'

Louise stopped, her eyes betraying the fact that she hadn't known this.

'Thanks for the heads up,' she said. 'But don't let Harry Farrell lead you where he needs you to go. Some secrets are best left dead.'

Before Laura could ask more questions, Louise was walking away, disappearing into the crowd with the sort of skill that spoke of serious training.

Kyle appeared at her elbow.

'What did she want?'

'To warn me about Sebastian,' Laura said, watching Louise vanish into the flow of returning evacuees. 'And something about identities.'

'Warn you how?'

'I seriously don't know.'

AS THEY MADE THEIR WAY BACK INTO ELECTRONIC ZONE, Laura's mind was racing; Louise's warnings about Sebastian and Harry echoed her own growing doubts about Silver's contradictory stories and mysterious knowledge. If his entire identity was manufactured, who had done the manufacturing? And why?

'Right then—' Raj said as they settled back around his workstation, though he was frowning at his equipment. 'That's bloody odd. My laptop's completely dead.'

'Dead how?' Frank asked, moving to examine the setup.

'Won't turn on at all. Was working perfectly when we left.' Raj pressed the power button repeatedly, checked the connections, tried unplugging and reconnecting everything. 'It's like something just fried the whole system.'

Kyle examined the laptop more closely.

'Could be a power surge during the evacuation? Sometimes when buildings lose power suddenly...'

'Maybe,' Raj said, though he sounded doubtful. 'But this isn't just a power issue. Look.'

He opened the laptop carefully.

'The screen's got these weird burn marks around the edges. And there's this smell...' He sniffed. 'Like ozone. You get that sometimes with electrical damage, but this is different.'

'Or an electromagnetic pulse,' Frank said quietly, making Laura look at him sharply.

'EMP?' Kyle asked. 'Like from films?'

'Smaller scale, but yes. Portable devices exist. Completely fry electronics within a certain radius.' Frank was examining the laptop more carefully. 'Though they're not exactly available at Currys.'

Laura felt a chill that had nothing to do with the London weather.

'The man I saw outside – one of the men who were watching our house. Do you think...?'

'I think we're dealing with people who have access to sophisticated equipment,' Frank replied grimly, seemingly now a believer. 'The question is whether this was targeted at stopping us from seeing that video, or just unfortunate timing.'

Raj was almost in tears.

'Two days' work, just gone. Everything on Harry's phone – the messages, contacts, financial records, all of it.'

'You didn't have backups?' Kyle asked in growing horror.

'Course I had backups. On the laptop. Which is now a very expensive paperweight, and in the process of becoming the brick it now is, factory reset the phone,' Raj slumped in his chair. 'I'm sorry, Mrs Carlyle. I know how important this was.'

Laura patted his shoulder gently.

'It's not your fault, Raj. And we did learn some things before this happened.'

'Such as?' Frank asked, making notes in his book.

'Harry confirmed The Calendar exists. He was investigating their infiltration of intelligence services. He was tracking someone with the initials S.S. who was receiving regular payments and showed signs of memory problems. And he made that video specifically because he thought he might be killed for what he'd discovered.'

'Plus Louise's warning about Sebastian,' Kyle added. 'His identity being false somehow.'

'The woman who approached you during the evacuation?' Frank asked sharply. 'I thought she was just asking what was going on?'

'She's the one I met at David's flat. She looked completely different though – professional, confident. Nothing like the nervous girlfriend act she was putting on before.'

Before Frank could ask more questions, his phone rang. He answered it, moving away from them towards the shop window.

'Young... yes, I'll hold.'

He walked to the far end of the shop, speaking quietly. Laura could see his expression growing more serious as the conversation continued.

'Right. Yes, I understand... give me the address... no, I'll handle it myself.'

He returned, pocketing his phone with a grim expression.

'That was my contact at Records. I asked them to dig

deeper into a particular situation after our conversation yesterday.' Frank's jaw was set in a way Laura recognised from their younger days. 'They found something. We need to go.'

'Go where?' Laura asked.

'To see someone named Phillip, who might have answers about what's really going on here.' Frank was already heading for the street. 'Come on. Kyle, I'm guessing you can get home from here? This is a "one guest" situation.'

He didn't wait for confirmation. Outside Electronic Zone, Frank hailed a taxi with the expression of a man done waiting for answers.

'Where are we going?' Laura asked as they climbed into the back.

'Greenwich,' Frank told the driver, showing him the address on his phone, then turned to Laura. 'To meet someone who's been expecting regular visits from Sebastian Silver for the past two years.'

'What do you mean?'

'We'll find out when we get there.' Frank's expression was grim. 'But Laura, I think there's more to Sebastian's story than he's told us.'

THE JOURNEY TO GREENWICH TOOK FORTY MINUTES THROUGH afternoon traffic. Laura watched London pass by – the familiar mixture of ancient and modern, elegant Georgian terraces giving way to Victorian suburbs, then the gradual shift towards the historic riverside borough where the Royal Observatory had once mapped the world's time.

The taxi finally pulled up outside an elegant Victorian building surrounded by well-maintained gardens. The building looked like an upmarket hotel or private club, the sort of place that charged enormous fees to ensure absolute discretion. A discreet brass plaque by the entrance gave the name.

TIDWORTH HOUSE – PRIVATE RESIDENTIAL CARE.

'A care home?' Laura asked, staring up at it.

'More of a specialised facility,' Frank said, showing his warrant card to the receptionist in the marble-floored lobby as they walked through. 'Detective Chief Inspector Young. We're here to see one of your residents. Doctor Matthews contacted me. Official police business.'

The receptionist, a middle-aged woman with the professionally calm demeanour of someone trained to handle difficult situations, checked her computer.

'He's in his room. Twenty-three. Second floor.'

'We'll announce ourselves,' Frank said firmly.

They took the stairs to the second floor, walking down a corridor that could have belonged to any expensive hotel except for the discreet medical equipment visible through open doorways and the particular hush that suggested serious treatment was happening behind closed doors.

'Room twenty-three,' Frank said, stopping outside a door marked only with a number. He knocked gently on the door.

'Come in,' came a voice from inside. Familiar, yet somehow completely different.

Frank opened the door, and they stepped into a comfortable room furnished more like a hotel suite than a medical facility. Armchair by the window, small kitchenette, photographs on the mantelpiece showing faces Laura didn't recognise.

And sitting in the armchair, wearing a comfortable cardigan and soft trousers, was Sebastian Silver.

This wasn't the man she'd seen before, even though it was clearly the same person. Everything about him was different – his posture, his expression, even the way he held himself.

'Yes? Can I—' he began, then stopped. 'Ah.'

His voice carried a distinct Boston accent that made Laura's stomach drop.

'Laura Carlyle, meet Phillip Morris,' Frank said matter-of-factly. 'The man from Harry's tape. You see, Sebastian Silver doesn't exist, but the fingerprints I took from his cane match Phillip here. From what I've been told, Phillip's not well. He had a bit of a breakdown recently, didn't you, Phillip?'

'I don't know what you mean,' Phillip replied as he rose from the chair, his Boston accent thick with confusion.

'Up until a few years back, Phillip was an accountant in Boston,' Frank continued, passing Laura the photograph. It showed a slightly younger version of Sebastian at a baseball game with a woman, both of them smiling. 'I only got the highlights on the call, but a couple of years ago, it all went wrong. He moved to London with his job, but his wife passed away, the economy crashed, and he was made redundant. He started to have... episodes.'

Frank gestured around the room.

'So he moved in here. Then a few months back, possibly five or six according to the doctor, things changed, didn't they, Phillip? You started wearing a suit. Started changing your name.'

'But what about the sword cane? With the taser thing?' Laura protested.

'Is an illegal weapon and easy to buy off the internet,'

Frank replied as he turned to Phillip. 'And we'll be having that off you, too.'

Phillip quietly picked up the familiar walking cane and passed it to Frank without a word.

'Why?' Laura asked, staring at this diminished version of the man she'd trusted. 'Why the charade?'

Phillip sat on the edge of his bed, suddenly looking very small and vulnerable.

'Because it's all that I have,' he mumbled. 'When I'm Sebastian Silver, I'm so alive. I... I can't explain it – when I'm Sebastian, I feel more... real. Without him, I feel... fake.'

Laura stared at him, her world tilting on its axis.

'Fake. Well, you certainly fooled me, Mister Morris. So, well done.'

16

THE CARE OF PHILLIP MORRIS

FRANK STOOD IN THE DOORWAY FOR A MOMENT, WATCHING Laura absorb the truth about the man she'd trusted with her life. His expression softened slightly, slipping to reveal a genuine concern for an old friend navigating an impossible situation.

'I'll leave you both to have a proper conversation,' he said quietly. 'But afterwards, we're all going to the station for detailed statements. No arguments.'

'Of course,' Laura replied, though her voice sounded distant to her own ears.

'There's a doctor who'll want to chat to you, the one who called me. Doctor Matthews. She'll want to speak with you about Phillip's condition.' Frank paused at the door. 'I'm going to nip outside for a smoke. Take your time, but don't take too long. There are still people out there who apparently want both of you dead.'

After he left, silence settled over the room like a soft blanket. Phillip remained perched on the edge of his bed, hands folded in his lap, looking rather like a schoolboy called to account for some minor mischief. The transformation from Sebastian's commanding presence was so complete that Laura found herself wondering if she'd imagined their entire partnership.

'I'm terribly sorry,' Phillip said finally, his Boston accent making him sound younger somehow. 'I know this must be confusing for you.'

'Confusing is one word for it,' Laura replied, settling into the armchair by the window. 'Though I have to say, you're taking this rather calmly.'

'Oh, I remember everything Sebastian did,' Phillip said matter-of-factly. 'Every conversation, every decision, every time he put you in danger.'

His voice grew smaller.

'I'm so very sorry about that last part.'

'You really do remember it all?'

'Every goddamned thing,' Phillip said with a rueful laugh. 'It's rather like having the most vivid dream of your life, except you know it really happened. When I'm Sebastian, I feel like I could take on the world. When I'm myself...'

He gestured helplessly at his cardigan and slippers.

'You feel ordinary?'

'I feel useless,' Phillip corrected. 'Sebastian walks into a room and immediately spots the exit routes, identifies potential threats, reads people like open books. I walk into a room and wonder if I've forgotten to zip my pants.'

Laura couldn't help smiling.

'That's rather harsh on yourself.'

'Is it? Sebastian saved your life. I can barely work up the courage to ask for extra cookies at teatime.' Phillip picked at his cardigan again. 'The strangest part is knowing I have all that information locked away somewhere in my head. When

Sebastian examined that microwave contraption in David's flat, I knew – somehow – that the cables were wrong and it was CIA tech. But ask me now how I knew that, and I haven't the foggiest.'

'What did you see?'

'That's just it – I can't explain it. Sebastian would have spotted it instantly, understood exactly what it was and how it worked. Phillip sees kitchen equipment that might explode if you put metal in it.'

Laura found herself genuinely curious about the mechanics of his condition.

'Yet the knowledge must come from somewhere.'

Phillip brightened slightly.

'Oh, it does. I've read everything, you see. Thirty years of spy novels, intelligence memoirs, technical manuals, operational histories. Most people watch television after work. I read about tradecraft.'

'Extensively, I'd imagine.'

'Obsessively might be more accurate. Le Carré, Fleming, Deighton, plus every declassified document I could find online. When I was an accountant, I spent my evenings learning about dead drops and surveillance detection routes.' He looked sheepish. 'Rather sad, really.'

'Not sad at all. Fascinating.'

'Sebastian can access every bit perfectly, as if he'd lived it rather than just read about it. He walks into dangerous situations without breaking a sweat, makes decisions in seconds, trusts his instincts completely.' Phillip's voice grew wistful. 'Sometimes I wonder what it would be like to feel that confident all the time.'

'Is that what Sebastian does? Feel confident?'

'Among other things. He notices everything I miss, understands connections I can't see, reads people's motivations like they're wearing signs.' Phillip smiled sadly. 'Rather like having a more capable version of yourself taking over whenever life gets complicated.'

Laura studied his face – the same features as Sebastian, but everything else utterly different. Even his posture had changed, shoulders slightly hunched as if apologising for taking up space.

'Do you ever feel resentful? Of Sebastian, I mean?'

Phillip considered this carefully.

'Sometimes. It's rather like having a brilliant older brother who effortlessly excels at everything you find difficult. But then again, without Sebastian, I'd probably still be sitting in this room feeling sorry for myself and not helping anyone at all.'

'You helped me enormously.'

'Sebastian helped you. I just... observed.'

'That's not true, Phillip. Every decision Sebastian made, every insight he had, every moment of courage – that all came from you. Sebastian may have the confidence to access it, but the intelligence, the fundamental decency, the desire to help – that's all you.'

'You really think so?' Phillip looked genuinely surprised by this assessment.

'I know so. Sebastian's confidence is impressive, but confidence without character is just bluster. You have both – you just need different circumstances to show it.'

Laura frowned.

'How did you find the taser cane? With the sword?'

'eBay,' Phillip shrugged. 'A seller was selling the hip flask one, I asked if he had any others. He sold it off-site, which meant off-books, mainly because it was illegal.'

'And you were okay buying an illegal cane?'

'Oh, I didn't buy it,' Phillip smiled sheepishly. 'Sebastian did. He's way better at negotiation than I am.'

Before Laura could respond, there was a soft knock at the door. It opened to reveal a woman who looked like she'd stepped out of a 1950s baking advertisement – comfortably rounded, wire-rimmed spectacles, and the sort of maternal presence that suggested she could solve any problem with the right combination of tea and common sense.

'I'm Doctor Sarah Matthews,' she said, offering Laura her hand. 'And you must be the famous Mrs Carlyle we've heard so much about.'

'Famous might be overstating things.'

'Not according to our Phillip. Sebastian's been singing your praises for days.' Doctor Matthews settled into the second chair with the ease of someone who'd perfected the art of making small rooms feel welcoming. 'Now then, I understand you'd like to know more about our resident mystery man.'

'If that's not inappropriate.'

'Oh, perfectly fine. Phillip's given me carte blanche to explain his peculiar situation.' Doctor Matthews beamed at them both. 'Though I must insist on proper tea first. Hospital coffee is an affront to civilisation, and meaningful conversations require civilised refreshments.'

'That's very kind—'

'Nonsense. The least we can do is provide decent hospitality.' Doctor Matthews moved to the room's telephone and dialled an extension. 'James? Could we have the good service in Phillip Morris's room, please? We have a proper visitor... yes, the full treatment... excellent, thank you, dear.'

She rang off and turned back to them with clear satisfaction.

'James is our head of kitchen services, though that rather understates his capabilities. The man could cater a state dinner if required. He'll have everything arranged in just a few minutes.'

'You're very well organised here,' Laura observed.

'We have to be. Our residents come from established families and have rather specific needs, so we've found that attention to detail makes all the difference in their recovery.' Doctor Matthews settled back in her chair. 'While we wait for refreshments, tell me what you've observed about Phillip's condition. Not medically, you understand – I mean as someone who's actually worked with both sides of his personality.'

'Well,' Laura began carefully, 'Sebastian certainly seemed knowledgeable about investigative techniques…'

'Oh, he's that all right,' Doctor Matthews chuckled. 'Had me convinced he was the real thing when I first met him. Asked me about operational security protocols and threat assessment procedures with the sort of casual expertise that would put actual intelligence officers to shame.'

Laura wondered if that was hyperbole, or whether Doctor Matthews had treated intelligence officers in the past.

'And then you discovered…?'

'That our Phillip here has the most extraordinary memory for fictional detail I've ever encountered. Show him a spy novel, and a couple of months later he can quote entire passages about surveillance tradecraft.'

There was another knock at the door, and a young man in pristine kitchen whites entered pushing what could only be described as a tea trolley worthy of the Ritz. Silver service gleamed under the room's lights, delicate bone china was arranged with precision, and the scones were clearly still warm from the oven.

'Your timing is perfect as always, James,' Doctor Matthews said as he began arranging everything with the sort of flair that suggested years of experience.

'Doctor Matthews trains us well,' James replied with a grin, setting out plates and cups with balletic efficiency. 'I've included some of those lemon biscuits Mrs Barker likes, and the jam is from the strawberries we grew in the kitchen garden.'

'You grow your own strawberries?' Laura asked, impressed despite herself.

'Oh yes, we're quite self-sufficient here. Doctor Matthews believes in the therapeutic value of good food prepared with care.' James finished his arrangements and stepped back to admire his work. 'Will there be anything else?'

'I think we're absolutely spoiled for choice. Thank you, dear.'

After James departed, Doctor Matthews began the tea service.

'Right then,' she said, spooning leaves into the pot with careful attention to proportions, 'where were we? Ah yes, Phillip's remarkable ability to absorb and synthesise fictional intelligence work into something remarkably convincing.'

'But he seemed to know things – about The Calendar, about surveillance techniques...'

'Oh, he does know things,' Doctor Matthews agreed, adding the almost-hot water to the pot and setting a timer, almost as if ignoring the fact that the subject of the conversation was in the room. 'Phillip has an almost encyclopaedic knowledge of intelligence procedures from popular culture.

Combined with his analytical mind and attention to detail, Sebastian can appear remarkably authentic.'

'You're saying he's essentially playing a character?'

'A character he's unconsciously created from thousands of hours of research and observation,' Doctor Matthews corrected gently, beginning to warm the cups. 'The remarkable thing is how complete and consistent Sebastian has become. Most people with dissociative conditions struggle with fragmented personalities. Phillip has created someone rather impressive. As for the real life threats, Phillip doesn't just read fiction, Mrs Carlyle. He's found countless redacted documents on the World Wide Web, so the chances are he's read some about this Calendar you talk of.'

She smiled.

'After all, he does like his conspiracy websites and podcasts.'

Laura thought back to the photograph she'd seen – Harry, James, and the third man identified as Sebastian, and the newspaper clippings of Sebastian in the background. Had Harry and James – *her* James, not this white-clad server – known him as Phillip back then? Had he written Sebastian's name on the photo later on, encouraging Phillip's fantasy, adding credibility to the Sebastian persona...

'That explains something,' she said suddenly. 'Sebastian working out complex calculations. He said he was "good with numbers".'

'Oh yes, Phillip's always been exceptional with mathematics,' Doctor Matthews confirmed, pouring the perfectly steeped tea into delicate cups. 'Part of what made him such a successful accountant – you know, spotting patterns and all that. Sebastian simply has more confidence in displaying those abilities.'

She offered Laura a cup with the sort of ceremony that elevated tea service to an art form, before offering Phillip one. He refused, probably too nervous to drink right now but then, as if changing his mind on the spot, nodded and accepted.

'Now then, I'm curious about something myself. How did you find working with Sebastian? As someone who didn't know about Phillip's condition?'

Laura accepted the tea gratefully, thinking back over their partnership.

'He was... remarkably effective. Sometimes I wondered how he knew things he shouldn't have known or appeared in places at exactly the right moment. But he never felt false, if that makes sense.'

'Perfect sense. Sebastian represents everything Phillip wishes he could be – confident, capable, decisive. In many ways, he's more authentically Phillip than Phillip himself.'

'How do you mean?'

'Well, look at what Sebastian accomplished. From what your police friend said, he's helped investigate a murder, protected you from dangerous people, unravelled a complex conspiracy. Those aren't the actions of someone pretending to be clever – they're the actions of someone who genuinely is clever but normally lacks the confidence to show it.'

Phillip looked up from his scone, which he'd been systematically demolishing while they talked.

'Frank said all that?'

'Well, his words were a little more blunt and colourful, but I chose to take the words like that,' Doctor Matthews continued. 'But it's why I'm not entirely convinced that integrating the two personalities is the right approach. Sometimes people need different aspects of themselves for different circumstances.'

'You mean Sebastian should continue to exist?'

'I mean Sebastian serves a valuable purpose. He allows Phillip to access capabilities and confidence that he struggles to reach otherwise. As long as both personalities remain healthy and functional...' she shrugged. 'Perhaps the goal shouldn't be elimination, but cooperation.'

This was a fascinating perspective, and Laura found herself reconsidering everything she thought she knew about Phillip's condition.

'Doctor Matthews, can you tell me about Phillip's background before he came here? The breakdown he mentioned?'

'Certainly. Phillip came to us just over a year ago in quite a state – wife dead, job gone, having what he described as a complete nervous breakdown.' Doctor Matthews refilled Laura's cup with the sort of attention to detail that suggested this was far from routine hospitality. 'But in the last six months he'd also had this rather interesting visitor who seemed terribly concerned about his welfare.'

'Harry Farrell.'

'Exactly. Lovely man, though clearly carrying the weight of the world on his shoulders. Said he and Phillip had worked together years back at some consulting firm in Boston.'

'And Harry took an interest in Sebastian?'

'Oh my word, yes. You'd have thought he'd discovered a long-lost relative.' Dr Matthews offered Laura a scone with obvious pride in the kitchen's work. 'Harry would arrive with boxes of materials – old photographs, declassified documents, intelligence memoirs. Like a grandfather sharing war stories, except the grandchild was a fictional character.'

'What sort of materials?'

'Everything you can imagine. Operational manuals, case studies, even old surveillance photographs from his time in the service – CIA, I think he mentioned once. Harry would sit right here for hours, testing Sebastian's knowledge, asking detailed questions about tradecraft and spy stuff.'

Phillip looked up from his methodical destruction of baked goods.

'Harry understood what it was like to live two different lives. Said most intelligence work required you to compartmentalise your identity just to function.'

'He told Sebastian that?'

'Oh yes. And me, when we spoke. Harry said the trick was knowing which identity to trust in which situation, and when to let one take over from the other.' Phillip's expression grew thoughtful. 'He seemed quite fascinated by Sebastian's methods, the way he could work through complex scenarios.'

'What sort of scenarios?' Laura asked, finding herself genuinely absorbed in this glimpse into Harry's last months.

'Hypothetical operations, mostly. Harry would present Sebastian with surveillance challenges or infiltration problems, then sit back and watch him work through the solutions.' Phillip smiled slightly. 'I think Harry was testing whether Sebastian's knowledge was purely theoretical or if it could be applied in practice.'

'Give me an example,' Laura said.

Phillip set down his teacup, his expression becoming more animated as he accessed these memories.

'Well, one time Harry described a scenario where you needed to observe someone in a crowded public space without being detected. Sebastian talked him through sight lines, timing patterns, the importance of blending with natural crowd movements. Then Harry complicated it – what if the target had counter-surveillance training? Sebastian explained about using multiple observation points, relay systems, how to identify if you'd been spotted.'

'And Harry's reaction?'

'He seemed genuinely impressed. Said Sebastian's instincts were remarkably sound...' Phillip paused. 'He also said Sebastian's approach reminded him of someone he'd worked with. Harry was quite mysterious about this other person. Said they'd been invaluable during complex operations but had paid quite a price for their service.'

'Did he say who it was?'

'No, but he seemed genuinely fond of whoever it was. There was genuine sadness when he talked about them...'

Doctor Matthews patted Phillip's arm as he trailed off, studying Laura's face.

'I had the impression this person might have been connected to your husband somehow,' she added. 'Harry mentioned James several times during his visits, when I was in the room.'

Laura nearly choked on her tea.

'James? My James?'

'I believe so, yes. Harry said James had worked with this man on several joint operations.'

The implications of this settled around Laura like fog.

'Doctor Matthews,' she said carefully, 'where exactly does Phillip spend his time when he's being Sebastian? I mean, obviously he can't stay in this room when he's... transformed.'

Doctor Matthews and Phillip exchanged glances that suggested this was a topic they'd discussed before.

'Ah yes, the famous gatehouse,' Doctor Matthews said with obvious amusement. 'Phillip discovered it during one of his walks around the garden. Victorian estate, you see – they built little cottages for the gardening staff.'

'It's been empty for years,' Phillip added. 'Just sitting there gathering dust and spiders.'

'Until Sebastian made it habitable,' Doctor Matthews continued. 'We've allowed it because it gives Phillip a sense of independence and purpose.'

'What sort of purpose?' Laura asked, though she suspected she already knew.

'Oh, you know Sebastian,' Phillip said with a rueful smile. 'Always preparing for contingencies. He's made the place rather... well, rather organised.'

'Organised how?'

Doctor Matthews chuckled.

'Let's just say Sebastian believes in being prepared for any eventuality. It gained the full Boy Scout treatment.'

'Nothing too dramatic,' Phillip said quickly. 'Radios, mobile phones, that sort of thing. Sebastian worries about staying in touch during emergencies.'

'And by emergencies, you mean...?'

'Oh, anything really. Sebastian has a rather active imagination when it comes to potential threats.' Doctor Matthews's tone was indulgent. 'Though I must admit, his preparations have been remarkably thorough.'

'How thorough?'

Phillip shifted uncomfortably.

'I may have acquired rather more supplies than strictly necessary. Sebastian doesn't like being caught unprepared.'

'What sort of supplies?'

'Food stores, medical supplies, backup power systems...' Phillip trailed off, looking embarrassed. 'It sounds rather mad when you list it all out.'

'It sounds like a bunker,' Laura observed.

'A very civilised bunker,' Doctor Matthews corrected cheerfully. 'Sebastian has excellent taste in emergency preparedness. Proper tea service even in apocalyptic circumstances.'

Despite everything, Laura found herself smiling. *Trust Sebastian Silver to prepare for the end of the world with style.*

'Does he spend much time there?'

'When he's active, yes. Sebastian considers it his operational headquarters.' Doctor Matthews's expression grew slightly more serious. 'Though we keep a careful eye on things. Phillip has the only key, and Sebastian's activities are entirely benign. Just... comprehensive.'

'How comprehensive?' Laura pressed.

Phillip looked genuinely embarrassed now. 'Well, there might be enough supplies for several weeks. And backup communications systems. And detailed maps of London with various routes marked. And possibly some basic medical equipment.'

'And surveillance gear,' Doctor Matthews added helpfully. 'Nothing illegal, mind you. Just the sort of thing you could buy online if you were sufficiently motivated.'

'Sufficiently paranoid, you mean,' Phillip corrected.

'Sufficiently prepared,' Doctor Matthews countered firmly. 'Considering recent events, Sebastian's caution appears to have been entirely justified.'

Laura filed this information away carefully. A private, well-equipped workspace where Sebastian could plan and prepare sounded like exactly what they might need if this investigation continued to escalate. More importantly, it suggested that Sebastian's preparations hadn't been entirely theoretical – he'd been ready for exactly the sort of situation they now found themselves in.

Doctor Matthews rose, gathering the tea things with efficient grace.

'You're welcome to visit again, Mrs Carlyle. Phillip enjoys having guests, and I suspect Sebastian will have more to tell you once he returns.'

'When will that be?'

'When Phillip puts his hat back on,' Doctor Matthews said simply. 'Though I'd recommend having some specific questions ready. The Sebastian persona can be rather... focused.'

THEY MADE THEIR FAREWELLS, LAURA PROMISING TO RETURN soon. As they reached the corridor, she looked back to see Phillip standing in his doorway, watching them go with the wistful expression of someone watching an adventure sail away without him.

'Mrs Carlyle?' he called softly.

'Yes?'

'When you see Sebastian again... could you tell him I'm grateful? For letting me feel brave, even if it was just pretend.'

Laura's throat tightened.

'It wasn't pretend, Phillip. Everything Sebastian accomplished, that was you. All of it.'

'That's very kind of you to say.'

'It's not kindness. It's fact.'

As they walked towards the stairs, Frank, now back from his cigarette break fell into step beside her.

'Well? What's the verdict?'

'I think Phillip Morris is a genuinely lovely man who's built himself the most extraordinary coping mechanism I've ever encountered,' Laura said. 'And I think Sebastian Silver, fictional or not, knows more about staying alive than the rest of us put together.'

'Are you planning to continue this partnership?'

Laura paused at the top of the stairs, looking back towards Phillip's room.

'Frank, that man – both versions of him – has saved my life, potentially solved Harry's murder, and asked for nothing in return except the chance to feel useful. Fictional spy or not, I'd rather have Sebastian Silver watching my back than anyone else I can think of.'

'Even if he's not real?'

'Especially because he's not real,' Laura said with a smile. 'Real spies have their own agendas. Fictional ones just want to do the right thing.'

As they descended towards the lobby, Laura thought about masks and pretence, about the different selves people wore for protection or necessity. She'd spent decades being the perfect diplomatic wife, then another fifteen years as the respectable widow.

Perhaps it was time to discover what Laura Carlyle might accomplish if she stopped worrying about being perfectly proper and started focusing on being perfectly effective.

That said, there was something about masks and pretence that niggled at her, somehow. As if there were a blatant clue she'd missed.

Ah, well. It'll turn up, eventually.

Outside Tidworth House, Greenwich hummed with its usual mixture of purpose and chaos. But as Frank's car pulled away, Laura caught a glimpse of movement at an upstairs window.

Phillip, still watching, still hoping, still caught between the ordinary man he was and the extraordinary man he could become with the simple addition of a hat.

And somewhere in that gentle, damaged, remarkable person was the key to everything – if she could just figure out how to help him believe in himself as much as he believed in Sebastian Silver.

17

INTERVIEW

Frank's police station at four o'clock in the afternoon felt like any government office, with institutional tea, photocopying and printer noises, and the quiet desperation of people filling out forms in triplicate. Laura followed Frank through corridors lined with health and safety notices that no one had read since 1987 and had likely been carried over from the old building.

'Interview Room Three,' Frank said, opening a door that looked like it had been decorated by someone who thought beige was an exciting colour choice. 'Nothing too dramatic. Just need everything official.'

The room contained a table, four plastic chairs designed by enemies of human comfort, and a recording device that probably predated decimal currency, although Laura was probably being a little overly harsh there. Digital recordings could still be corrupted, so maybe analogue was still good for backup, after all. Through the single window, Laura could see Kyle, still in the station's car park, deep in conversation with a uniformed constable beside Frank's car. She'd called him on the way back and hadn't been surprised to find him waiting for her.

'Making friends?' she asked.

'I believe PC Williams is explaining proper vehicle maintenance procedures,' Frank said. 'Your grandson has questions about everything from tyre pressure to radio protocols.'

'He's always been curious.'

'Curious enough to qualify for the force by teatime, at this rate.'

Laura settled into one of the chairs, immediately understanding why police interviews were so effective – after five minutes on these seats, anyone would confess to anything.

'Before we start,' she said, 'what happened to Sebastian's trilby?'

Frank produced the hat from the evidence bag, handling it like unexploded ordnance.

'Officially? Not evidence of anything except questionable fashion sense.'

'But you know what it does to Phillip.'

'I know what Doctor Matthews claims, as I've read her report now.' Frank set the trilby between them. 'Whether that's medicine or performance art remains to be seen, when I interview him later.'

Laura stared at the hat.

Such an ordinary thing to have such extraordinary effects.

'What would you do? If you needed information only Sebastian could provide?'

'I'd ask myself whether I trusted the man more than I feared his imaginary friend.'

Before Laura could work out whether that was helpful or just confusing, the door burst open, and Aunt Celia swept in carrying what looked like a military-grade thermos flask and wearing an expression that could freeze boiling water.

'Detective Chief Inspector Young,' she said with the sort of politeness usually reserved for traffic wardens. 'I trust you're not interrogating my niece without proper refreshments.'

Frank blinked.

'Mrs Harrington? How did you—'

'Kyle telephoned. Naturally I came at once.' Celia set down her thermos with the authority of someone planting a flag. 'Earl Grey, proper strength. Two sugars for Laura, none for you unless you ask nicely.'

'You can't just—'

'I told reception I was Laura's solicitor. Amazing what confidence and a good handbag accomplish.' Celia arranged herself in the remaining chair as if she'd bought the building. 'Now then, shall we proceed? I assume you have questions about Laura's recent foray into practical detection.'

Frank looked between them, visibly recalculating.

'This is supposed to be official—'

'Then make it official properly,' Celia interrupted, producing a small notebook. 'Date, time, persons present. I may be retired from the diplomatic service, but I remember procedure.'

'You can't just—'

'Detective Chief Inspector, my niece has been solving murders whilst you were shuffling papers. The least you can do is provide adequate tea service.'

Laura watched Frank surrender to the inevitable and activate the recording device.

'Interview with Mrs Laura Carlyle,' he said through

gritted teeth. 'Also present: Mrs Celia Harrington, who apparently thinks police stations are social clubs.'

'I think they're undernourished institutions,' Celia replied, producing paper cups from nowhere. 'Which I'm rectifying.'

She paused as if waiting.

'Well, go on then!' she exclaimed. 'What's keeping you! Do I have to do everything?'

Frank stared back, and Laura actually felt sorry for him.

'Maybe I should begin?' she offered.

FOR THE NEXT HOUR, LAURA WALKED FRANK THROUGH THE entire investigation – Rebecca's visit, the enhanced photographs, David's murder, the break-in at his apartment, the confrontation with Calendar operatives, Mister Monday. She kept to facts, avoiding speculation about Sebastian's true nature whilst building a comprehensive picture of what they'd discovered.

Frank scribbled notes, occasionally pausing to ask for clarification or to circle something with particular emphasis.

'The surveillance photographs from David's apartment,' he said, looking up from his notepad. 'You mentioned multiple passports for Louise. How many exactly?'

'Four photocopies that we found. Russian, Polish, Italian, and one other I can't recall. All with her photograph but different names.'

'Professional grade forgeries?'

'They looked authentic to me, though I'm hardly an expert, and as I said, they were photocopies.'

As if on cue, Celia produced the folded sheets of A4, sliding them over the table.

'Of course you took evidence from a crime scene,' Frank muttered.

'It wasn't a crime scene any more,' Celia argued. 'Your people had gone by the time Laura arrived. If they didn't find these, that's just shoddy work on your part.'

'And the digital storage device Sebastian retrieved?'

'Lost when the laptop was destroyed at Electronic Zone,' Laura lied. In truth, she hadn't seen it since Sebastian Silver had picked it up, but she wasn't going to snitch on him anytime soon. 'Along with everything else we'd discovered about Harry's investigation.'

Frank made another note.

'Convenient timing on that electromagnetic pulse.'

'Wasn't it just?'

Celia leaned forward slightly.

'Detective Chief Inspector, I'm curious about something. When Laura first approached you about Harry Farrell's death, why were you so quick to dismiss her concerns?'

Frank's pen stopped moving.

'The official determination was natural causes—'

'Yes, but Laura's hardly known for flights of fancy. In forty years of friendship, I've never known her to pursue conspiracy theories or imagine mysteries where none existed.'

'Mrs Harrington—'

'It's a legitimate question. If an old friend with Laura's reputation for analytical thinking approached you with concerns about a suspicious death, wouldn't you at least look more closely at the evidence?'

Frank set down his pen, his expression uncomfortable.

'There were... suggestions from higher up that the case was straightforward. American diplomatic personnel, clean medical examination, no obvious signs of foul play.'

'Suggestions,' Celia repeated. 'From whom?'

'I can't discuss internal communications—'

'You mean someone told you to treat it as natural causes regardless of evidence? Maybe CIA? Or perhaps The Calendar themselves?'

'I mean there was pressure to process the case efficiently and move on to other matters.'

Laura and Celia exchanged glances. The implications were troubling – if The Calendar had influence within official channels, or if the CIA had wanted to protect their old asset, it explained both the rushed investigation and Frank's initial reluctance to take her concerns seriously.

'That's rather concerning,' Laura said quietly.

'Which is why I'm willing to work with you now,' Frank replied. 'Even if it means bending procedures and trusting fictional spies. So, in your assessment, this Calendar organisation poses a genuine threat?'

'They've murdered people to protect their secrets. I'd call that threatening.'

'And you believe Sebastian Silver has knowledge that could stop them?'

Laura glanced at the trilby.

'I believe Sebastian understands how they think. Whether that comes from experience or imagination hardly matters if it saves lives.'

'Even if helping him means encouraging what might be a serious delusion?'

'Doctor Matthews doesn't consider it harmful. If anything, it gives Phillip confidence he otherwise lacks.'

Celia sipped at her tea.

'The real question, Detective Chief Inspector, is whether you'll accept unconventional help, or insist on official channels that have been spectacularly useless so far.'

Frank's jaw tightened.

'Official procedures exist for good reasons—'

'Official procedures called Harry's death natural causes and missed an entire criminal network,' Celia said sweetly. 'Laura accomplished more in two or three days than your department managed in a month.'

'Laura also contaminated crime scenes and nearly got herself killed.'

'Results matter when people are dying.'

Frank's mobile rang before he could respond. He answered with obvious irritation.

'Young... what? When?... keep everyone back, I'm coming.'

He rang off, looking grim.

'Another case I'm working on.' Frank gathered his notes. 'We're done for now. But we're not finished here.'

'Naturally,' Celia said, packing away her tea service with military efficiency. 'Though next time, provide better biscuits. Is my niece arrested?'

'Of course not.'

'Then we shall retire to Queen's Gate,' Celia motioned for Laura to rise with her. 'You may call on us there later.'

THEY WALKED BACK THROUGH THE CORRIDORS TOWARDS reception, where Kyle was visible through the glass doors, still chatting with PC Williams whilst examining what appeared to be a breathalyser.

'Your grandson has remarkable enthusiasm for police equipment,' Frank observed.

'He gets it from his grandmother,' Celia replied. 'Harrington women have always been interested in how authority functions.'

Frank nodded. Even though he'd only known Laura while married, he would have known Harrington was her maiden name.

'And how to work around it when necessary?'

'When justice requires it.'

Frank stopped at the reception desk, apparently wrestling with something. Finally, he picked up the trilby and offered it to Laura.

'Unofficial advice? You'll need all the help you can get. Even if it comes from unconventional sources.'

Laura accepted the hat, surprised by its weight.

'You're returning this?'

'I'm releasing personal property with no evidential value,' Frank said carefully. 'What you do with it is your choice.'

'Thank you.'

'Don't thank me yet. When this goes sideways, I'll deny everything.'

As they approached the exit, Kyle looked up from his impromptu police tutorial with obvious disappointment.

'Finished already? PC Williams was just explaining drug testing protocols. Did you know they can detect cannabis use from up to thirty days ago? Fascinating stuff.'

'I'm sure it was,' Celia said dryly. 'Though I hope you're not planning a career change.'

'Actually, I was thinking about it. PC Williams says they're always looking for graduates.'

'Over my dead body,' Laura said firmly. 'Your mother would never forgive me if I let you join the police force whilst she's in Japan.'

'Why not? You've practically joined yourself.'

'I have not joined the police force.'

'No, you've just been investigating murders, breaking into crime scenes, and fighting international conspiracies,' Kyle grinned. 'Much more exciting than being a proper police officer.'

Frank cleared his throat.

'Kyle might want to continue his education whilst I walk Mrs Carlyle out. Learn about security procedures.'

Kyle's face lit up like Christmas morning.

'Could I see the custody cells? PC Williams mentioned they've got some interesting stories about famous criminals who've been held there.'

'We'll see what can be arranged.'

As Kyle disappeared back into the building with PC Williams, chattering about fingerprinting techniques, Celia shook her head.

'That boy's entirely too enthusiastic about criminal procedures for someone who's supposed to be studying economics.'

'He gets it from his grandmother,' Frank observed, mimicking Celia's earlier response. 'Laura's the same way – always asking questions other people wouldn't think to ask.'

'You're in a hurry,' Laura added. 'The other case you're working on. I can find my own way out.'

'No offence, but I want to prove to myself you're out of the building and out of my hair for the moment.' Frank gave a soft smile. 'Even if it means more hassle down the line.'

Laura now found herself on the pavement with Frank, watching London's early evening traffic whilst Celia remained visible through the glass doors, apparently giving PC Williams detailed instructions about Kyle's continued education.

'Your aunt's quite formidable,' Frank observed.

'She once made the Serbian ambassador cry at a dinner party by asking pointed questions about his country's human rights record.'

'Remind me never to get on her bad side.'

'Too late for that, I'm afraid. She's convinced you've been neglecting your duties regarding Harry's death.'

'And what do you think?'

Laura considered this carefully.

'I think you're doing your best within a system that's not designed for cases like this. But I also think some problems require unofficial solutions.'

'Is that your diplomatic way of saying I'm useless?'

'It's my diplomatic way of saying you're constrained by procedures that don't account for organisations like The Calendar.'

Frank hailed a taxi with perhaps more force than strictly necessary.

'You know, when we were younger, I always thought you were wasted as a diplomatic wife.'

The taxi pulled up, and Frank opened the door for her.

'You're being remarkably accommodating about all this,' Laura said.

'I'm being practical. This Calendar business is beyond normal police procedures. If your fictional spy can help stop them, I'll overlook certain irregularities in how you've conducted this investigation.'

'Such as?'

'Breaking and entering, evidence tampering, assault with various household items.' Frank's smile held no warmth. 'Officially, I know nothing about any of that.'

'And unofficially?'

'Unofficially, I'm grateful someone's finally taking this seriously enough to do something about it. Go back and get *Sebastian Silver, superspy*. I'll make sure your aunt and grandson get home okay.'

'One thing,' Laura paused. 'A legitimate question, I promise.'

Frank straightened. 'Go on.'

'Brian, the man who was shot,' Laura continued. 'When we met him under the name Mister Friday, he had a syringe, like the one that Harry and possibly David were killed with. Why did they shoot him when they could have just poisoned him? It wasn't any kind of message.'

'Ah, I can actually answer that,' Frank smiled with the look of someone finally able to show off. 'Brian's bloodwork came back. His toxicology reports showed he had an incredible resistance to most forms of poison. All I can think is perhaps these mysterious men build a tolerance to the chemicals they use, in case they accidentally ingest? Either way, if he had been poisoned, the chances are that after a small nap, he'd have shrugged it off.'

As Laura settled into the taxi, Frank caught the door before she could close it.

'Laura, be careful. These people have killed multiple times to protect their secrets. They won't hesitate to expand that number. And you *haven't* had this tolerance build up.'

'I understand the risks.'

'Do you? Because once you put that hat on Phillip's head, there's no going back. You'll be committed to whatever comes next, wherever it leads.'

Laura looked down at the trilby in her lap, then back at Frank's genuinely worried face.

'I was committed to this the moment Rebecca Farrell knocked on my door asking for help. Everything since then has just been... clarification.'

'Clarification?'

'Understanding what I'm actually fighting, and what I'm willing to do to win.'

Frank studied her face for a long moment.

'Laura? Trust your instincts. They've kept you alive this long.'

The taxi pulled away, carrying her through London's evening traffic towards Tidworth House and the most unusual partnership of her life.

AFTER AROUND FIFTEEN MINUTES, HER MOBILE RANG; REBECCA Farrell's name appeared on the screen.

'Rebecca? How are you managing?'

'Mrs Carlyle, I'm so sorry to bother you, but I was hoping you had some updates.'

'I do, but I want to confirm one more thing before I come back to you, if that's okay?'

'Okay, of course.' Rebecca sounded a little crestfallen at this. 'Did you find this mysterious Sebastian fellow?'

'I did.'

'And has he helped find out what happened to Harry?'

Laura went to answer, but the niggling feeling she'd felt before tugged at her.

'Rebecca, Harry's belongings. How did you get them?'

'The belongings? They came from the police.'

'Did you sign for them?'

'Of course I did. You don't get given things without signing. Did Sebastian tell you anything?'

Laura froze as Frank's earlier words came back. As far as the police were concerned, there'd never been anything signed.

'Rebecca, where are you now?'

'At home. Why?'

'I thought you were going away?'

'I waited in case you had information. Was I wrong to do that?'

'I want you to pack a bag and go stay with friends or family for a few days. Don't tell anyone where you're going and don't use your credit cards.'

'You're frightening me, Mrs Carlyle.'

'Good. These people have killed to protect their secrets. I don't want you to become their next target.'

'What are you going to do?'

'Take them down.'

'Do you have Harry's files?'

Laura paused.

'You gave me them, remember?'

'Oh, I meant the ones on the phone. You said you had someone looking at it?'

'Ah. I'll explain that one when I see you next.'

After Rebecca rang off, Laura sat back in the taxi seat, her mind racing. The Calendar was escalating its tactics – from surveillance to direct threats to attempted murder. How long before they moved beyond threats entirely?

But there was something wrong. How had Rebecca known Laura had opened the phone, or was even doing that? All she'd done was ask to borrow it.

Now you're getting paranoid, Laura.

But it's not wrong to be paranoid when so many red flags are showing.

The trilby sat beside her on the seat, looking perfectly innocent. Such a small thing to represent such enormous consequences.

Her phone beeped, and this time it was a message from Frank.

Did you take Kyle?

What do you mean? I'm on my way to Greenwich. You saw me get in the car.

You're not with Kyle?

No.

You didn't come back for him?

She didn't have time to reply. A second later, the phone rang. Frank.

'What's going on?' Laura asked. 'Kyle's with you, remember? You said you'd get him and Celia home.'

'No, he's not. I had to go to a briefing for the other case, but I was just told that Kyle left through the back exit five minutes ago. Got a message on his phone and said he was "meeting his grandmother outside". I have a witness who says he climbed into a black taxi waiting outside, and it drove off. Someone was inside, Laura. Someone who obviously isn't you.'

The world seemed to tilt sideways.

'It wasn't me,' Laura whispered.

'Oh, Christ,' Frank replied. 'Laura, Kyle's been taken.'

Laura wanted to scream. Somewhere in the city, her grandson was in the hands of people who'd proven they'd kill to protect their secrets.

Laura clutched the trilby tighter, knowing with absolute certainty that only one person had the knowledge and ruthlessness to get Kyle back alive.

And that person existed only when an accountant from Boston put on a hat.

18

THE GATEHOUSE

THE TAXI PULLED UP OUTSIDE THE CARE FACILITY AS THE CLOCK tower chimed five. Laura clutched Sebastian's trilby against her chest like a life preserver, which wasn't entirely inaccurate given the circumstances.

She paid the driver with shaking hands, Frank's words still ringing in her ears.

Kyle's been taken.

The Calendar had her grandson.

They'd killed Harry and David, shot their own operative, and now they had Kyle. The only person who might be able to save him was sitting in a care facility, nothing more than an accountant from Boston who'd lost his wife and his mind in roughly equal measure.

Her mobile buzzed. An unknown number.

> Bring what we want. Midnight. Location to follow. No police or the boy dies.

Laura stared at the message.

What they wanted? What did they want? Harry's secrets?

Her phone rang again – Frank.

'Laura, where are you? We need to coordinate—'

'I'm handling this.'

'You can't handle this alone! These people are—'

'Professionals. I know,' she cut him off. 'So is Sebastian.'

'Sebastian's a patient in a care home!'

'Sebastian,' Laura said, surprising herself with her certainty, 'is exactly who we need right now, and don't forget you sent me to get him.'

'That was before—'

She ended the call and switched the phone to silent. Yes, she was making a mistake, keeping Frank at arm's reach. But right now, she wasn't thinking like the analytical puzzle-solver she'd been the last few days.

Now, she was thinking like a grandmother.

THE RECEPTIONIST BARELY GLANCED UP AS LAURA SIGNED IN.

Good.

The last thing she needed was questions about why she was visiting twice in one day, or why she looked like she'd been dragged through a hedge backwards. She took the stairs rather than the elevator, needing the time to work out exactly what she was going to say.

How did one ask someone to risk their sanity for a stranger?

She found Phillip in his room, sitting exactly where she'd left him. He was staring out at the front garden and street beyond; hands folded in his lap like a schoolchild waiting for detention. The late afternoon light made him look smaller, more fragile. Other residents moved about in the background – an elderly woman watering plants, a man in a wheelchair reading by the windows. Normal people living normal lives whilst her world fell apart.

'Phillip.'

He blinked, the process of focusing on her face clearly requiring effort, in a way like swimming up from deep water.

'Mrs Carlyle. You've returned rather sooner than expected.'

'They have Kyle.' She forwent pleasantries and instead showed him her phone. 'They want to make the exchange at midnight.'

Phillip took the mobile carefully, reading the message twice. Colour drained from his cheeks.

'I don't understand. What could they possibly want from you?'

Laura held up the trilby. Such an ordinary thing; felt and silk and a bit of wire in the brim to hold the shape... yet she'd seen what it could do.

'I don't think it's from me. I think it's from *him*.'

Phillip's gaze fixed on the hat. Fear flickered across his features – not the manufactured anxiety of someone playing a role, but genuine terror.

'I know what I'm asking.' Laura sat down across from him, the chair's familiar squeak a tiny anchor of normalcy. 'It's monstrous, really. Asking you to risk who you are for a boy you barely know. But Kyle is twenty years old, and he's probably scared out of his mind right now, because these people have killed already and won't hesitate to add to that. But Sebastian Silver is the only person I know who might be able to bring my grandson home alive.'

Phillip stared at the hat in her hands.

'What if I lose myself completely this time? What if I put

this on and Phillip Morris disappears forever? What if I become Sebastian and never find my way back?'

It was a fair question. Laura could hear piano music drifting from somewhere deeper in the building, the gentle murmur of other residents going about their evening routines. Normal sounds from a normal world that seemed very far away from murdered intelligence officers and kidnapped grandsons.

'Then Celia and I will help you find your way back,' she said quietly. 'We'll sit with you and tell you stories about Boston, about your life before London. We'll remind you that Phillip Morris is a good man who deserves to exist, even if he's not always confident about it.'

'But what if that's not enough?'

'Then at least we'll have tried.' Laura leaned forward. 'Phillip, I've seen what Sebastian becomes when he puts on that hat. I've watched him think through complex problems, handle dangerous situations, keep me safe when any sensible person would have run away screaming. That's not magic. That's you.'

Phillip shook his head.

'Sebastian knows things I don't know. Can do things I could never do.'

'Like what?'

'Like yesterday, when we were examining those photographs. Sebastian looked at them and immediately understood what had happened, how Harry had been killed. I could stare at those images for hours and never see what he saw in seconds.'

Laura considered this. Sebastian had been impressive, certainly. But...

'Or maybe Sebastian just has the confidence to trust what

Phillip already knows. You're an accountant, Phillip. You're used to looking at details, finding patterns, working out what the numbers really mean, and you've read every spy book known to man. Sebastian just applies those same skills to different problems.'

'You think so?'

'I think Sebastian is who you'd be if life hadn't knocked you down so hard. If your wife hadn't died, if you hadn't lost your job, if you hadn't ended up alone in a foreign country with no support system...' Laura paused. 'I think the hat doesn't create Sebastian Silver. It just gives you permission to be confident again.'

Through the windows she could see the sun beginning to set, painting the sky in shades of orange and pink. Somewhere in London, Kyle was waiting.

Time was running out.

'They'll kill him, won't they?' Phillip's voice was barely audible. 'If we don't give them what they want.'

'Yes.'

'And you really think Sebastian can stop them?'

'I think Sebastian is our only chance,' Laura smiled, though her heart was beating too fast. 'Besides, we make quite a team, apparently. All three of us.'

'Three of us?'

'You, me, and Sebastian. According to Doctor Matthews, anyway.'

That earned her an almost-smile. Phillip picked up the hat, turning it over in his hands like it might bite him.

'You know, sometimes I think Sebastian talks about you when I'm... when I'm not listening properly.'

'What do you mean?'

'I remember fragments. Thoughts that don't feel like

mine.' Phillip looked up at her. 'Sebastian worries about you, Laura. Cares about you. More than he probably should, considering we've only known each other a few days.'

'He said that?'

'Not in words. But I can sense what he feels about things. His thoughts bleed through sometimes, even when I'm Phillip...' he paused. 'He thinks you're remarkable. Brave and clever and... and he'd never forgive himself if something happened to you because of this investigation.'

'Well then,' Laura said, trying to keep her voice steady, 'he'll want to make sure Kyle gets home safely, won't he?'

Phillip nodded slowly. Then, before he could change his mind, he placed the trilby on his head.

The change wasn't instant, but Laura could see it beginning almost immediately. Phillip's posture straightened, his shoulders squaring. His eyes sharpened, becoming more alert. The uncertain, gentle man seemed to fade away like morning mist, replaced by someone altogether more assured.

'Mrs Carlyle.' Sebastian Silver's voice was crisp, authoritative. No trace of Boston accent, no hesitation. 'How long do we have?'

'Six and a half hours until midnight.'

'Then we'd better collect some equipment.' He stood, adjusting the trilby with an ease that spoke of long practice. 'Follow me.'

'Where are we going?'

'Somewhere I've been preparing for exactly this sort of eventuality.'

Silver led her through corridors, and past common areas where residents sat reading or watching television. He moved with purpose, clearly knowing his way around the facility better than any patient should. At a door marked 'Staff Only', he produced a key from his waistcoat.

'How do you have—'

'One acquires useful items when one pays attention,' Silver said, leading her down a narrow hallway. 'The staff here are generally competent, but they're not trained for security concerns.'

The hallway led to a covered walkway, which connected to a square of grass, which in turn connected to a small Victorian building tucked behind the primary facility. It looked like a gardener's cottage from the outside.

Silver unlocked the door and gestured for her to enter.

'Bloody hell,' Laura breathed.

'Language, Mrs Carlyle,' Silver said, but he was smiling.

The single room had been transformed into something that wouldn't have looked out of place in a gentlemen's club, if gentlemen's clubs routinely prepared for international espionage. Bookcases lined the walls, filled with volumes on everything from surveillance techniques to European history. A large oak table dominated the centre of the room, its surface covered with maps of London, photographs, and what appeared to be surveillance notes written in Silver's precise handwriting.

Along one wall stood a glass-fronted cabinet containing walking sticks – dozens of them, each slightly different from the others. Near the window sat a comfortable leather armchair with a small table arranged for tea service, complete with proper china and what looked like genuine silver spoons.

'It's like a cosy headquarters,' Laura observed, turning slowly to take it all in.

'Functionality needn't preclude comfort,' Silver said, moving to the walking stick cabinet. 'I've always believed that pleasant surroundings contribute to clear thinking.'

He selected a stick with a silver handle shaped like a wolf's head.

'GPS tracker and small camera. Useful for surveillance work.' He returned it to its place and showed another with a plain wooden grip. 'Taser. Not my preferred option, but occasionally circumstances require... persuasion.'

'How many are there?'

'Twelve at present. Different tools for different situations. Thankfully, I have duplicates.'

'From eBay?'

'That's just what I tell Phillip.' Silver opened a drawer in the oak table, revealing an array of small devices organised in custom-fitted compartments. 'The fact is, I have other streams of acquisition. Communication equipment, lock picks, first aid supplies, emergency funds in various currencies. The sort of things one hopes never to need but appreciates having available.'

Laura inspected the collection. Each walking cane was beautiful in its own right, but clearly functional rather than decorative.

'How did you manage all this with no one noticing?'

'People see what they expect to see, particularly in institutional settings. To the staff, I'm an eccentric patient with expensive tastes and a walking stick collection.' Silver's smile was slightly rueful. 'They assume the books are part of some therapeutic reading programme, and the maps are evidence of travel fantasies. Doctor Matthews was happy for me to play spies in here. She simply didn't realise I was doing more than playing.'

Laura picked up one of the photographs from the table. It showed a man in his fifties leaving what looked like an office building. The image was sharp, professional quality.

'Are these surveillance photos?'

'Research on various Calendar operatives. Some recent, others from archived intelligence files given to me – Phillip – by Harry.' Silver joined her at the table. 'I've been building a comprehensive picture of their organisation for some time.'

'Why didn't you say anything?'

'Because I…' Silver paused. 'Actually, I don't know.'

The work was impressive in its scope and detail. Each photograph was labelled with dates, times, and locations. Maps showed movement patterns and meeting places. A large board on one wall displayed what appeared to be an organisational chart, with lines connecting various names and photographs.

'Who's this?' Laura asked, picking up a photo of a woman, white hair in a bob, sadly watering some geraniums.

At the question, Silver paused.

'You don't recognise her?'

'Should I?'

Silver took the photo, checking it again before once more turning it to face her.

'Laura, that's Rebecca Farrell.'

'No,' Laura shook her head. 'Rebecca has black hair, greying.'

Silver seemed to start at this.

'*That's* who that was at your door!' he exclaimed. 'I assumed she was one of your various committee women.'

'No, stop,' Laura was backing away now. 'This isn't funny,

Sebastian, Phillip, whatever your name is. I spoke to her. I went to her house.'

'I promise you, the woman who came to your door was not Rebecca,' Silver continued. 'If I'd known she claimed that role, I would have made my appearance sooner.'

There was a long, awkward moment of silence as Laura considered what Silver had stated.

'So who tasked me with finding Harry Farrell's killer?'

'That I do not know,' Silver said, and his voice carried enough regret to feel sincere. 'But the real Rebecca Farrell left London two weeks ago, after Harry's internment in Kensington.'

Laura stared at the woman in the photo. So, not only had someone taken Rebecca's identity, they'd also utilised her house, knowing she wouldn't be back.

It made sense now. The note saying to get the cat looked after. The possessions that had never been signed for by Rebecca but were apparently in her possession.

The knowledge of Sebastian Silver and the phone being opened.

'I don't like being played,' she muttered, as Silver continued to select items from various cases, each movement economical and sure. 'She has to be Calendar, right?'

'Most likely.' Whatever the source of Sebastian Silver's abilities, he certainly didn't move like someone unsure of himself.

'What exactly are you preparing for?'

'A rescue mission. Though I suspect The Calendar's true objective isn't Kyle.'

'What do you mean?'

Silver looked up from his preparations.

'Consider the timing, Mrs Carlyle. They could have taken

Kyle at any time over the past few days. His university schedule is predictable, his security non-existent. Why now? Why demand an exchange when they could simply have grabbed him and disappeared?'

Laura felt understanding dawn.

'Because they want something specific. Something they believe I have access to.'

'Precisely. And what do you have access to that they might want?'

'You.' The word came out as barely a whisper. 'They want you.'

'Very likely. The question is whether they want Sebastian Silver the operative, or something else entirely.'

'What do you mean?'

Sebastian was quiet for a moment, his gaze distant.

'There are things I remember, fragments about The Calendar that feel important. Names, places, operational details. But I can't tell if these are real memories or simply reconstructions based on research. And Harry used to ask me if I ever remembered names, lists, secret operatives. I couldn't answer him, as I had no knowledge of what he meant.'

He moved to the organisational chart on the wall, pointing to a section marked with question marks.

'There's someone The Calendar calls Mister Sunday. According to what I've learned, he was their leader until approximately fifteen years ago, when he disappeared under mysterious circumstances.'

'And you think Kyle's kidnapping is connected to this Mister Sunday?'

'I think tonight will provide answers to questions we haven't even thought to ask yet.' Sebastian turned back to her.

'But one way or another, we'll solve this Sunday cypher and have Kyle home by morning.'

Laura went to reply but then shuddered as a thought crossed her path.

'My husband died fifteen years ago,' she said. 'You're in the background of several news clippings, watching him. Was that anything to do with you?'

Before Silver could respond, they heard footsteps on the gravel path outside, and he was beside her instantly, finger to his lips.

'Expecting anyone?' he whispered.

Laura shook her head.

The footsteps stopped outside the door. A key rattled in the lock.

'Phillip? Are you in here?' A familiar voice called out. 'I saw the light on and thought you might need assistance.'

'I thought you had the only key?' Laura whispered.

'*I* thought I had the only key,' Silver whispered back.

The door opened to reveal James, the orderly who'd served tea earlier that day. He stepped into the gatehouse, then stopped short when he saw Laura and Silver together.

'Oh. I didn't realise you had company, Phillip.'

'James.' Silver's voice was carefully neutral. 'What brings you here this evening?'

'Making my rounds. Doctor Matthews asked me to check on our residents, and I noticed the light.' James's gaze swept the room, taking in the equipment, the maps, the walking stick collection. Something shifted in his expression – mild curiosity transforming into something altogether more dangerous. 'Quite the setup you have here.'

Silver stepped slightly in front of Laura.

'Just organising some old belongings.'

'Old belongings,' James smiled, but it was cold, predatory. Like a cat that had cornered a particularly interesting mouse. 'Is that what we're calling them?'

The atmosphere in the room changed, and Laura backed towards the door, every instinct screaming *danger*.

'I should probably head back to the main building,' she blurted.

'Oh, I don't think so.' James pulled something from his pocket – a needle-less syringe filled with clear liquid. 'You're both exactly where you need to be.'

EVERYTHING HAPPENED FAST AFTER THAT.

James lunged towards Silver, aiming the syringe at his mouth. Silver caught his wrist, spinning him around, but James was stronger than he looked and broke free, stumbling backwards towards Laura.

'Stay back!' Silver shouted, but James was already moving again, this time successfully grabbing Silver's arm and forcing the syringe towards his mouth. Laura watched in horror as the clear liquid disappeared past Sebastian Silver's lips – and James stepped back, breathing hard, a look of satisfaction on his face.

'Mister Sunday sends his regards,' he whispered.

Silver staggered, one hand going to his throat, the other reaching out towards Laura as if trying to tell her something vital. His trilby slipped sideways, and she could see the moment when confusion flickered across his features – Sebastian Silver fading, Phillip Morris beginning to surface, *both* of them dying.

'Sebastian?'

He was already falling, legs giving out beneath him. He hit the floor hard, convulsed once, then went still. The trilby rolled away across the wooden boards, coming to rest near the door like a discarded prop.

Laura knelt beside him, checking for a pulse with trembling fingers. His skin was growing cold.

'Fitting, really. Full circle,' James said conversationally, watching her desperate attempts at resuscitation.

'Call an ambulance!'

'I don't think so.'

Laura rose, grabbing a walking cane as a weapon, her face scrunched in anger.

'You *murderer!*' she screamed in anger.

'Oh, I think you'll find this was a poor, troubled man having a cardiac arrest, or a stroke of some kind,' James was moving towards the door when voices erupted from outside – multiple people approaching fast.

'Phillip? Where are you?' Doctor Matthews's voice, sharp with concern.

'We're in here!' Laura shouted. 'James just killed him!'

James cursed under his breath, looking around the room frantically. There was nowhere to hide, no other exit, and a furious pensioner about to bash his skull in with a cane if he stayed. The footsteps were almost at the door.

'Mrs Carlyle?' Doctor Matthews called again, much closer now.

James made his decision, shoving past Laura and bolting through the door just as Doctor Matthews appeared on the path with two orderlies behind her. There was a moment of confused shouting as James pushed past them, calling something about an emergency in the main building.

'What on earth—' confused, Doctor Matthews began,

then saw Laura returning to Silver's still form. 'Dear God, what's happened?'

'James,' Laura gasped. 'James poisoned him.'

Doctor Matthews was beside them instantly, her medical training taking over. One of the orderlies was already on his radio calling for an ambulance.

But Laura could see on the doctor's face what she already knew in her heart.

Sebastian Silver was dead.

And Kyle was still missing.

19

THE WAKE

LAURA PUSHED THROUGH THE FRONT DOOR OF THE QUEEN'S Gate house at twenty past eight, feeling rather like she'd aged a decade in the past few hours. The familiar scent of home – beeswax polish and the faint lavender Celia insisted on using despite Laura's repeated protests that it made the place smell like a geriatric ward – should have been comforting. Instead, it felt like walking into a museum of her previous life.

'Laura?' Celia appeared in the hallway, took one look at her niece's face, and immediately headed for the kitchen. 'Right. Tea. Sit.'

'Sebastian's dead.' The words came out flat. Laura couldn't manage anything more dramatic – if she started crying now, she might never stop, and Kyle was still out there somewhere.

Celia's hands stilled on the kettle.

'Dead how?'

'Poisoned. Same way they killed Harry and David.' Laura slumped onto one of the kitchen chairs, the one with the slightly wonky leg that Kyle always forgot about. 'James – the orderly from the care facility – appeared at the gatehouse and injected something into Sebastian's mouth. He collapsed and that was it.'

'The orderly was Calendar?'

'Apparently. Though frankly, I'm losing track of who's supposed to be which day of the week, or even if there's multiple days.' Laura rubbed her temples, where a headache was building with the persistence of a determined woodpecker. 'God, Celia, I convinced Phillip to put on that hat. I practically sent him to his death.'

'Nonsense,' Celia said briskly, filling the kettle with more force than was strictly necessary. 'You asked for help saving Kyle. Sebastian chose to give it.'

'I manipulated a mentally ill man into—'

'You gave a remarkable man the chance to be heroic. There's a difference, and you know it.' Celia's voice had gone sharp. 'Don't you dare diminish what he did by wallowing in misplaced guilt.'

Laura wanted to argue, but the fight had gone out of her. Sebastian Silver was dead, Kyle was still missing, and she had absolutely no idea what to do next. The Calendar had texted wanting to meet at midnight, but what was the point? They'd wanted Sebastian, and now he was gone.

'The Calendar texted,' she said instead. 'They want to meet at midnight. Exchange Kyle for... for whatever they think I have.'

'Which is what, exactly?'

'I haven't the faintest idea. Sebastian thought they wanted him, but he's dead now, so...' Laura trailed off, then added quietly, 'There's something else. Sebastian showed me a photograph. The real Rebecca Farrell. White hair, completely different from the woman who came to my door.'

Celia paused in her tea preparations, sugar spoon halfway to the cup.

'The woman who started this entire investigation?'

'Was fake. Calendar operative, presumably.' Laura accepted the tea gratefully, wrapping her hands around the warm china. 'Which means this entire investigation was orchestrated from the beginning. They wanted me to find Sebastian or at least wanted Sebastian to find me. They used me to flush him out.'

'Rather elaborate way to locate one man.'

'Unless that one man was outstanding at hiding.' Laura sipped her tea, thinking. 'I should have guessed. The 1776 in the email address, that lead us to David Revere and Louise, bringing in Keith who'd encourage my curiousness... I was played, Aunt Celia. And now the game has changed the rules.'

She sipped the tea, looking up at the ceiling light.

'Sebastian had gaps in his memory, but he knew things. About The Calendar, about intelligence work. Things an accountant from Boston shouldn't know.'

'You think he was one of them originally?'

'I think there's a lot about Sebastian Silver that we never understood.' Laura glanced at the kitchen clock – eight-thirty. Time crawled towards midnight like a reluctant witness. 'Maybe he found some real world document that explained the truth about them. Conspiracy hunters stumble into real-life situations all the time.'

'They also sit in basements and talk about conspiracies,' Celia muttered. 'We should probably call Frank. Though knowing Frank, he'll want to turn it into some elaborate police operation with helicopters and tactical units.'

'They said to come alone. If they see police—'

'They'll kill Kyle anyway if they don't get what they want. At least with police backup, you'd have a fighting chance.'

Before Laura could respond, there was a sharp knock at the front door. Celia raised an eyebrow.

'Bit late for Eleanor's social calls.'

Laura went to answer it, finding Frank on the doorstep, his face flat and unreadable. Behind him stood a uniformed constable she didn't recognise, who looked young enough to be Kyle's study partner.

'Laura.' Frank's voice was carefully neutral in that way that meant he was about to deliver bad news. 'We need to talk.'

'If this is about Sebastian—'

'It's about Kyle.' Frank stepped into the hallway without invitation, the constable following like a nervous shadow. 'We know about the ransom demand.'

Laura's heart sank as she led them back to the kitchen.

'How?'

Frank looked sheepish.

'I'd had your phone tapped,' he muttered. 'When you were in the station.'

Laura went to shout, but it was pointless. If anything, it saved them time now.

'How much do you know?'

'Enough to know you're planning to meet them alone at midnight. Which absolutely isn't happening.' Frank took a seat at the kitchen table. 'I've lost one civilian in this case already. I'm not losing another.'

'Frank—'

'No arguments. We do this properly, with backup, with a plan that doesn't involve you walking into a trap like some sort of amateur sleuth from a detective novel.'

Laura stared at him. Frank was right, of course. Meeting The Calendar alone was essentially suicide with extra steps. But Kyle was her grandson, her responsibility. She couldn't just hand him over to police procedure and hope for the best.

'What are you proposing?' she asked finally.

'We wait for them to specify the location, then we set up surveillance. You go in wearing a wire, we stay close enough to intervene when things go sideways.'

'You mean if, right?'

'Of course. If. That's what I meant.'

'And if they detect the wire?'

'Then we hope they want whatever you're carrying more than they want revenge.'

It wasn't exactly a confidence-inspiring plan, but it was better than walking into a trap with nothing but good intentions and Celia's emergency umbrella. Laura was about to agree when her mobile rang.

Unknown number.

'Mrs Carlyle?' The voice was electronically distorted, like something from a bad science fiction film. 'I trust you received our message about the midnight meeting.'

'I did.' Laura glanced at Frank, who was already making frantic hand gestures at the constable. 'But I'm afraid I don't understand what you want from me.'

'Come now, Mrs Carlyle. Don't play dumb. The same thing we wanted from Sebastian Silver before he was eliminated.'

'You know Sebastian's dead?'

'Yes. One of our lower level Thursdays performed his

duties adequately. Though he seemed to take particular satisfaction in the assignment.'

There was something personal in the way they spoke about Sebastian's death, and Laura felt a chill that had nothing to do with the kitchen's draughty windows.

'What do you want?' she asked again. 'If not the man himself?'

'Information. Sebastian Silver had access to certain classified materials that belong to us. We want them back.'

'Sebastian was mentally ill,' Laura said, trying to keep her voice steady whilst Frank scribbled notes. 'Whatever he thought he knew came from books and films. Spy novels and old documentaries.'

'How wonderfully naïve of you, Mrs Carlyle. Sebastian Silver may have been delusional, but his research was remarkably thorough. He found documents that should have remained buried. We want to know what he discovered and who else he might have shared it with.'

Laura felt something click into place.

'That's why you sent the fake Rebecca. You needed someone to investigate, to flush Sebastian out of hiding.'

'Partly. Though you're rather more important than you might think, Mrs Carlyle. After all, it was your husband's death fifteen years ago that started this whole untidy business. We thought it rather poetic to involve his widow in the cleanup.'

The kitchen seemed to tilt around Laura.

'James? What does James have to do with this?'

'Everything. Though I suspect you'll work that out, eventually. You always were the clever one in the family. We even named our orderly "James" in your late husband's honour. A small tribute to the man who caused us so much inconvenience, and a reminder to Mister Silver – or, rather, Mister *Morris* – every time he heard the name called.'

The mockery in the distorted voice made Laura's blood run cold. They weren't just using her; they were enjoying it. Fifteen years of grief, and it had all been a lie.

'You killed him,' she hissed.

'That's an allegation never claimed,' the voice almost *tutted* at her. 'Your husband was becoming inconvenient, though. Too many questions, too much investigation into matters that didn't concern him. We simply redirected his attention. Permanently.'

Frank was making increasingly urgent gestures, clearly wanting her to keep the caller talking. Laura took a shaky breath.

'I want to see Kyle first. Proof that he's alive and unharmed.'

'You're hardly in a position to make demands, Mrs Carlyle.'

'Then we have nothing to discuss.'

A pause. Muffled voices in the background, as if the caller was consulting with someone else.

'We'll provide proof when we meet. The Globe Theatre at midnight. Main stage. Come alone.'

'How do I get in? It'll be closed—'

'Good God, were the stories we heard of you make believe?' the voice mocked again. 'If you can break into a murder scene, you can break into a fake Theatre.'

'Fake?'

'Of course. The real Globe was several streets away. This is a pretty facsimile, which from a distance looks just like the real thing, but up close reveals the flaws. Just like the late Mister Silver, actually.'

'I want to talk to Kyle now.'

'Midnight, Mrs Carlyle. The Globe Theatre. Don't disappoint us. We want the list.'

The line went dead.

Laura looked at Frank.

'Globe Theatre's an interesting choice. Multiple levels, lots of hiding spots.' Frank was already making notes. 'We can position people in the galleries, cover all the entrances and exits.'

'Come on, Frank! You're not that subtle. They'll spot your people from the other side of the Thames.'

'Not if we're careful. The Globe's complicated – plenty of places to hide surveillance equipment. And tonight's show will be on right now, so I can get Southwark police to assist us here.'

Laura stared at the phone in her hands, processing what she'd just learned.

'Laura?' Celia's voice seemed to come from very far away. 'You've gone rather pale.'

'They killed James,' Laura said numbly. 'They as good as stated it. The Calendar killed my husband.'

The kitchen went silent. Frank stopped taking notes, the constable shifted uncomfortably, and Celia went absolutely still in that way that meant she was preparing to do something drastic.

'Said he was asking too many questions, becoming inconvenient.' Laura laughed, but it came out bitter and wrong. 'All these years, I thought it was just a terrible accident. Mechanical failure, they said. But it was murder.'

'Laura—'

'And Sebastian found out. Maybe that's why they wanted

him dead. He was getting close to the truth about what really happened fifteen years ago.'

'Laura, there's no proof of this,' Celia whispered. 'They could be saying this to get an emotive reaction from you.'

'They said they wanted a list. But what list?'

Before Laura could continue though, there was a noise from the back of the house; a metallic scraping sound like someone trying to force the kitchen door with tools that weren't quite up to the job.

Frank was on his feet immediately, hand moving to his jacket.

'Stay here,' he ordered, moving towards the back door.

The scraping sound came again, more urgent this time. Then a familiar voice, weak but unmistakable.

'Laura? Celia? Are you there? Please tell me you're there.'

Laura's heart stopped. She knew that voice.

'Sebastian?'

Frank had his hand on the door handle, his extendable baton drawn.

'Stay back,' he warned.

But Laura was already pushing past him, throwing the door open.

Sebastian Silver stood in the narrow mews behind the house, leaning heavily against the brick wall like a drunk tourist who'd lost his way. His clothes were torn, his trilby askew, his face pale as yesterday's milk, but he was unmistakably, impossibly alive.

'Hello, Laura,' he said, and promptly collapsed.

THEY GOT HIM INTO THE KITCHEN, FRANK AND THE CONSTABLE supporting him whilst Celia fussed with blankets and emergency tea. Silver – *or was he Morris without the hat?* – looked dreadful, skin grey, hands shaking like autumn leaves... but definitely breathing.

'How?' Laura demanded, kneeling beside the chair where they'd settled him. 'We watched you die. Doctor Matthews checked for a pulse.'

'The poison,' Silver said, his voice weak but growing stronger with each word. 'It should have killed me. Would have killed anyone else, certainly.'

'But?'

'But I've been exposed to it before. Multiple times, apparently. My body has built up a resistance over the years.' He looked up at Laura, his eyes sharp despite his physical condition. 'Which can only mean one thing.'

'What?'

'I *was* Calendar, Laura. I had to be one of them. My body recognised the poison because I'd been inoculated against it as part of my training.' Sebastian's voice was growing stronger, more confident. 'Which means everything I remember about intelligence work, about The Calendar organisation – it's not fantasy. It has to be memory.'

Laura felt like someone had just told her the kitchen was actually a spaceship.

'You're saying you really are a spy?'

'I'm saying that maybe I was. Before the breakdown, before Phillip Morris, before the care facility... before all that, I was Calendar.'

He paused, meeting her eyes.

'It makes sense. I was their leader. I was Mister Sunday.'

The kitchen went so quiet that Laura could hear the

upstairs radiator ticking and the sound of Mrs Kowolski's television through the basement ceiling.

'Mister Sunday,' she repeated slowly. 'The one who disappeared fifteen years ago.'

'The one who turned traitor, according to Harry's research, which he shared with me.' Sebastian's smile was bitter as week-old coffee. 'I've been hunting myself without realising it. The irony is rather overwhelming.'

'What happened?' Laura asked. 'How did you end up as Phillip Morris?'

'I'm not entirely certain. The memories are... fragmented. Like trying to remember a dream that someone else had.' Silver rubbed his temples. 'I remember there was a confrontation, perhaps? Then nothing. I woke up in a hospital in Boston. I was their leader, so I knew all their secrets. I had... there was a list. They wanted it, I hid it. They couldn't kill me outright – too many safeguards, too many people who would ask awkward questions. But they could make me forget.'

He paused, frowning.

'Or maybe I was Phillip before I was Sebastian?' he asked. 'Maybe Phillip is the real me? Sebastian is the dream? I don't know any more. Harry Farrell found me somehow, started visiting me at the care facility. He claimed he was my old friend but knew me by both names. He'd bring photographs, documents, anything that might trigger my memory. He was trying to help me remember who I really was.'

'So they killed him,' Laura said quietly.

'They tried to. But Harry was cleverer than they gave him credit for. He'd been preparing for this for months, maybe years. He knew they'd eventually move against him.'

'What do you mean?'

Silver looked up at her, his eyes fully alert now.

'Think about it, Laura. If I survived the poison because I was Calendar, and the woman who came to your door was fake...'

'Then Harry Farrell might be alive too,' Laura finished. 'That's what you're thinking.'

'Not quite,' Silver shook his head. 'I'm thinking he's alive, but also that he's not the man he claimed to be. With hindsight, I think he might have been my successor.'

'The next Mister Sunday? That's a hell of a leap of logic,' Celia replied, her usual prim manner temporarily forgotten. 'How do we find out?'

Sebastian Silver struggled to his feet, steadying himself against the kitchen table.

'Simple. We go to Kensington Cemetery and see if there's actually a body in the Farrell crypt.'

He looked around the kitchen, taking in Frank's police presence, the constable's obvious confusion, and Celia's carefully neutral expression.

'I don't suppose anyone fancies a bit of grave digging?'

Frank shook his head.

'You can't be serious. We're police officers. We don't rob graves.'

'Then don't think of it as grave robbing,' Silver said, straightening his jacket with something approaching his old dignity. 'Think of it as investigating a potential case of faked death and identity fraud.'

'That's still illegal without proper authorisation.'

'Frank,' Laura said quietly, 'they have Kyle. My grandson. The only family I have left.'

She stood up, reaching for her coat.

'I'm going to that cemetery whether you help me or not.

But I'd rather do it with police backup than on my own with just an umbrella and good intentions.'

'It's past nine o'clock,' Celia pointed out. 'The cemetery will be locked tighter than Parliament.'

'I have skills,' Silver said quietly.

'Like breaking and entering,' Frank replied, remembering what else Silver had been up to in the last couple of days.

'Covert entry,' Sebastian corrected. 'There's a legal distinction.'

'Not to the Crown Prosecution Service, there isn't.'

Laura looked between them, frustrated by the bureaucratic complications.

'Then what do you suggest? We meet The Calendar at midnight and hope they honour their word about Kyle?'

'We go to the cemetery,' Frank said finally. 'Unofficial investigation. If anyone asks, we were following up on an anonymous tip about suspicious activity.'

'And if we find the crypt empty?'

'Then we call in every favour I've got and go get your grandson.' Frank checked his watch. 'But we need to move fast.'

Silver nodded, testing his strength.

'I can manage. Though I should probably change clothes first. These are rather distinctive after being dead for an hour or so.'

'There's some of James's old clothes in the wardrobe upstairs, up the top, second room on the right,' Laura said. 'Should fit you well enough, although they're not exactly the most stylish, being fifteen years out of date.'

As Sebastian Silver headed for the stairs, Laura turned to Frank.

'Are you certain about this? Your career—'

'My career can go hang,' Frank said grimly. 'These people have killed too many good people. And they made me look a fool.'

Celia rose from her chair, smoothing down her skirt with the air of someone preparing for battle.

'Well then, I suppose we'd better get moving. Can't have Kyle missing his morning lectures.'

'You're not coming,' Laura said immediately.

'Try to stop me,' Celia replied with her sweetest smile. 'I've been looking forward to a proper adventure for years. And someone needs to keep you all from doing anything unnecessarily stupid.'

'I think the boat's already sailed *way* past that island,' Frank muted. 'Let's just hope we get there before it sinks.'

20

GRAVE ROBBING

The clothes fitted well enough, though Laura suspected James had been more substantial than Sebastian Silver. The charcoal suit hung loose on Silver's frame, but the trilby sat at its customary angle, restoring dignity to a man who'd spent a small chunk of the evening being dead.

'Much better,' Celia declared, critiquing him. 'Though James would have worn a pocket square with that suit.'

'I'll endeavour to remember that for future resurrections,' Silver replied, testing his walking cane against the kitchen floor. 'Shall we go disturb the peace of the dead?'

'That's dramatic,' Celia observed, pulling on her sensible coat with the air of someone preparing for battle.

'Given recent events, I think dramatic is appropriate,' Silver replied. 'The dead have been unusually active lately.'

Frank checked his watch – it was half-past nine. The cemetery would be locked, patrolled, and generally unwelcoming to midnight visitors.

'How exactly do you propose we get inside?' he asked.

'The gates will be chained, and I'd prefer not to explain grave robbing to my superiors.'

Silver adjusted his trilby.

'Leave the locks to me. Some skills prove remarkably persistent.'

'You can handle cemetery gates?' Frank asked.

'I have certain capabilities that remain accessible. Though the precise provenance of such knowledge remains unclear.'

Laura found this more reassuring than false bravado; Sebastian's confidence felt genuine this time.

THEY MADE AN UNLIKELY PARTY THROUGH KENSINGTON – A police detective regretting his life choices, an elderly lady treating grave robbing as a social engagement, a widow in her best coat, and a man dressed in someone else's Sunday best – although using the word "Sunday" there felt off, somehow.

The young constable had been sent back to the station by Frank, possibly because it was past his bedtime.

'When Harry was visiting you,' Laura asked, 'did he seem familiar?'

Silver's expression became thoughtful.

'There are echoes. His voice, his manner – something resonates, but the specifics remain elusive.'

'Like trying to remember a dream?' Celia suggested.

'More like having a word on the tip of your tongue. The recognition is there, but the context has been obscured.'

Laura studied his expression. The confidence seemed genuine, which made her trust his capabilities even if his memory remained fragmented.

'You survived that poison,' she pointed out. 'That suggests your training was thorough.'

'Indeed. Physical conditioning has a persistence that memory lacks.' Silver adjusted his walking cane. 'Whatever my previous occupation, it involved certain specialised skills.'

The cemetery gates loomed ahead, impressive ironwork that had been keeping the living out and the dead in for over a century, while security lighting cast everything in harsh shadows.

'Right,' Silver said, approaching the gates with what appeared to be confidence masking uncertainty. 'Let's see if muscle memory counts for anything.'

From his jacket pocket, he produced a leather case containing various small tools.

'Is that a lock-picking set?' Frank demanded.

'It's a gentleman's travelling kit,' Silver corrected. 'For those occasions when one finds oneself accidentally locked out of places one has every right to be.'

'We don't *have* every right to be here.'

'We have moral authority,' Celia declared. 'Sometimes that's more important than legal technicalities.'

Silver began working on the lock with movements that started tentatively but became more assured. It took several minutes – longer than a professional might have required, but much faster than someone learning from scratch.

'Whatever your previous occupation,' Celia observed, 'you clearly weren't just an accountant.'

They slipped through, and Silver repositioned the chains to look secure.

'Right then,' he smiled. 'Let's go hunt a body.'

Kensal Green was impressive even at night – grand mausoleums, elaborate angels, and monuments that spoke of Victorian confidence.

'It's peaceful, isn't it?' Laura observed, surprised.

'Death generally is,' Celia replied pragmatically. 'It's the living who make things complicated.'

Silver had grown quieter as they walked, occasionally adjusting his trilby, but more out of nervous habit than need.

'This place feels significant,' he muttered. 'Though I cannot place why.'

They found the Farrell crypt without difficulty – a modest stone structure with wilted flowers and Harry's name freshly carved. Even though he was born American, it seemed he had a family plot somehow.

'Recent stonework,' Celia observed, examining the plaque. 'This wasn't prepared months in advance. Someone was in quite a hurry.'

Silver examined the crypt door.

'This lock is modern. Much more sophisticated than the cemetery gates.'

The lock took longer, his hands less certain. When it finally clicked open, he looked more puzzled than pleased, as if unsure why things were harder now.

The interior was small, simple, and contained exactly what they'd expected to find.

A *coffin.*

Harry Farrell's mahogany casket rested on the stone platform, precisely where it should be. Brass handles gleamed dully in the torchlight, and a small brass nameplate confirmed this was indeed the last resting place of *Harold Marshall Farrell.*

'Well,' Celia said after a moment. 'That's exactly what we expected to find.'

'Too exactly,' Silver said, studying the coffin. 'This placement is almost theatrical.'

Frank played his torch beam around the small space.

'Looks like a normal burial to me.'

'Then we need to look inside,' Laura whispered.

'Laura—' Frank began.

'We have to know.' Laura's voice was steady. 'If Harry faked his death, there won't be a body in there, right?'

Silver approached the coffin, running his hands along the edges.

'The lid isn't sealed. These screws are barely finger-tight.'

'That's not normal, is it?' Celia asked.

'Decidedly not,' Silver replied. 'Coffins are sealed for obvious reasons. This has been prepared for easy access.'

'Open it.' Laura felt her heart hammering.

Silver looked at Frank, who shook his head firmly.

'This is desecration of a grave. I can't be part of this.'

'What did you think would happen?'

'I don't know! This is all well outside my comfort zone right now!' Frank snapped.

'Then look away,' Laura said. 'But we're opening it.'

Silver's hands moved efficiently, removing the loosened screws. The coffin lid lifted easily.

Inside was exactly what they'd feared finding.

Nothing.

No body. No remains. Just empty silk lining and the lingering smell of artificial flowers.

'Well,' Celia said after a stunned silence. 'That's definitive.'

Laura stared into the empty coffin; all their suspicions had just been confirmed in the most dramatic way possible.

'It's one thing to suspect someone's faked their death,' Frank said grimly. 'Quite another to open their coffin and find it empty.'

Silver's torch beam caught something tucked behind one of the silken folds inside – a small object, deliberately hidden but positioned where someone searching thoroughly would eventually find it.

'What's that?' Laura asked.

Silver retrieved it carefully. It was a USB drive with a note attached in handwriting.

For S. Silver – the truth you need to remember. H.F.

'Harry left this specifically for you,' Laura said, studying the note. 'He knew you'd come here.'

'He knew we'd figure out the coffin was empty,' Silver corrected, turning the drive over in his hands. 'This was always meant to be found, but only after we'd discovered his deception.'

'Elaborate way of passing along information,' Celia observed.

'Unless the information is something he couldn't risk transmitting through normal channels,' Frank suggested. 'Something that needed to be discovered in a specific context.'

'Well,' Celia said practically, 'standing in a crypt speculating won't tell us what's on it. We need to get back home and see what Harry wanted you to remember.'

THEY MADE THEIR WAY BACK THROUGH THE CEMETERY, EACH lost in his or her own thoughts. The empty coffin had confirmed their suspicions, but it raised far more questions than it answered.

'So, Harry faked his own death,' Celia said as they reached the gates. 'The question is why go to such elaborate lengths.'

'And where is he now?' Laura added. 'If he's alive, why take Kyle, if it even was him? What does he actually want?'

Silver was unusually quiet as he secured the cemetery gates behind them.

'Sebastian?' Laura prompted. 'What are you thinking?'

'I'm thinking that whatever's on this drive is going to change things,' he said slowly. 'Harry wouldn't have gone to these lengths for anything trivial.'

BACK AT QUEEN'S GATE, THEY SETTLED IN THE SITTING ROOM whilst Silver connected the USB drive to Kyle's laptop.

'Are we certain this is safe?' Frank asked. 'Could be malware.'

'Given that Harry already knows where we are and there's a chance he's the one who already has Kyle, additional surveillance won't make things worse,' Silver replied.

The device contained two files – a video message and a photograph.

'Video first,' Silver said. 'If we're going to hear Harry's version of events, we might as well get it over with.'

He pressed the play button, and a moment later Harry Farrell's face appeared on screen – but this wasn't the frail man they'd expected and had seen on a half-watched video on Raj's laptop in Electronic Zone. This Harry looked healthy, alert, and pleased with himself.

Laura's chest tightened before he'd even begun speaking.

'Hello, Sebastian,' Harry began conversationally. 'If you're watching this, reports of my death have been greatly exaggerated.'

Silver went very still beside Laura.

'I imagine Laura Carlyle is with you. I hope she's been useful in helping you remember who you really are.'

'What does he mean?' Celia asked quietly.

'I have no idea,' Silver replied, though his voice carried less certainty than usual.

'You see, Sebastian, I needed someone to help me find you,' Harry explained. 'Someone with the right connections, the right motivation, and just enough intelligence to follow the breadcrumbs I left behind. Mrs Carlyle has been perfect for the role.'

Laura felt sick. 'He's been manipulating me from the beginning.'

'I've been planning this for months,' Harry continued. 'Ever since I realised what you really are, what you used to be. Oh, you hide it well behind that carefully constructed persona, and it's been a goddamned chore visiting you every week, hoping this would be the day, this would be the time you'd remember what I needed you to reveal... but I remember the real Sebastian Silver.'

Silver's hand moved unconsciously towards his trilby.

'Do you remember me yet, old friend?' Harry asked, leaning closer to the camera. 'Do you remember what we did together, what we built? Or are you still hiding behind that convenient amnesia?'

'Of course I recognise you,' Silver said slowly, more to

himself than to the man on the screen. 'You've been visiting me for months. But this isn't the frail, concerned friend who brought Phillip photographs and documents. This is someone else entirely.'

'The Calendar has split, Sebastian,' Harry continued, obviously unable to hear the other side of the story. 'There are those who want to preserve the old ways, those pathetic traditionalists clinging to obsolete methods. And then there are those of us who understand that times have changed, that opportunities exist for those bold enough to seize them.'

'This is a recruitment video,' Frank said grimly.

'I lead the progressive faction now,' Harry explained, his pride evident. 'We could use someone with your particular expertise, your unique perspective on how organisations like ours should operate.'

Silver's expression was controlled.

'He's speaking as if we have a shared history. There are resonances. But the details remain inaccessible, and the Harry who came to see me seemed genuinely concerned about my welfare. This version... this feels like performance.'

'But I suspect you'll need proper motivation to make this decision,' Harry continued with a bitter smile, unaware of the conversation. 'My former colleagues at the traditional Calendar can be so... persistent in their recruiting methods. I do hope young Kyle Carlyle remains safe while they try to use him as leverage to find me. They think I have your list, you see. The one that started this whole damned problem. So, old friend, how about you do me a favour, rummage around in your broken-ass brain and find the goddamned thing for me, before they decide you're as useless to them as Brian was? There's a good boy.'

And with this, the video ended, leaving them in shocked silence.

Laura stared at the blank screen, trying to process what she'd just learned.

'Well, if he mentioned Kyle, that's one thing that helps,' Silver said. 'Kyle was taken a couple of hours ago. Harry left this for me tonight. Which means he knew I didn't die, and he's still around.'

'But he still doesn't explain how we get Kyle back!' Laura snapped. 'And we've got just over an hour until the deadline! What list is he talking about!'

'I don't know, but it might involve the photograph,' Silver said quietly. 'We should look at the image file that was on the drive.'

The image showed the aftermath of Harry's supposed death – paramedics loading a stretcher into an ambulance. From the distance and angle, it was obviously another image taken by David, but there, clearly visible among the medical team, was a face that made Laura freeze.

'That's Brian,' she said. 'Mister Friday. The man who tried to kill us in the car park. The man who Frank found dead in his house.'

'So, Brian was working with Harry all along,' Celia observed. 'Helping stage the fake death.'

'Until someone decided he was no longer useful or found out he was playing both sides.'

'How do you know he played both sides?'

'Because he was with Mister Monday when we saw him in the lobby,' Silver added. 'The man who believed he'd killed Harry Farrell, as seen in the other photos. I'd say Monday saw this photo, realised Brian had betrayed him, and that, not his failure to stop us, was what led to his untimely demise. As Harry said, *"before they decide you're as useless to them as Brian was".'*

Laura was staring at the photograph, pieces clicking into place.

'David took this picture. That's why he had to die – he recognised Brian in the EMT uniform, didn't he?'

'Most likely,' Frank agreed. 'David was being paid to photograph Harry, including at the church, but he captured more than his handlers expected.'

'And when David tried to use this evidence for blackmail, maybe directly to Harry, knowing he wasn't dead...'

'Harry eliminated the threat,' Silver finished. 'Or, he made sure someone else saw this and allowed the other side of The Calendar to do his dirty work.'

'Surely fake Rebecca wouldn't have shown me the email?' Laura frowned.

'She might have if it helped sell the story,' Frank suggested.

'But why involve me?' Laura asked, her voice stronger but carrying an edge of anger. 'Why not approach Sebastian directly?'

'Because I was hiding, even if I didn't realise it,' Silver said slowly. 'And apparently hiding well enough that even someone who claims to know me couldn't find me inside Phillip that easily.'

'So he used me as bait.'

'It appears so.'

Frank was taking notes.

'We need to consider that if Harry's been planning this for months, he'll have contingencies.'

'Meaning?'

'Meaning we need to be very careful about how we

proceed. Harry's demonstrated he's willing to kill to protect his operation, and he's not doing whatever the other side wants. Kyle's life depends on our not underestimating him.'

Silver nodded.

'Harry's assessment is likely accurate. Whatever our previous association, he understands my operational patterns.'

'So, what do you suggest?' Laura asked.

Silver was quiet for a moment. When he finally spoke, his voice carried determination.

'We approach this systematically. Harry expects certain responses based on previous experience. If we can identify those patterns, we can anticipate his next moves.'

'How do we identify those patterns?'

'By exploring the evidence. Harry's methodology, his choice of venue, his timing. Every operational decision reveals preferences and training. We simply need to decode the message.'

Laura looked around the sitting room – at Celia with her practical concern, at Frank with his police training and growing frustration with legal limitations, at Silver with his fragmented memories and uncertain capabilities.

'Then we'd better get started,' she said. 'Kyle's depending on us.'

'Where do we begin?' Celia asked.

Silver was quiet for a moment, his hand resting on his trilby. When he looked up, there was something different in his expression – not confidence exactly, but determination.

'We begin by assuming Harry's told us the truth about one thing – that he knows me better than I know myself. Which means his expectations about how I'll respond are probably based on actual knowledge of how I used to operate.'

'And?'

'And if that's true, then perhaps I can work backwards from his expectations to figure out what I'm supposed to know – in particular whatever this list is, that's somewhere deep inside my head.'

Laura wasn't entirely certain this logic was sound, but it was better than sitting around waiting for Harry's next move.

'Right then,' she said. 'Let's see what the old Sebastian Silver would have done in this situation.'

21

THEATRE NIGHT

The Globe Theatre sat on the South Bank of the Thames between the Millennium Bridge and Tate Modern, a testament to one man's determination to resurrect Elizabethan drama. Built through public funding and Sam Wanamaker's tireless advocacy, it was as close to the original Globe as modern scholarship could manage. Not that it was the original, of course – archaeologists had found those foundations several streets away when a housing project went up on Park Street. The car park even had the real Globe's layout etched into the cobblestones, a rather poetic touch that Laura doubted the current occupants would appreciate.

The theatre normally hosted performances that drew tourists and Shakespeare enthusiasts alike, but tonight's show had long since ended. The doors were closed to the public, the building dark against the London sky. Laura and Celia stood at the main entrance, surveying their options whilst the usual collection of late-night tourists and after-hours London wanderers moved along the South Bank path. The entire area had a distinct quality at this hour – less purposeful, more mysterious. Street lamps cast long shadows, and the Thames moved past with its ancient indifference to human drama.

Laura found herself thinking about all the performances this theatre had hosted, all the tragedies and comedies played out on its stage. Tonight felt like both – a tragedy in the making, but with elements so absurd they bordered on farce. A widow and her elderly aunt, breaking into a replica Elizabethan theatre to negotiate with international assassins for the release of a university student, based on a long-missing list hidden in an amnesiac with an identity disorder. Shakespeare himself couldn't have written something quite so unlikely.

'Are we supposed to break in?' Celia asked, walking along the theatre's perimeter. 'Do we knock? Present our credentials? Send a calling card?'

Laura pointed towards a gate that led into a courtyard beside the Globe. The gate was closed, but the lock had been left conspicuously aside – the sort of detail that suggested someone wanted them to find it.

'I'd say that way.'

The courtyard was dimly lit, the building officially closed, but there was enough illumination to guide them past the Globe's distinctive, white-daubed exterior. The whole setup felt rather like a stage production itself – dramatic lighting, ominous setting, and the distinct sense that someone was orchestrating events from the shadows.

'No time like the present,' Celia said, and they entered through what appeared to be an exit door.

The Globe had been designed as a sixteenth-century theatre, which meant no proper seats in the central area – just the 'pit' where groundlings would have stood to watch performances. The wealthier patrons would have occupied the galleries around the sides, looking down at both the stage and the common folk below. *Rather like a cozy mystery,* Laura thought with grim amusement – everyone watching everyone else, waiting to see who would be revealed as the villain.

At this time of night, however, there was no crowd, just the echoing emptiness of the auditorium. That wasn't entirely true – on the stage, presumably left over from whatever performance had run earlier, Kyle sat in what appeared to be a throne-like chair. Laura's heart leaped when she saw him, and she started forward, but Celia grabbed her arm.

'He hasn't been released,' she hissed. 'If he had been, he'd be coming to us. He's been told to stay put, so we should too.'

Laura forced herself to remain calm, though every instinct screamed at her to run to her grandson. The two women paused in the middle of the auditorium, surrounded by the ghosts of four centuries of theatrical drama.

'We're here,' Laura called out, her voice carrying clearly in the circular space. 'Let's get this over with.'

Movement from stage right caught her attention, and three suited men emerged from the shadows. The first was unmistakably familiar – the man she'd seen in the photograph outside St. Bartholomew's Church, the one who'd confronted her in David's building lobby, and who had almost certainly killed David as well.

Mister Monday.

'Mrs Carlyle. Mrs Harrington, I believe,' he said pleasantly, as if they were meeting at a garden party rather than a midnight hostage exchange.

Celia squared her shoulders with the sort of dignity that had once made junior diplomats quake.

'You must be the enigmatic Mister Monday I've heard so

much about. Are your little friends also days of the week? I understand there's a vacancy for a Friday.'

'There are many Fridays, Mrs Harrington. Just as I am not the only Mister Monday in the organisation. Think of them as ranks – an army has several captains, majors, corporals. Days of the week are simply our version of that system. Monday is the highest rank, descending through to Saturday.'

'And Sunday?' Laura asked.

'We've had our share of Mister Sundays, but there's usually only one at a time,' Mister Monday nodded. 'I believe you've met two of them – or at least encountered Harry Farrell and Sebastian Silver.'

'Harry Farrell and Sebastian Silver,' Laura repeated, filing away the information.

Mister Monday smiled at her tone.

'Wait, was Silver a Sunday? I can't recall – it would have been before my time. But Harry Farrell was indeed a Sunday until he turned against us.'

'Now we're getting somewhere,' Laura said. 'Tell me what happened. Perhaps we can work out a reasonable solution to this situation.'

'You don't even know what you're negotiating for,' Mister Monday laughed. 'You're here to beg for your grandson's life, and you haven't even considered what we actually need.'

'Oh, I believe I know exactly what you need,' Laura stepped forward with more confidence than she felt. 'The thing is, we kept thinking it had changed, but it was always the same, wasn't it?' She glanced around the Globe's circular galleries. 'I'm guessing there are more of you here than just the three visible ones. Perhaps one on each level, all watching, each with their little syringe ready. It really is becoming rather a predictable method, you know. You should consider diversifying.'

Mister Monday's smile widened.

'Yes, we know that Sebastian Silver is no longer of this world. Our man James eliminated him. New strain, very strong and quick, only the current days of the week have a resistance, I'm afraid. It was a last resort, you understand.'

He looked over at Kyle and patted the boy's shoulder almost affectionately.

'You can go. This meeting was never really about you.'

Kyle looked confused, which was entirely understandable given the circumstances.

'But you haven't been given anything. What do you mean? This is supposed to be a prisoner swap, right? Gran gives you something, you give me, but she hasn't given you anything. So, why are you releasing me unless...'

He froze.

'Unless you intend to kill us all, anyway.'

Mister Monday said nothing, which was answer enough.

'Go be with your grandmother,' he said quietly. 'I'm giving you a last gift. Don't refuse it.'

Kyle didn't need a second invitation. He rose from the throne and made his way quickly to the auditorium, where he embraced both Laura and Celia with the sort of fierce relief that made Laura's throat tight. She held him for a moment longer than necessary, breathing in the familiar scent of his aftershave and the faint smell of fear-sweat that clung to his clothes. He was trembling slightly, though trying to hide it.

'Are you hurt?' she whispered.

'No, Gran. Just scared.' His voice was steady, but she could hear the effort it took. 'They weren't cruel, just... dismissive. Like this was routine business.'

Laura felt a surge of both relief and fury. Relief that he was unharmed, fury that he'd been put through this ordeal at all. But there would be time for both emotions later. Right now, she needed to focus on ensuring they all survived the next few minutes.

'Harry Farrell was one of us,' Mister Monday continued conversationally, 'until about fifteen years ago. Then he changed. Don't misunderstand – he was still a member of The Calendar, still our Sunday for a time. But there was rot inside him. Five years ago, he stepped down, claiming his wife was ill.'

'And you let him do this?' Laura asked.

At the question, Mister Monday actually laughed.

'You make it sound like joining The Calendar is a life sentence. We have many operatives who retire, just as MI5 or the CIA do. We're not monsters, even if we're perceived that way.'

'So, what happened?'

'It was a ruse, Mrs Carlyle. Harry Farrell stole information. You see, he'd spent those ten years building a network of moles and spies within the organisation, deliberately aimed at bringing us down. When we discovered this, we initially thought it was some sort of insurance policy – if we killed Harry, the information would be released. But as we investigated further, we realised this wasn't defensive. Harry had created his own version of The Calendar, a more extreme version.'

He gestured to his companions.

'It was around then that Phillip Morris appeared on the scene – a Bostonian accountant with personality issues who believed he was Sebastian Silver. Initially, we thought he was simply delusional. But Harry had been visiting him at the residential home, providing him with stories, memories. You see, there was a list – a very specific list of Calendar operatives embedded in governmental security services. Agents in MI5, CIA, Mossad, even the FSB. Fifteen years ago in Prague, Sebastian Silver hid it, giving it to someone he trusted. We have no idea to whom he gave it, how, in what format, or even why. We knew, however, that in every meeting they had together, Harry Farrell was trying to obtain that information.'

'But why?' Celia asked practically. 'Surely it's fifteen years out of date by now.'

'That list showed junior members of government who are possibly now leaders of nations,' Mister Monday replied. 'Sleeper agents ready to step forward the moment we call upon them.'

At this, Laura laughed – not from amusement, but from the sheer audacity of it all.

'But you don't know who they are, do you? You've lost the list. This isn't about preventing exposure to the world. This is simply about the fact that there's a list out there with all these people who could help you, and you haven't got a blasted clue who they are.'

She turned, looking around the Globe's circular galleries as she spoke.

'All of you sitting here in your little black suits, looking like an undertaker's convention. And none of you even knows if this list still exists. That's why you wanted Sebastian remembering. You wanted him to remember who he gave it to, why he did it.'

She paused, pieces falling into place.

'Prague, fifteen years ago. My husband died shortly after. Is that why I'm here? You think James was involved?

For the first time in the conversation, Mister Monday's composed mask slipped slightly.

'We knew from records that Sebastian Silver had a connection to you, had known you in his previous life. Harry, when visiting Sebastian, seemed to believe this as well and had actively encouraged him in your direction. This was why Sebastian was watching your house.'

Laura felt something cold settle in her stomach. The pieces were falling into place now, forming a picture she didn't want to see. *James's death, which she'd mourned as a random tragedy for fifteen years, might have been something else entirely.*

The thought was almost too large to process – that his death had been connected to this world of shadows and secrets, that she'd been living a lie all these years.

'Let me understand this correctly,' she said slowly, working through the implications. 'Fifteen years ago, Sebastian Silver was part of The Calendar, as was Harry Farrell. But Sebastian was secretly working against you, and he passed this mysterious list of naughty secret people to somebody. You never found out who, but this list has been held quietly for fifteen years. On this list are people who could now be government officials, but you don't know their identities because you don't have the details any more. Harry Farrell wants to create his own version of The Calendar organisation, and he's been trying to get from Sebastian the information you all want.'

'We believed Silver gave the list to your husband,' Mister Monday replied. 'It makes sense that you would know where it is. The speed with which you've taken to this investigative life suggests that you have—'

'I have boredom,' Laura snapped, surprising herself with the vehemence. 'Fifteen years of being a widow, running women's committees and charity flower shows. I live with my grandson when he's not with his mother, and my aunt, who feels I could do better no matter how well I perform.'

'She's not wrong there,' Celia added helpfully.

'I have felt constrained for over a decade,' Laura continued, 'and the moment I step out of my comfort zone, the moment I find something I realise I can actually do, you assume it's purely because I already know something? How dare you! How dare you make assumptions about a woman you've never met! How dare you believe that I've spent fifteen years hiding a secret I didn't want or even care about! My husband died in a road accident! He wasn't murdered, and Sebastian Silver wasn't involved!'

'Are you certain of that?' Mister Monday asked quietly.

'Perhaps I should ask him directly.'

'Let's do that.' Mister Monday looked at his men, almost chuckling as he spoke. 'I know a man with a Ouija board.'

'You don't need one,' a fresh voice spoke from above, and a spotlight suddenly illuminated the top row of seats.

Even in a prisoner exchange, it seemed Sebastian Silver couldn't resist a touch of theatricality.

'You're dead,' Mister Monday's eyes widened. 'You were killed.'

'I was poisoned, I'll grant you,' Silver replied from his elevated position. 'However, the reports of my death, as you can see, are nothing more than a blatant lie provided by amateurs.'

'That's not how the quote goes,' Celia muttered.

'I don't think literary accuracy is our primary concern just now,' Laura whispered back.

Sebastian pointed down at Mister Monday, the tip of his cane aimed directly at his adversary.

'You forgot I was trained, Monday – and your man didn't stay around long enough to check, just like you didn't when you thought you'd killed Harry. Now I might not remember everything about what happened back then...' he tapped his trilby. 'Memory issues. But one thing I do know is that if I were rumoured to be Mister Sunday, and I didn't die when poisoned, something that was supposed to be foolproof... it means if I'm still alive, then Harry didn't die either. Which you already know, as you killed Friday for helping him. And that time you didn't risk the poison.'

'Because he was immune to the new strain!' Mister Monday exclaimed. 'You and Farrell weren't!'

'Apparently, someone's been overstating the potency of your new murder liquid,' Silver shrugged as he looked around the Globe's circular galleries. 'So, we seem to have a dilemma. You want to kill us for a list that no longer seems to exist, and a dead man who's in the wind. We want to end you. Do we fight, or do we negotiate?'

22

THE FINAL PERFORMANCE

'What have you done?' Mister Monday demanded, though his voice had lost much of its earlier confidence. The composed assassin who'd seemed so in control was fraying at the edges.

Silver smiled down from the gallery, his trilby perfectly positioned despite the evening's adventures.

'Harry Farrell tried to convince me I was once some sort of super spy – all very dramatic and exciting. But the thing is, if I were anything like you people...' He gestured at the black-suited figures scattered around the theatre. 'Well, frankly, the thought of wearing funeral attire every day would send me straight back to the care facility. Dreadfully depressing, all that black.'

'The Sebastian we've observed is rather helpful,' Laura called up from the auditorium, surprised by how steady her own voice sounded after everything they'd been through. 'Puts others first but never asks for help himself. Bit of a hero complex, really. Harry was counting on that – expecting Sebastian to turn up here alone, unprepared, probably with some sort of an elaborate plan that would fail spectacularly.'

'Exactly. So I thought about how Phillip Morris would handle this situation instead,' Silver continued, his voice carrying clearly in the circular space. 'Phillip assumes he can't manage things alone. Rather sensible attitude, actually. However, guess what! It seems that when you combine the two personalities, you get someone who's perfectly comfortable asking for backup. Like the various members of the Intelligence community who'd been waiting in the galleries for the last hour or so.'

Kyle squeezed Laura's hand.

'Gran,' he whispered, 'are those really intelligence agents up there?'

'I rather hope so, darling,' Laura whispered back. 'Otherwise we're about to be very disappointed.'

'You called the police?' Mister Monday's voice carried genuine amusement now.

'Oh, heavens no,' Laura laughed, the sound echoing strangely in the Globe's circular architecture. 'Can you imagine trying to explain all this to Detective Chief Inspector Young? "Well, you see, there's this international conspiracy called The Calendar, and they're named after weekdays, and my friend has a magic hat that makes him competent..." He'd have us sectioned. Well, he would have if he hadn't seen it firsthand. But then there's his boss, and his *boss's* boss...'

There were subtle sounds from the galleries above – footsteps, quiet voices, the sort of careful movement that suggested people taking position. Laura thought that Shakespeare would have appreciated the irony of genuine drama unfolding in his reconstructed theatre.

'We went to people who already knew about you,' Laura

continued, warming to her theme. 'David Revere was CIA, apparently. Following Harry around, possibly even working with him. But MI5 was watching David, and they were rather put out when you killed him. Something about paperwork and jurisdictional disputes. You see, you said no police, but you didn't mention not bringing intelligence services. Bit of an oversight on your part, really. Rather like saying no dogs allowed but forgetting to mention *wolves*.'

'Sebastian, are you quite finished up there?' Celia called from beside Laura, her voice carrying across the auditorium. 'Because this is all very theatrical, but I'm eighty years old and standing on concrete. Medieval audiences were clearly made of sterner stuff.'

Sebastian rapped his cane against the gallery rail.

'Quite right, Mrs Harrington. Time to end this nonsense.'

What happened next was so unexpected that Laura found herself thinking she was watching a performance, rather than real life. There was a taut cable running from Sebastian's gallery to one of the stage pillars – probably for hanging decorations during performances, and Sebastian removed his belt, looped it around the rope, and zip-lined down to the stage like some sort of aged action hero.

He landed with rather less grace than intended though, stumbling slightly but keeping hold of his cane.

'Well,' he said, straightening his knocked trilby with careful precision, 'that was more dignified in my head.'

'Sebastian Silver, international man of mystery,' Celia observed dryly. 'Very impressive. Do you do bar tricks as well?'

'I save those for special occasions,' Sebastian replied, advancing on Mister Monday with renewed confidence. 'Though I'm afraid your colleagues are going to be rather busy shortly. The people in the galleries are the sort who ask questions in small, windowless rooms in black sites.'

'You think you can take me?' Mister Monday asked, backing away across the stage.

'Oh, I wasn't talking about you – you're yesterday's jam. Sticking around past your sell-by date and someone else's problem now,' Sebastian said, looking around the stage area with the sort of theatrical timing that suggested he was rather enjoying himself. 'Harry? I know you're here. You never could resist a dramatic finale.'

There was movement from the side of the stage, and a figure stepped into the light. Even with his face partially concealed by the shadows, Laura recognised him immediately.

'How did you know?' Harry Farrell asked, moving into the spotlight to reveal features that were very much alive.

'Because you're an old ham who wouldn't miss his curtain call,' Sebastian replied. 'Though I must say, the whole "mysterious death" performance was rather elaborate. Very you.'

Laura felt her breath catch. Harry looked worn down, tired in a way that spoke of years spent looking over his shoulder. But he was undeniably alive, and hearing his voice made the reality of his deception hit home.

'You betrayed us, Sebastian.' Harry's voice was flat, angry. 'You gave our list to James Carlyle.'

Laura felt her stomach drop.

'You're certain it was James?'

'There was no one else it could have been,' Harry said, his eyes never leaving Sebastian's face. 'Prague, fifteen years ago. You were supposed to be one of us, Sebastian. Instead, you handed over everything to a diplomat! Names, positions, operational details. Years of work gone because you decided to play white knight.'

Harry drew something from his jacket – not a gun, but a vicious looking blade, longer than a usual combat knife, more the length of a military bayonet.

'I've been searching for that information ever since. Do you have any idea what those people could accomplish now? Junior civil servants who are now ministers, analysts who run departments, clerks who became ambassadors?'

'And you want to use them,' Sebastian said.

'You're *damn right* I want to use them!' Harry's voice rose, echoing in the theatre's circular space. 'The Calendar spent years rebuilding, and I've been trying to find the evidence to bring them down, gain an advantage here. But you hid it too well, Sebastian. Even from yourself.'

Laura watched this exchange with growing unease. The hurt in Harry's voice was real, but so was the anger. Whatever had happened fifteen years ago, it had destroyed a friendship and set events in motion that had led to this moment.

'So you used me to remember,' Sebastian said. 'Fake your death, manipulate Laura into investigating, force the list to surface.'

'The Calendar sent the fake Rebecca,' Harry said, looking across the stage at Mister Monday. 'I've been trying to protect you from them. They want the list as much as I do, but for very different reasons.'

'Oh, come on,' Mister Monday drawled, obviously enjoying the moment. 'You want to rule the world, we want to rule the world, how are they different?'

'You kill people!'

'You killed David.'

'*You* killed David!'

'Through information *anonymously given by you!*' Mister Monday snapped. 'Don't tell me it wasn't you trying to pull strings! And then there's the Mister Friday you killed!'

'When did I kill a...' Harry frowned. 'Wait, Brian? I didn't kill him!'

'No, we did,' Mister Monday replied calmly. 'After we realised you'd turned him. But again, in making him your asset, you did as much as pull the trigger!'

'Rubbish!' Harry waved the blade angrily. 'I just wanted this to end properly!'

'End properly?' Silver stepped forward, his cane held loosely in his hand. 'Harry, whatever justification you've built in your mind, this stops now.'

Silver's walking cane extended with a soft click, revealing the beginnings of a blade that caught the stage lights.

'You think this is over?' Harry shouted. 'You think removing a few Calendar operatives solves anything? There are cells in every major capital. People in positions of power who've been waiting fifteen years for activation orders.'

'Then we'll find them too,' Silver said, drawing his own sword with a whisper of steel.

'Will you? Or will you retreat to your comfortable delusion that you're just Phillip Morris, accountant, and none of this is your responsibility?'

The first clash of steel echoed through the theatre. But this wasn't the dramatic duel Laura had expected from such a prestigious theatre stage. Both men were clearly skilled, but they were also in their sixties, and the fight was more about positioning than flash.

Harry's blade was shorter, but this meant he moved in close, forcing Silver to fight at a disadvantage as he pressed his attack, forcing Silver back towards the rear of the stage.

'The Sebastian Silver I knew would have finished this by now. But you're not him any more, are you? You're some sort of compromise, neither spy nor civilian. Where's your comfy cardigan, *Phillip?*'

Silver parried, but his response was slower than it should have been. Harry's blade caught him across the forearm, drawing blood that stained his borrowed jacket sleeve, and then with a second, ornate flick, he took Silver's trilby right off his head, sending it stage left.

There was a moment of silence as Silver stepped back.

'Ah, there you are, Phillip,' Harry smiled darkly.

'You're right,' Silver said quietly, his breathing slightly laboured. 'I'm not the Sebastian Silver you knew.'

His hand moved towards his trilby, and for a moment Laura thought he might transition back to Phillip and needing to gain it back to continue. But instead, he straightened, his grip on his sword firming.

'I'm someone better.'

Instead of continuing the swordplay, Silver – or was it Phillip now – simply dropped his weapon and stepped inside Harry's guard, using the "sheathe" of his cane to strike down at Harry's wrist with surprising force.

Surprised and not expecting the action, Harry gave a yelp of pain as his own extended blade fell from his hand and to the floor – but it didn't hit the ground, instead caught deftly by Silver, who now brought it back up.

'The old Sebastian Silver would have killed you,' Silver said, the blade now pressed against Harry's throat. 'The new one believes in due process.'

As if summoned by his words, figures began emerging from the galleries. Not Calendar operatives, but people in sensible clothing who moved with the sort of quiet competence that suggested they carried proper identification and asked pointed questions for a living.

Louise appeared at their head, no longer the nervous young woman who'd posed as David's girlfriend – now she was there as an operative of something larger – MI5 or MI6, but definitely one of the "MI's".

'Harry Farrell,' she said formally, 'you're coming with us.'

'Or what?' Harry looked around at the assembled operatives, then back at Silver. 'You think this is over? You think arresting me solves anything?'

'We're not arresting you,' Louise smiled. 'We can't. How can we arrest a dead man? And you *are* dead, Harry. We have witnesses and everything. They held a funeral. Your wife's already received her insurance payout.'

Two operatives moved across the stage as Harry stumbled backwards, away from them.

'Dead men don't get due process,' Silver continued, picking up and sheathing his sword cane. 'Goodbye, Harry.'

As the operatives moved to secure Harry and the remaining Calendar operatives, including Mister Monday who accepted this end with surprising grace and a smile that insinuated he wasn't worried about his immediate future, Laura felt Kyle's hand slip around her shoulders. The immediate crisis was over, but she had a distinct feeling that her quiet life in Queen's Gate would never be quite the same.

Silver was still on the stage, looking down at her with an expression she couldn't quite read. The trilby, now picked up and placed back on the head was slightly askew, and she wondered whether he was still Sebastian Silver or whether the momentary loss meant he was beginning the slow transition back to Phillip Morris.

There was a commotion at the door, and Frank Young

and some officers entered through the rear entrance and exit. Louise looked over, but a simple nod from Frank showed her he wasn't there to step on any toes.

'Just mopping up, in case there's anyone left,' he said, simply.

'There's nobody left.' Louise turned to face Frank, but then paused, looked back at Mister Monday and smiled. 'Actually, you have this one. He killed Harry Farrell. I believe you have video and photographic footage of this, as well as confirmation of the poison in David Revere. Who he also killed.'

'I didn't kill Harry Farrell!' Mister Monday exclaimed, the smile fading as he realised his last act wasn't the one he'd prepared for. 'He's standing up there!'

'I assure you, there's no such man here,' Silver said, looking around with mock concern and making a point to look past the now in custody Harry. 'But Harry Farrell's dead, so unless he's Hamlet's Ghost... of course, I believe you to be the type of man who robs graves, so I very much expect to find Harry Farrell's body gone, when the police go to look for it.'

As Frank Young and his officers gratefully took the arguing Mister Monday, Louise – if that was even her name – walked over to Laura.

'There is a list,' she said. 'And fifteen years ago, he gave it to your husband. That is, someone did. We don't have an official report, as this was the day before James Carlyle's accident.'

'Was it an accident?' Laura asked and was not surprised to see a noncommittal shrug from the MI5 operative.

'We don't know,' she replied. 'We also don't know what he did with the list, or even if Sebastian ever had it. As for the sleepers? They're not looking to "out" themselves any time soon. But if your man in the hat remembers anything? Let me know first.'

And, this stated, Louise waved her hand and, almost as if magicians performing a trick, the operatives and their charges melted into the shadows, leaving Laura, Celia, Kyle and Frank in the auditorium, with Silver on the stage, and Mister Monday being dragged off by uniformed officers.

'Well,' Celia said, readjusting her handbag with an expression that suggested she'd had quite enough drama for one evening, 'that was more excitement than I've had since the church fete committee tried to ban the coconut shy. Shall we go home? I'll put the kettle on.'

Silver smiled at that, and Laura realised that whoever he was – Sebastian, Phillip, or some combination of both – he was exactly the sort of person who would appreciate the offer of proper tea after saving the world.

'That,' he said, 'sounds absolutely perfect.'

EPILOGUE

Two Weeks Later.

Laura's morning post contained the usual assortment of London nonsense – two parking tickets that couldn't possibly belong to her (she didn't even own a car), three charity luncheon invitations from committees who'd apparently decided her recent adventures qualified her as a "woman of action", one particularly sniffy letter from the Queen's Gate Residents' Committee regarding "irregular foot traffic and unexplained police presence", and a handwritten note from Eleanor Jenkins requesting "clarification about recent events" in the sort of careful script that suggested diplomatic training, or a significant amount of googling.

The parking tickets were particularly galling. One claimed her non-existent vehicle had been illegally parked outside Harrods at 3:47a.m. on Tuesday, while the other ticket was for a space in Camden that she was fairly certain she'd never even visited. *London bureaucracy,* she reflected, *carried on regardless of international conspiracies or personal trauma.*

She set the lot aside and watched Kyle field his seventh phone call of the morning from his position on the conservatory floor, laptop balanced on his knees and the sort of weary expression that suggested fame wasn't quite what he'd expected.

'No, I can't give details about ongoing investigations,' he was saying to what sounded like another journalist. 'Yes, it was properly terrifying. No, I don't know if there'll be a film. No, I can't put you in touch with Sebastian Silver – mainly because I'm not entirely sure who Sebastian Silver actually is myself.'

Kyle had developed quite an impressive repertoire of polite refusals over the past three days. Laura particularly enjoyed his response to the request for "behind-the-scenes photographs" – 'Well, there was quite a lot of being unconscious and tied up, which doesn't photograph particularly well.'

Sebastian Silver looked up from his newspaper – he'd been reading the same page for twenty minutes, though Laura suspected he was actually listening to Kyle's increasingly creative ways of saying 'absolutely not' to interview requests. The trilby sat securely on his head, and she'd noticed he'd been checking it periodically throughout the morning, a gesture that was becoming less anxious and more habitual.

'Still feeling integrated?' she asked quietly.

'More each day. It's rather like having access to two different libraries in the same building. I know where everything is, but sometimes I have to remember on which floor I left a particular book. That said, I do worry whether I'll fade away without a hat. Maybe I need to curate a new collection of different items of headwear to go with my canes.'

He nodded over at Kyle, and Laura noticed it was a gentle one, as if still scared of the trilby sliding off.

'Popular lad,' he observed.

'Traumatised lad,' Laura corrected, noting the way Kyle's hands still shook slightly when his phone rang. 'Though I suppose that's not as marketable for the press.'

'The attention will die down, as Keith's exposé, like all others, has a limited shelf life before the next scandal emerges,' Silver said.

Laura nodded, grimacing. The deal for Keith's help had been the exclusive, and she'd gone through with her word – which had led to all of this.

'Hopefully,' she replied. 'Or we could all fake our deaths.'

'That's so last month's news,' Silver smiled, then paused. 'Actually, there's something we should discuss. About what happens next.'

Laura's stomach did something unpleasant. She'd been dreading this conversation for two weeks now – the one where Sebastian announced he was well enough to return to his proper life, wherever that might be. The arrangement they'd fallen into, with him staying in James's old study and the three of them navigating round each other like a family that had somehow assembled itself by accident, felt too good to be permanent.

'You'll want to go back to the facility,' she said.

'Actually, I was hoping I might stay. If you'll have me.'

Kyle's phone conversation stopped mid-sentence. Even Celia, who'd been clattering about in the kitchen with what sounded like enough crockery for a state dinner, went quiet.

'Stay?' Laura repeated, because apparently her conversational skills had abandoned her entirely.

'Doctor Matthews thinks it would be beneficial for my continued integration. Stable environment, people who understand both sides of my personality.' Silver folded his paper with unnecessary precision. 'And there's the fact that you now have a basement flat free.'

Laura nodded at this. Mrs Kowolski had handed in her notice the moment the case was over, complaining of the continuous noise at all hours. When Laura had explained it was because of Kyle being kidnapped, and how it had all been in the news, Mrs Kowolski had simply stated "not my monkey, not my circus", whatever that meant, and walked out, never to be seen again.

Laura would not be missing Mrs Kowolski any time soon.

'Well, that's definitely an upgrade from the camp bed in the study,' she said. 'And you could move your gatehouse items down there.'

'That would be splendid. I'll pay the correct rent, of course,' Silver smiled.

'How?' Celia asked. 'I mean that with all respect, Mister Silver, but you were being held in the clinic as a charity case. This is a desirable residential property.'

'He received two grand a month in pensions,' Kyle suggested.

'And the basement flat is a desirable postcode, and easily worth more than that,' Celia argued.

'A price that could be massively discounted for the man who helped save Kyle,' Laura argued.

'Who also has a valid case of being the one who put him in trouble in the first place,' Celia bristled.

'I'll pay the going price,' Silver stated quickly to stop any kind of argument. 'I have healthy savings, a pension – even if it's for a fake person – and the stipend I'm given monthly. Also, there's the matter of our partnership, and any monies made through that.'

'Partnership?'

Kyle held up his laptop screen, which displayed a newspaper headline in letters large enough to be seen from space.

Queen's Gate Detective Agency Solves International Conspiracy.

'Okay, so yes, Keith's been busy,' Laura said weakly.

'Rather good branding, actually,' Sebastian said. 'And we do seem to work well together.'

Before Laura could form a coherent response to this development, there was a knock at the front door. Realising this was a moment to catch her breath, she went to answer it, leaving the others to discuss fictional detective agencies. It was likely another journalist, or perhaps Mrs Reynolds with more requests to meet "Mister Brosnan", but instead, Laura faced a woman in her sixties with the sort of understated elegance that suggested expensive education and good breeding.

'Mrs Carlyle,' The woman smiled. 'It's good to see you again.'

'I'm sorry, have we met?'

'You met me as Doctor Sarah Matthews. You might remember me better if I wore the glasses I did last time? I believe it's time we had a proper conversation.'

Laura blinked. This woman looked nothing like the frumpy and harried medical professional she'd met at the care facility. This person belonged at embassy receptions or charity galas, somewhere important people discussed important things over excellent wine.

'You look… different.'

'I wasn't entirely myself when we met before,' the onetime Doctor Matthews winked. 'May I come in? There are things you should know.'

Laura led her through to the morning room, closing the door behind them. Doctor Matthews glanced around, taking in the family photographs and the comfortable furniture with the sort of look that suggested she was noting exits and sight lines.

'Okay,' Laura started. 'If I can't call you Doctor Matthews, what can I call you?'

'My name is Sarah Matthews, but for most of my career I was known as Mockingbird.'

The room suddenly felt very quiet.

'You're Calendar,' Laura said, her hand moving instinctively towards her phone.

'*Was* Calendar. Just as Phillip – Sebastian – was.' Mockingbird's voice remained calm.

'This is about Sebastian, isn't it?' Laura said.

'Among other items of note.' Mockingbird settled into the chair Laura indicated. 'There are things you should know about his situation. About all our situations, actually.'

Something in her tone made Laura sit up straighter, as Mockingbird continued.

'We both served, and we both left when we discovered what the organisation had become.'

'You worked together.'

'We spent three years developing what we called the

Sunday Cypher. Extracting endangered assets, protecting witnesses, providing safe houses for defectors. Everything The Calendar was supposed to be doing before it became corrupted.'

Laura felt pieces clicking into place.

'Sunday. Because Sebastian was Mister Sunday.'

'Exactly. Sebastian was Mister Sunday – but not the Sunday you've heard about. The Calendar wanted people to believe Sunday was its ultimate authority. In reality, Sunday was its biggest problem.'

Mockingbird paused, choosing her words carefully.

'Almost twenty years ago, Sebastian discovered The Calendar had been compromised. The entire organisation was rotten. Selling intelligence, assassinating inconvenient people, manipulating markets. Over the next few years we gathered evidence, prepared to bring down the network, and Sebastian discovered a list of assets placed in positions of trust across the globe. They found out before we could act.'

'What happened?'

'The confrontation was... unpleasant. Sebastian tried to pass it to a trusted asset – your husband – in Prague, but in the process was ambushed, badly hurt, and suffered significant trauma, especially when his friend and contact James Carlyle died the following day. His mind... well, it simply broke under the stress. I extracted him, but he was completely dissociated. He'd created an entirely new identity – Phillip Morris, a quiet accountant who just wanted a simple life.'

Laura leaned forward.

'You helped him disappear.'

'I helped him heal. The Phillip Morris identity wasn't a cover – it was his mind protecting itself. I made sure he had documentation, a place to live in Boston, a chance to build something real.'

'And it worked.'

'For many years. Sebastian, as Phillip, found genuine happiness. Met a wonderful woman – Helen – and was truly at peace.'

Laura saw where this was heading.

'She died.'

'Losing Helen began breaking down the barriers between his personalities. He started remembering fragments of being Sebastian while still being fundamentally Phillip. That's when I brought him to London.'

Laura thought about the care facility, about Mockingbird – then as Doctor Matthews's careful attention to Sebastian's condition.

'You've been protecting him.'

'We've been protecting each other. The facility gives us cover – I'm just a doctor treating trauma patients. No one looks too closely at a psychiatric facility.'

'And Harry Farrell?'

'Harry... that was pure chance. He was looking for data, following threads, and found us.'

'Did he recognise you?'

'Harry Farrell never saw *me*,' Mockingbird smiled. 'He saw Doctor Sarah Matthews, a frumpy woman with glasses. I had the "Clark Kent" disguise on, it seemed. But he recognised Sebastian was integrating naturally. At the time I thought he was still an ally, and after he'd visited a few times, we thought with the right catalyst – someone like you – Sebastian might be strong enough to face his past and help finish what we'd started.'

Mockingbird stood, smoothing her skirt.

'I learned from the Globe debriefs he was working with Brian – Mister Friday, and that he made sure the syringes with the new toxins were replaced with the old batch – this meant that Harry could "die" and recover with nothing more than a headache. Of course, this gave us the fortuitous advantage of meaning—'

'That James had the old toxin too,' Laura finished, understanding. 'So Harry making sure he could fake his own death effectively saved Sebastian.'

Mockingbird smiled.

'I wanted you to know the truth before you decide what comes next. Phillip will need support as he continues integrating. And there are others like him – former operatives who need the sort of help traditional channels can't provide.'

She moved towards the door, then paused.

'Your husband would be proud of what you've accomplished, Mrs Carlyle. He always said you were destined for more than charity committees.'

'You knew James?'

Mockingbird nodded.

'As I said, he was the one Sebastian gave the list to.'

'Is that what killed him?'

'I have no idea, if I'm being brutally honest. It could, after all, have been a simple accident,' Mockingbird replied sadly. 'And I also don't know who was on the list Sebastian found, as this is a part of his past he doesn't seem to want to return to.'

She shook Laura's hand.

'The Calendar is hurting right now, but they're not dead. With luck, they now believe Silver's just a thorn in their side rather than a threat, and with Harry now gone too... you should be fine. Stay safe, Miss Carlyle.'

'It's Mrs—'

'It's been fifteen years, Laura,' Mockingbird smiled. 'Live a little for once.'

She smiled, nodded a farewell and then walked out of the room without another word.

After she left, Laura sat alone in the morning room for a long time, processing what she'd learned. Outside, she could hear Kyle still fielding phone calls and Sebastian Silver's quiet voice offering suggestions.

Her family, she realised. *Not the one she'd planned, but the one she'd somehow assembled.*

When she finally rejoined them in the conservatory, Silver looked up from his newspaper.

'Everything all right?' he asked.

Laura reached for her notebook.

'I think,' she said slowly, 'we do need to discuss the future.'

'So,' Kyle said eventually, 'are we actually doing this? The detective agency thing?'

Silver folded his newspaper properly this time.

'It would give us purpose. And there are people who need help that official channels can't provide.'

'We'll need business cards,' Kyle said, warming to the idea. 'And a proper phone line. I could build a website.'

'We'll need protocols,' Celia said, appearing in the doorway with a fresh pot of tea. 'Can't have people thinking we're amateurs.'

Laura looked around at her unlikely family – Kyle with his laptop and his new understanding that the world was more dangerous than he'd thought, Celia with her encyclopaedic knowledge and increasingly sharp questions about their visitors, Sebastian Silver with his careful integration of two lifetimes of experience.

'The Silver Detective Agency,' she intoned. 'It does have a certain ring to it.'

'We'd be helping people,' Silver said. 'People caught between worlds, carrying secrets they can't share, dealing with threats they can't officially acknowledge.'

'And there'd be proper cases to solve,' Kyle added. 'Not just charity committee politics.'

'But I have one request,' Silver said, frowning. 'A name change.'

'What, you want Silver in bigger letters?' Celia raised an eyebrow. 'Perhaps a little trilby above your name?'

'The opposite,' Silver smiled. 'I think The Carlyle & Silver Detective Agency rolls off the tongue far easier.'

Celia went to argue, paused, then nodded.

'Well, it's better than Keith's blasted headline,' she muttered, pouring the tea.

Laura reached for her notebook. It wasn't the quiet retirement she'd planned, but then again, quiet had never really suited her, anyway.

'Right then,' she said. 'Let's start with a proper business plan.'

Outside, Mrs Reynolds walked her Yorkshire terrier past Laura's house and noted with approval that the distinguished silver-haired gentleman who looked like Pierce Brosnan was back.

Such a well-dressed man.

And after all that unpleasantness with police cars and journalists, it was nice to see things returning to normal.

Well, as normal as things ever got in Queen's Gate.

Which, all things considered, was probably normal enough.

Want the next Carlyle & Silver Cozy Mystery? CLICK HERE on digital, or turn the page...

Laura Carlyle & Sebastian Silver
will return in their next cozy mystery

SILVER and the Christmas Caper

Coming December 22nd

ABOUT THE AUTHOR

Jack Gatland is the pen name of *#1 New York Times Bestselling Author* Tony Lee, who has been writing in all media for thirty-five years, including comics, graphic novels, middle grade books, audio drama, TV and film for *DC Comics, Marvel, BBC, ITV, Random House, Penguin USA, Hachette* and a ton of other publishers and broadcasters.

These have included licences such as ***Doctor Who, Spider Man, X-Men, Star Trek, Battlestar Galactica, MacGyver,*** BBC's ***Doctors, Wallace and Gromit*** and ***Shrek***, as well as work created with musicians such as ***Ozzy Osbourne, Joe Satriani, Beartooth, Pantera, Megadeth, Iron Maiden*** and ***Bruce Dickinson.***

As Tony, he's toured the world talking to reluctant readers with his 'Change The Channel' school tours, and lectures on screenwriting, story craft and comic scripting for festivals and conferences such as *Raindance* in London and *Author Nation, The Global Publishing Summit* and *20Books* globally.

A Freeman of the City of London and an introvert West Londoner by heart, he lives with his wife Tracy and dog Darcy, just outside London.

Feel free to follow Jack / Tony on all his social media by clicking on the links below, to engage, discuss Declan and put the world to rights.

www.jackgatland.com
www.hoodemanmedia.com

Visit Jack and Tony's Reader's Group Page
(Mainly for fans to discuss his books):
https://www.facebook.com/groups/jackgatland

Subscribe to Jack's Readers List:
https://bit.ly/jackgatlandVIP

www.facebook.com/jackgatlandbooks
www.twitter.com/jackgatlandbook
ww.instagram.com/jackgatland

Want more books by Jack Gatland? Turn the page...

Printed in Dunstable, United Kingdom

78013646R00201